DRAGON
BREATHES FIRE

I Delyth

Er cof annwyl am
Moelwyn Jones (1943–2015)

GLYNDŴR

DRAGON
BREATHES FIRE

MOELWYN JONES

With grateful thanks to my family:
Dylan, Bethan, Ffion, Gwennan and Catrin,
and also to my wonderful friend, Iris Cobbe,
for all their support.

Delyth Jones

First impression: 2018
© Moelwyn Jones family & Y Lolfa Cyf., 2018

Cover image: iStockphoto

ISBN: 978 1 78461 606 9

Published and printed in Wales
on paper from well-maintained forests by
Y Lolfa Cyf., Talybont, Ceredigion SY24 5HE
e-mail ylolfa@ylolfa.com
website www.ylolfa.com
tel 01970 832 304
fax 832 782

1

CHRISTMAS 1401 PROVED a merry and a restful one despite the stark isolation of our small fortress of Dolbadarn amid the snows and frosts of Snowdonia. The carpenters and masons had worked wonders on the ancient stone structure during the summer; the buildings and defensive walls had been restored and we actually had well-constructed wooden roofs and snug-fitting doors to keep out most of the draughts which had chilled us to the core the previous Yuletide. The renovated old fireplaces and the additional new ones kept us warm, and the generosity of the people of the surrounding valleys ensured a plentiful supply of firewood and basic foods. We frequently sent out hunting parties which often returned with various meats for the table such as rabbit, deer and wild boar from distant woods.

My garrison consisted of thirty of my personal guard under the command of Rhys Gethin. I had sent the remainder of *Y Cedyrn* and the men of the previous garrison to spend Christmas with their families or with friends. It had been a hard summer and everyone was in need of rest and a break from the tensions of war. The evenings were full of good cheer, with my old friend Gruffudd Llwyd orchestrating the entertainment and highlighting many an evening with his own magnificent poetry which he sang in his rich baritone. His voice had matured and mellowed with age like a fine French wine and we were fortunate indeed to have the privilege of listening regularly to such a wonderful singer and bard.

One night, as I lay in bed with Mared sleeping peacefully by my side, I reflected on all that had happened since the battle of Hyddgen. It had become pretty clear to me that one day soon I would be involved in a confrontation with my cousin Hywel Selyf at Nannau, his family's large and noble home not far from the town of Dolgellau, snuggling in the hills to the south of Snowdonia.

I have always had a great deal of affection for Dolgellau and its surrounding area as several of my relatives and friends live there. Hywel was the eldest son of my father's younger brother, Meurig. He was three years older than me but we took an instant dislike to each other. Even when we were small boys he was intensely jealous of my standing as the natural claimant to leadership of the royal house of Powys. He believed that, as he was older than me, he should be senior in all things. The fact that my father was the eldest son of Gruffudd Fychan ap Madog, and therefore the current successor, mattered not a jot in Hywel's young mind. Initially, he was physically bigger and soon began to enjoy bullying me. Fortunately, we lived in the March and a fair distance from Nannau, so we did not see each other very often. I remember dreading summer holiday time when I would be bundled off to Nannau, or Hywel would descend on our Sycharth home to make my life hell. As we grew older the bullying got progressively worse. Then a strange thing happened. When I turned twelve, I began to grow rapidly and I quickly realised that I would soon be as big, if not bigger than my tormentor.

One bright morning during my thirteenth summer, I was riding on horseback along the last stage of the journey to Nannau where I was supposed to 'enjoy' a fortnight's holiday with Hywel and the Selyf family. My father had sent me with a guard of six archers led by one of his oldest captains, Aled ap Gwyryd, now becoming rather elderly at forty-eight, but who had taught me so much about archery, swordsmanship and hand-to-hand combat this past twelve-month. He had always been a kind of favourite uncle to me and I dreaded the moment when I would have to wave him goodbye as he and his troop left me at Nannau. Shortly before we got there Aled moved his horse up beside mine.

'Why do you frown so, Master Owain, are you not going to Nannau to enjoy yourself?'

'Yes, yes, of course I am,' I responded, forcing a smile which would not have convinced anyone.

There was a short silence as we cantered along. Then, old Aled cleared his throat. 'Tell me, Owain – if your father put you in charge of a hundred men – archers and pikemen, and you came upon a bigger English force whose leader bade you stop and told you that you were now on an English lord's land and not your father's, what would your reply be? Would you bow and say that you would go back to check with your father? Or would you tell him straight that the land was your father's and that they, the English, were trespassing and should leave at once?'

'I would tell them that they were trespassing and should leave at once!' I answered hotly.

Aled nodded and smiled.

'A good answer, my boy, a good answer. But what would you do if this trespasser were to laugh and say that he was bigger than you and that his force was bigger than yours, and if you did not get your young arse out of his sight he would kill you on the spot?'

I grinned. 'Why, I would politely tell him "Yes, sir" and I would lead my men back the way we had come with our heads held low. Then, after putting a hundred yards between us, I would issue sharp orders to my archers to wheel and fire their arrows straight down the enemy's laughing throats. After two or three salvoes I would order a charge with our pikemen in the lead, followed by the archers with drawn swords... there would not be much laughter then...'

Aled was smiling broadly. 'An excellent answer, my son. However, there is a lesson there for you to learn. That is the way you must conduct yourself in all walks of life. I do not mean that you should go around killing everyone who disagrees with you. What you must always do, though, is be prepared to stand up for yourself. Often, a suitably timed word or sentence will be enough to indicate that you are no pushover and people will respect you for it. There may be other times when you have to deal with some obnoxious individual who needs rather more than words... something a little more... er... physical perhaps, to convince him that you are not a man to be trifled with.'

Here Aled paused, smiled and gave me the slowest, longest wink I had ever seen. I blushed. Then, before I could recover, he gave me an exaggerated going over with his eyes and murmured, 'Hmmmm... yes, those shoulders look a good deal broader than they did last year, and, yes, you have become a fair bit taller too...'

He laughed lightly again and, without another word, dropped back a pace to his customary position as leader of the escort.

It was a warm summer's day and much too sunny, really, for fishing. Fortunately, the little steam running through the grounds of Nannau was quite heavily wooded along both banks and, at one point, the canopies were actually entwined and branches from trees on both sides mingled in some profusion. The resultant cool and shady stretch of stream was a pleasant spot for fishing. Hywel was being his usual hateful self, stealing the worms I was using as bait, nudging me as I prepared to cast the line of my snood, and the like. I refused to be drawn and got on with my preparations as best I could. After what seemed an age he eventually gave up, scowling with irritation, and wandered a few yards away and sat by the stream.

Breathing a sigh of relief, I settled down to fish, for Nant y Creir was regarded as one of the most bountiful streams in the area. I soon became aware of small splashing sounds and realised that Hywel was casually chucking pebbles into the rock-strewn pool in which I was fishing. I turned to look at him and saw that he was eyeing me, with his face creased in a maddening smirk. In that moment I was consumed by a cold rage which I had never experienced before. Aled ap Gwyryd's words came rushing back to me… 'There may be times when you have to deal with an obnoxious individual who needs rather more than words…'

I rose slowly to my feet, dropped my snood and strode purposefully towards my tormentor. He was saying something but I could not hear his words, nor did I want to, for I was in a world of my own. My heart was pounding in my ears but I felt no fear. The time had come, and no matter what happened next, my relationship with the bully was about to change forever. As I approached I saw Hywel's face move through a series of expressions, as if in slow motion, from the usual supercilious grin to mild surprise, to a certain concern, then to alarm. He began to back away but it was already too late for that. I was moving quickly, both fists bunched, knuckles white. Without a word I raised my right arm and swung it, using my shoulder to inject as much of my body weight as I possibly could into the punch, just as old Aled had taught me. My right fist landed with a sickening smack on the bridge of his nose, sending waves of pain shooting up my arm. I heard the shattering of bone and gristle, then my cousin was lying flat on his back, stunned. There were several moments of silence while his senses returned, then he began to wail as the pain of his rapidly swelling, broken nose became his main focus. He staggered to his feet and I gasped as I saw that his nose was now flattened to one side of his face, changing his countenance completely. He staggered away a few yards before turning back, sobbing.

'Just you wait… I'm going to tell my father… he… he will kill you for this…'

I sat for a while beside the stream. Now that my temper had evaporated I felt sickened and shocked by the damage I had inflicted on him; but in truth I did not regret my action for he had pushed me well beyond the realms of reason and deserved all he got. I was not looking forward to facing the fury of my aunt and uncle, however.

My fate turned out to be worse than I had ever imagined. Meurig, Hywel's father, met me at the door, red-faced and yelling with rage. Before I could say a word he clouted me hard across the head so that I slumped, semi-conscious, at his feet. I was then vaguely aware of being half-carried by two of the servants to a wooden post near the stables. My shirt was torn off me and I was turned towards the post with my wrists tightly bound behind it.

'So, you fancy yourself as quite a man do you, attacking my son, causing permanent damage to his face? But a man has to face the consequences of his actions. You are going to be punished for viciously injuring Hywel for no reason. Stand up properly like a real man. You will now be horsewhipped and I intend to carry out the punishment myself.'

I had once seen a man being punished with a horsewhip in the town of Oswestry. He was a homeless cripple who had stolen a loaf of bread. The town crier informed the crowd who had gathered that the thief would be subjected to twenty lashes. He bravely took the first seven lashes without making a sound. Then, as the knotted whip progressively tore the skin off his back, he began to scream, each lash eliciting a louder and more agonised scream than the previous one. At the end he collapsed onto his knees mumbling and sobbing incoherently.

I felt myself go cold as a terrible fear gripped me. Then I heard the crowd, including family and servants, shouting and urging my uncle to lash me as hard as he could, excited by the prospect of seeing a fellow human being hurt and humiliated. I was thirteen years old and I could not believe what I was hearing. I swore to myself that I would not give them the satisfaction of hearing me scream like the poor cripple in Oswestry. I tried to bolster my courage as I visualised my father's anger when he heard of this outrage. He would surely kill this monster brother with his bare hands.

Just as I was relishing this thought, I heard the horsewhip sing and I was struck with unbelievable force across the shoulder blades. I felt the pain of the blow and nothing else for a second or two. Then I was engulfed in a much worse agony as my scourged flesh parted from my body in a bloody mess of tortured strips. I gritted my teeth and only just managed to maintain my silence before the whip savaged me again in more or less the same place. I was gnashing my teeth together now, searching frantically for some method of holding back the screams that were lining up to escape my convulsing throat. By the eighth lash I was mentally screaming in the hottest fires of hell but still I managed, through some miracle, to maintain my silence. The crowd had fallen silent now too at the sight of the bloody horror of what had been my unscathed back only minutes before. I thought I heard some voices calling for a halt to the inhuman punishment. Meurig ignored those calls and I counted eleven strokes before slipping away into dark and blissful night; a still place, cocooned in welcome shadows, free from pain and torment.

When I recovered consciousness sometime later I was lying on my side in my guest room bed with my back heavily bandaged. I had no choice but to stay there for more than a week, nursed tirelessly by a now very concerned aunt Alys. I had to lie on my side or face down, for it would have been unbearable to attempt lying on my back. My bandages were changed every day and a special salve coated painfully onto my badly-damaged flesh before the application of fresh bandages. The healing process was slow and it was not until the sixth day that I attempted to stand and take a few tentative steps towards the window before collapsing from weakness onto the floorboards. I had to be gently carried back to bed. A few days later, though, I was feeling a lot stronger and I knew that I had turned a corner and would soon be well enough to ride.

When old Aled and the escort eventually came to take me home, my back was still bandaged but otherwise I was recovering steadily and delighted to be going home. I had seen neither my uncle nor Hywel at all during my recovery but everyone else, including the servants, now treated me with a new respect. I heard that Meurig had administered fifteen strokes before his wife, Alys, had rushed forward to stop him from punishing me further, for by now I was hanging from the pole unconscious and she feared for my life.

Aled and his men did not arrive until after dark and they dined with Meurig and other members of his family, with no mention made of Hywel's broken nose or of my whipping. The following morning when we left Nannau, Hywel was nowhere to be seen and his father and I studiously ignored each other during the farewells. I made a point, however, of quietly thanking aunt Alys for stopping my punishment when she did and for her careful nursing which had helped me so much during my recovery. My actions had badly disfigured her son, yet when I left, my aunt had a tear in her eye.

I did not report on my calamitous holiday to Aled for several hours so that he would not be tempted to take matters into his own hands and return to Nannau to confront my uncle. I eventually told him the whole sorry tale. Afterwards he asked to see my back, and what he saw left him seething with anger.

'Meurig ap Gruffudd, like his son, is a bully,' he snarled. 'He is also a monster, for a normal man would not inflict such cruelty on a thirteen-year-old boy, especially his own kin. I tell you, there will be big trouble when your father gets to know of this.'

In fact, my father never did get to hear of it, for when we eventually returned to Sycharth we learned that he had collapsed two days before and was seriously ill. Apparently he had been assailed by terrible chest pains, and before collapsing had lost the ability to speak. He never recovered full consciousness and, within a week, he was dead.

Still wide awake, despite revisiting my calamitous holiday of long ago, I got up to relieve myself in the corner closet, and once back in bed I reviewed my attack on Abbey Cwm-Hir a short while before we returned to Dolbadarn. The abbot had been spending more time in composing and sending detailed accounts to Bolingbroke of our numbers, our activities following the defeat of the Anglo-Flemish army and our growing support, than in saying his prayers. With 300 men of Gwynedd and my elite guards I had ransacked the abbey and left the worthy abbot in no doubt about my views on traitors to the Welsh cause, be they men of the cloth or of the sword. He will, I feel sure, think twice before engaging is such activity again. We followed this up with attacks on Bishop's Castle, which we destroyed before taking New Radnor castle near Llandrindod Wells and ravaging the east of Radnorshire. Sixty survivors of the English garrison at New Radnor were lined up in front of the castle and beheaded in retaliation for Henry's slaughter of innocent civilians and children during his invasion of north Wales the previous year. Even now the memory of that mass execution brings the bile to my throat. War, however, is a bloody, ruthless business and the enemy cannot be allowed to get away with acts of wanton cruelty without experiencing the same treatment in their turn.

The previous winter's inhospitable stay at Dolbadarn had given me time to think of our requirements if we were to stand a chance of defeating Bolingbroke. One area where he had a marked advantage was in information gathering. Over the last two centuries both the King and the Marcher

Lords had built up an almost ubiquitous network of spies and informers which had almost been our undoing in some of the skirmishes of the previous autumn. While I had completely outwitted them as to my own whereabouts – thanks largely to the loyalty and meticulous planning of a few loyal and quick-thinking advisers – the enemy often had detailed information of our military targets and plans which was as disconcerting as it was dangerous. Conscious that we were in urgent need of a similar versatile and efficient spying capability, I had sent a messenger to my sister Lowri's husband, Robert Puleston, at their home in Flintshire. Robert was a quiet, reserved landowner of Marcher stock with a disarming smile, who came across in conversation as a harmless, friendly, ostensibly stolid individual. However, his closest friends knew him to be a brave warrior, skilled with the sword, who also possessed a very sharp and incisive intellect.

Years before, he had accompanied me on one of King Richard's military campaigns in Scotland. When we returned from fighting the Scots we had struck up a close friendship, for I had found him a totally loyal and far-thinking companion-in-arms. He was present at my proclamation as Prince of Wales, and when several of the others present had second thoughts and subsequently sought the King's pardon, I had asked him to do so as well. At first he had been shocked, but when I told him that his intellect would be of much more use to me than his sword and that by distancing himself from me he would be far less likely to be suspected of aiding me later on, he relented. It also meant that he, Lowri and other family members would be able to lead 'normal' lives as apparently loyal subjects of the crown.

Robert arrived in Snowdonia several days later, dressed

as a common drover, accompanied only by Idris, the young messenger I had sent. It was bitterly cold and the mountains were encased in a thick layer of snow. The two shivering travellers were ushered into our private apartments and seated in front of the welcoming log fire. Then they were treated to steaming hot bowls of *cawl* which they both consumed with obvious appreciation. Robert and I had not met since shortly after my proclamation and there was much to talk about. Following the King's pardon, life had returned, more or less, to normal although some of his lands in Cheshire, confiscated last autumn by the King, had still not been returned to him. However, we celebrated the news that Lowri was pregnant with the couple's second child.

Later, after young Idris had left us, I shared my thoughts on setting up an effective spy network and Robert listened, first of all in surprise but soon with obvious pleasure, honoured that I had chosen him as my prospective spymaster.

'Why, Owain, I cannot believe that you have chosen me for such a task. I am highly honoured, brother-in-law. It will be a fascinating project and immensely important to the success of our cause.'

Robert stood up and paced around the room, his face alive with enthusiasm.

'I will give it my immediate attention. If you give me a few days I will be in a position to suggest a form and a clear-cut role for this organisation within the context of your aspirations and objectives. I already have important contacts at court and in Parliament, as well in the Marches of course. I will have to rely on your local leaders in the other parts of Wales to provide me with a few key figures in their respective localities to begin with. I will then be able to build my network with care and the utmost secrecy. Yes, by God, this will be a role I shall fulfil with great interest and pleasure.'

'I had hoped you would accept this responsibility, for I know of no other who is as qualified to make a success of it.' I smiled. 'In fact your enthusiasm for the task is quite infectious. Let me know when you are ready to present your vision for the *Cysgodion* (Shadows). In fact, that might be an appropriate name for the new organisation. I will convene a meeting which will also include one, or maybe two, of my key advisers who will need to know of your work in any case. Thereafter, the only people who will know the extent of your work and the identity of your agents will be you – and me.'

'I will bid you goodnight now, my Prince. I have much thinking to do.'

Robert left me with a broad grin on his face and, despite his exhaustion after the cold journey from Flintshire, there was a jaunty swagger to his gait as he strode out of the room.

Several days later I had lunch with Robert; the family physician, Ednyfed ap Siôn, and Gruffudd Llwyd. Again we sat at a modest table in my private quarters and the conversation was light and jovial, for Ednyfed and Gruffudd had, as yet, no idea that we would be launching our top secret intelligence gathering service in a meeting after the meal. I had chosen those two with care because between them they represented the shrewdest and most level-headed advisers at my disposal. They would have no difficulty in realising the significance and importance of creating such a body to help us. Unlike some of my young commanders, they would be well aware of the necessity for influencing the minds of men in positive ways and the huge advantages of learning about enemy plans and strategies as soon as they were hatched, not to mention the distribution of false information at key moments to our opponents, regarding our own intentions.

'As I'm sure you have guessed,' I said after we had eaten our fill and recharged our tankards with ale, 'you have been asked to join Robert and myself for lunch because we wish to seek your opinions on an exciting, new and secret development. Robert will be in charge of it and I have asked him to begin working on it and to develop the principles and organisation needed to make it an effective aid to our struggle for freedom.'

I saw Ednyfed give Gruffudd a questioning look and Gruff's shrug of the shoulders in response. Then Robert cleared his throat and began outlining his vision of our projected spying organisation. He had hardly completed three sentences before our two advisers started grinning broadly. Robert halted, his annoyance at being taken so lightly etched on his face.

'Forgive me, Robert,' Ednyfed broke in quickly, 'Please don't take offence but Gruff and I are not finding you amusing. It is simply that the project you are describing has been in our minds for several weeks and we, too, have been giving its organisation a great deal of thought.'

'Why have you not informed me and included me in your discussions!' I asked, failing to keep the edge from my voice.

'Your pardon, my Lord, but we wanted to present you with a properly thought-out set-up so that you would have a prepared project to ponder,' Gruffudd offered soothingly.

Robert chuckled at our strained faces and suddenly we were all relaxed again, eager to compare notes. As it turned out, the two planned spy rings were remarkably similar in their proposed objectives and structures. The only obvious difference was that Ednyfed and Gruff had given little thought to a leader, or spymaster. However, both were fulsome in their support for Robert Puleston in that role for exactly the reasons I had selected him. We discussed the setting up of the *Cysgodion* and agreed that Robert would be given free rein to develop and hone the new body into an efficient and resourceful espionage tool. We also decided that we would never reveal its existence to anyone else and that the defining title, *Cysgodion*, would only ever be used among the four of us. And so, a key arm of our revolt was born although, officially, it never existed.

After the others had left – Robert to brave the frost and snow with an escort of six archers on the return journey to his Flintshire home, and Gruffudd and Ednyfed to their respective duties – I had the fire banked up with more dried logs and sat on the settle. I studied the glowing red inferno at the heart of the fire and stared, fascinated, at the eager yellow flames dancing and growing as they licked the edges of the doomed logs, causing the wood to spit out crackling embers, as if in defiant desperation, which burst into pinpoints of red before vanishing up the chimney. Soon I could see the tortured forms of fleeing humans desperate to get away from the embers of their homes and the vicious swishing of sword blades dripping with blood. Yes, I was remembering the terrible events of the previous autumn and wondering if I could have done anything to halt Bolingbroke's second and most cruel chevauchée yet into Wales, had the *Cysgodion* been set up a year earlier.

At the beginning of September, Robert Puleston heard

from a friendly contact at court that Henry had sent out summonses to twenty-two English counties to attend a general muster at Worcester on October 1st. His plan was to gather the largest English army ever seen and launch a major invasion of Wales to bring the rebellion to an end once and for all. Like his previous invasion of north Wales, this would be another chevauchée but this time setting off from Worcester via Hereford with extra support from the Hereford and Shrewsbury garrisons.

Chevauchée was a method of warfare Henry had seen practised by the French. Instead of seeking military targets and living off the land with food stolen from terrified civilians, the invading army would instigate all-out violence on everyone in its path, including the butchering of unarmed men, women and children. Every dwelling or other building of any value would be razed and all crops either stolen or burnt if surplus to requirements. This ruthless mode of warfare resulted in the depopulation of large areas and untold hunger and suffering for the 'lucky' survivors. The psychological impact was often to make those survivors hate their own nobles and military who would be blamed for leading them to such a fate.

We were warned by our informants – before Henry had even set forth from Worcester – that the English army was huge. It consisted of 70,000 armed men and almost 10,000 support personnel. We realised that facing such a host in a set-piece battle would be suicidal for, at best, in 1401 the largest army I could muster would have been fewer than 10,000 armed men. In addition, the English would have several squadrons of heavy cavalry and cannon, while we had neither. Traditionally, we in Wales had relied on lightly-armoured foot soldiers and light cavalry, with a heavy dependence on speed of movement and the lethal accuracy of the longbow; all of which perfectly suited guerrilla tactics in the mountainous terrain and wooded valleys of our country. Unfortunately, we would not be able to stop the mass killings and destruction which Henry would inflict upon large swathes of mid Wales as he led his army through Powys, probably across to the west coast. On the other hand, in order to bring the rebellion to an end he would have to either catch me or kill me. I was confident that with my thorough knowledge of the country and my faith in our own military capabilities, there was little danger of that.

The downsides of huge armies are many. They are slow-moving and cumbersome; they require enormous amounts of food; they have long, vulnerable baggage trains; and they have to ensure that they are properly supported by a whole array of craftsmen, armourers, cooks, waiting staff, porters, stable boys, trumpeters, drummers, bow-makers, fletchers, gunners and blacksmiths. Then there are physicians and their assistants to tend to the wounded and, among the camp followers, the inevitable mobile taverns and brothels with accompanying whores. All this baggage, human and otherwise, can be very vulnerable to surprise attacks, ambushes and all manner of guerrilla tactics, particularly in the hills and forests of Wales. The lack of well-maintained, wide roads is a curse for such an army, particularly in bad weather. Heavy rain can quickly turn poor roads and tracks into a morass in which thousands of heavily-laden men and animals can succumb to fatigue, considerable physical discomfort and loss of morale. If this is compounded by frequent surprise attacks, a significant number of soldiers have to march wearing full armour and with rainwater seeping through chinks and fastenings into undergarments, chafing and sores can develop quickly making life singularly unpleasant for marching and riding, let alone fighting.

As soon as we heard that the great army was on the move I gave Rhys Gethin command of 600 mounted and lightly-armoured archers drawn from Gwynedd and Powys. Their orders were to harry the enormous English army with fast surprise attacks on its flanks, causing maximum damage and death. In addition they would use any means, whether starting rock falls in mountain passes, vicious ambushes, or unexpected attacks on the rear where most of the baggage trains, food wagons and pack horses would be, in the hope that some could be captured for our own use. I sent my brother Tudur as well, so that the force could be split when necessary to attack separate sections of the invading force at the same time. I also instructed them to strike unexpectedly at night as well as by day to deprive the English of their beauty sleep, create alarm and deliver death and injury. The harrying was to start in the Marches and continue wherever the grand army went within Wales.

They left Snowdonia in high spirits, determined to hassle the English army at every opportunity, making life as difficult as possible for them. I then sent messengers to my commanders in the south and west with as much detailed information as I could about the huge invasion force, telling them of Rhys Gethin and Tudur's mounted force and instructing them to raise similar forces in their own areas to engage the enemy using similar tactics. Rhys Ddu was the Commander in Ceredigion, Pembrokeshire and the western parts of Carmarthenshire, while Henry Dwn of Kidwelly was given charge of the eastern reaches of Carmarthenshire and Glamorgan, should Henry IV decide to turn south prior to returning to England. I was convinced that the invasion would not last for more than four weeks; the sheer cost of the operation would be prohibitive after that.

The first days of October 1401 were days of glorious autumn sunshine and the grand army began its invasion of Wales with great pomp as the citizens of Hereford celebrated its departure to war. The steady, inexorable beat of drums awoke the sleeping giant as it flexed its mighty muscles and began its lumbering progress into the Marches. The drums were joined by fanfares of trumpets as the ungainly mass stretched to form a seemingly endless line and the people of Worcester stared in amazement bordering on awe, for they had never seen such a massive army in their lives. They were extremely glad that it was King Henry's army and not that of an enemy. However, many shopkeepers were glad to see the backs of the soldiers, for they were all enlisted men, and at least a tenth of their number were felons, thieves, murderers and thugs who could escape a long prison sentence by joining up in the King's army for one year's service.

On the morning of the third day Henry took a south-westerly route into the Welsh hills. The change of direction coincided with a marked change in the weather, with the morning sunshine replaced around lunchtime by a wintry north wind and scudding cloud. In late afternoon the leading cohorts left a bare, windy valley for the welcome protection of a forest which gradually swallowed up the bulk of the army. As the baggage trains approached the trees, guarded on either side by two companies of longbowmen and 200 pikemen, it started to rain, the swirling wind driving the cold autumn rain into their faces.

Without warning, Rhys Gethin's bowmen, riding quick,

sure-footed mountain ponies came galloping over the low brows of the hills on either side, arrows notched at the ready. The English guards were caught completely by surprise. They were tired from three days of marching and some had already discarded their armour in anticipation of making camp at nightfall and eating a hearty supper before enjoying a well-earned night's rest. They had been convinced from the start that the Welsh would not dare attack such a powerful army, and to be attacked at this time of day was the last thing on their minds. The next ten minutes became a sudden, chilling nightmare for them.

The pikemen swung around to face the enemy with weapons at the ready but only a few archers managed to get their bows strung in time. The Welsh rode their ponies straight at the panicking defenders but, at the last moment, swung their mounts sideways and fired their arrows, before turning and loosing another volley into the enemy lines. At least a third of the defenders on both sides of the baggage trains fell, dead or mortally wounded as the horsemen galloped away before turning to attack again. Many of the surviving English archers had strung their longbows by now and released their arrows at the horsemen bearing down on them again, but fear and panic had set in and their volley was loosed too soon and from unsteady hands. Only a few made contact, causing some injuries but none of the Welshmen fell from the saddle. In seconds our forces were close enough to repeat their previous actions and two clouds of arrows enveloped the defenders bringing more pain and death. By now some of the baggage train drivers had managed to reach the trees, and guards at the rear, responsible for the last baggage train, gave up all pretence of fighting back and scuttled into the safety of the forest. With shouts of triumph, some of the Welsh horsemen raced up to the edge of the trees to face any possible counter-attack while the others secured their prize of one baggage train and two food wagons.

Meanwhile, the alarm had been raised and within ten minutes two squadrons of heavy cavalry came thundering out of the trees, some of the riders wearing little or no armour. They halted in the open area where the unexpected attack had taken place. The Welsh archers had disappeared, taking baggage and food wagons with them. For a moment or two they stared in shock at the bodies of dozens of their comrades scattered over an area of 200 yards. Several dismounted to help the injured, groaning in pain. The leader shouted an order to several riders to hurry to the ridges above in case the attackers were still in sight. The riders came back to report that the valleys on either side were soggy marshes while the higher ground beyond was heavily wooded. There was no sign of the Welsh attackers or their booty. Moreover, the marshy valleys were totally unsuitable for heavy cavalry; the destriers would soon sink to their fetlocks in the swampy ground. With darkness approaching it was useless to think of tracking and pursuing the Welsh on their swift and versatile ponies.

By the sixth day of October the grand army had reached the small town of Llandovery where they were joined by another English force led by Henry's son, Prince Hal. This force had also set off from Hereford but had travelled to Llandovery via Brecon where the garrison was besieged by some of my local forces. They had, sensibly, raised the siege and retired from the scene on hearing of the Prince's approach, for his force also included heavy cavalry and some cannon. When the two English armies met, both leaders were frustrated and annoyed. In addition to the theft of some of his baggage and food, Henry had suffered two more daylight attacks resulting in unacceptable loss of life and failure to inflict any real damage on the attackers. Worse still, Rhys Gethin and his men had launched an audacious attack in the middle of the previous night, stealing up on an area covered by half-a-dozen sentries and slitting their throats, before riding their horses through the camp killing, trampling, destroying and firing many tents. They had killed more than a hundred and injured many more before riding away without suffering a single fatality. The King was furious and ordered the officer of the watch to be stripped of his rank and given fifty lashes of the whip for dereliction of duty.

Prince Hal was angry and frustrated, having failed to engage the besiegers of Brecon. They had simply faded away into the surrounding hills before he reached the town. Little wonder that both were intent on finding someone to punish for their woes.

They soon discovered that the leading landowner in the Llandovery area was a grand old gentleman called Llywelyn ap Gruffudd Fychan, Lord of Caio. He was known as a man of gentle birth, renowned for his hospitality and generosity. It was claimed that his household used sixteen tuns or casks of wine annually. On the morning following Henry's arrival in Llandovery, a sympathiser of mine, Cynwil ap Erfyl, was arrested after his whereabouts were made known by collaborators. A scaffold was hurriedly erected outside the castle and local people were invited to attend the spectacle of Cynwil being hung, drawn and quartered. Naturally, the poor man was terrified; but equally determined to hide his fear from the English. Llywelyn ap Gruffudd Fychan was asked to attend the execution as the King's guest of honour, an invitation he could hardly refuse.

Henry, Prince Hal, several of his senior officers and his guest of honour sat on a raised dais. As Cynwil ap Erfyl was manhandled towards the scaffold, hands tied behind his back, the King instructed the prisoner and his escort to stop and face him. Cynwil turned but kept his head bowed and his eyes downcast.

'Young man, I have sentenced you to death on this day for supporting the arch traitor, murderer and thief, Owyn Glendourdy. I take it you are aware that I have chosen for you a slow and agonising way to die as befits your transgressions. However, it does not have to be like that. If you simply tell me where the traitor hides I will afford you a quick and easy death by giving you a proper hanging, which will be over within a minute. Should you reveal Glendourdy's hiding place, publicly repent and promise your loyalty to me for the rest of your life, I will let you live and allow you to walk away from this place a free man.'

For the first time, Cynwil raised his eyes and stared at the English King but said nothing.

'Well? What say you?' Henry asked impatiently.

There was another long pause as the young man stared at Henry. A slow, half-smile of disdain crossed his features.

'I say this.' The prisoner's voice was quiet and choked with emotion, yet clear enough for all to hear in the dramatic silence. 'You are not my king. My sovereign lord is Owain, Lord of Glyndyfrdwy and Cynllaith Owain; descendant of the royal houses of Powys Fadog, Deheubarth and Gwynedd – the one and only true Prince of Wales. I place my trust in God who will receive my soul knowing that I have been true to my Prince, my countrymen and my forefathers. You are no king, merely the murderer of a king. Now do your worst, for you will surely burn in the fires of hell.'

A long, low sigh like the wailing wind before a storm passed through the large crowd of onlookers, both English burghers and native Welsh. The lad had sealed his doom but even the English townspeople and soldiers stared at him in undisguised admiration. Prince Hal stared too in open-mouthed disbelief.

Henry, however, was apoplectic. 'Why you s-s-stupid b-b-bar-barbarian… How dare you speak to me like that? Executioner, I want this man to suffer the slowest and most painful death you can devise. If you don't fulfil my expectations – you too will suffer the same death.'

Llywelyn ap Gruffudd observed the drama with an expressionless face but his insides were in turmoil. His heart was filled with admiration for the youngster's selfless devotion to his Prince and inwardly he railed at the fates which had decreed such an inhuman death for a brave lad in the prime of youth. What was needed was more people like young Cynwil to come forward to support the rebellion. And what about himself? He was now an old man… too old to fight for Glyndŵr maybe… but certainly not too old to die for the cause. After all, he had led a genteel and comfortable life and he would not be around for much longer in any case. As he sweated, watching the brave young man being butchered slowly while still alive, and trying to shut out his anguished screams of agony, the grand old man decided that, come what may, Cynwil's ultimate sacrifice would not be in vain.

That evening, having invited themselves to Llywelyn ap Gruffudd's imposing hall in Caio, the King, Prince Hal and several of their leading knights applied themselves eagerly to the sumptuous feast and liberal supply of wine and ale provided by their host. Sometime during the evening Llywelyn leaned over to whisper in Henry's ear. He assured the King that he knew of my current whereabouts.

'I know all of Glyndŵr's favourite hiding places in this part of the world,' he whispered confidentially. 'I could take you there tomorrow if you like.'

'You would truly deliver your countryman into my hands?' Henry breathed. 'Sire, you are a true and valiant subject. When we capture the traitor, you shall be knighted on the spot.'

So the popular local squire voluntarily sealed his own fate, condemning himself to the horrors of a slow and cruel death in my name. I wonder if any of my most loyal followers have any inkling of the suffocating weight of guilt a nation's leader must bear; the self-doubts… the nightmares… the sleepless nights… the lonely, nagging pains and cares of responsibility… the shadow of men's curses, silent but ever present at his shoulder… Only Mared knows – and weeps for me, though she fondly imagines that I know not the depth of her love.

The Lord of Caio took the noble Bolingbroke on a wild goose chase, for he had no intention of betraying me or anyone else. Why would he when two of his sons were riding with Rhys Gethin at the time? It was not until the morning of the third day that Prince Hal voiced his doubts regarding Llewelyn's intentions to his father. When challenged the old man simply laughed in their faces.

'Ha! It took you long enough to realise what I was up to. You fools! Did you honestly think I, a Welsh nobleman, would betray a *Tywysog* of the blood to an English king… a usurper of the English crown and his whelp? My God!

You have a lot to learn, Henry Bolingbroke – about human nature, about national pride and about loyalty to your own people.'

Henry, white-faced and shaking with rage, rode up to Llywelyn and clouted him with his mailed hand across the face.

'And you, deceitful old man, have a great deal to learn about the nature of pain and death. I shall take great pleasure in teaching you many lessons on the subject when we get back to Landouvery and the scaffold. When you finally die you will welcome the grim reaper with open arms, if you still possess arms when he comes for you.'

In response the Lord of Caio spat the blood from broken teeth into the monarch's face and stared at him in defiance.

Llywelyn's execution the following morning was the strangest the King had ever witnessed. The light rain developed into a heavy downpour as the victim was led to the scaffold and the sky was soon rent by streaks of lightning and heavy peals of thunder. Only a small crowd had gathered to watch and there were no loud shouts or insulting chants. The Welsh onlookers had shock and desolation etched on their faces, and even the English burghers looked disturbed, for the old man was universally liked and respected in the area. As a result there was an eerie silence around the scaffold. Llywelyn himself seemed to have lost his voice and his writhing body and noiseless grimaces conveyed his suffering more eloquently than any screams would have done.

When Henry finally led the grand army westward leaving the blood-stained, broken body in pieces on the scaffold, the onlookers had long since left the scene in unspoken disgust. Bolingbroke had been left totally dissatisfied with the execution and the crowd's sullen refusal to participate in any way. His dark mood did not lighten as he thought over his plans for his ultimate destination. Neither human kindness nor forgiveness figured in his intentions. The rain had stopped but everyone marching westward was soaked to the skin, and the hundreds of soldiers ordered to wear full body armour were already feeling the initial chafing of wet skin in tender places.

During the next fortnight Henry visited his castles at Carmarthen, Cardigan and Aberystwyth, confiscating land from Welsh gentry along the route and burning their crops, before carrying away scores of children as captives. He captured many men suspected of being supporters of the rebellion and executed them without trial. He also left greatly strengthened garrisons in the castles of each of the three towns.

Nevertheless, Henry and his army were subjected to incessant, damaging attacks from the marauding mounted archers of Rhys Gethin and my brother Tudur, enhanced now by the forces of Rhys Ddu. I had sent word to the three that, once Henry reached west Wales, he was to be harried day and night to unsettle the slow and vulnerable invaders and to deprive them of sleep. My lieutenants carried out their orders with gusto, managing to steal significant numbers of tents and horses, as well as quantities of arms. These, and several wagonloads of food, were sent back to our bases in Snowdonia and eagerly received, for in many of our mountain encampments we badly needed the food and the horses. The precision of the archers caused consternation among the English troops and many were slain. I would dearly have loved to engage them in head-on battle, but I had to let my head rule my heart. All the forces I could muster would only amount to one tenth of Henry's army and we would have no answer to the power of heavy cavalry and the new, untrustworthy but potentially devastating, cannon.

The ancient and impressive monastery of Ystrad Fflur lies in the protective foothills of the Cambrian Mountains. Known to the English by its Latin name, Strata Florida, it is acknowledged as the most important Cistercian community in Wales. At least nine Welsh princes of the royal house of Deheubarth are known to have been buried there, including the Lord Rhys, its original benefactor, and their graves can still be seen to the eastern side of the south transept. It is rumoured that the remains of Dewi Sant (St David), the patron saint of Wales, are buried there, while those of renowned fourteenth-century bard, Dafydd ap Gwilym, lie beneath a yew tree within its hallowed walls. Ystrad Fflur is also famous as a centre of learning and a long line of Welsh abbots have established it as a great preserver of Welsh culture.

Unfortunately, Norman lords and English kings have always believed it to be a centre intent on fomenting rebellion among the Welsh, and it was to Ystrad Fflur that Henry Bolingbroke directed his massive army in his second major invasion of Wales.

On a Saturday morning in late October, Henry rode up to the great west door at the head of his troops and demanded entry. Knowing that resistance would be useless, the abbot, Llŷr ap Cadfael, ordered the two lay brothers at the gate to open the doors and to welcome the King of England with deference. Henry ordered a squadron of light cavalry to enter ahead of him, and the two lay brothers were rewarded for their welcome with instant death as they were skewered by the lances of the leading horsemen. The few choir monks and lay brothers near the entrance raced indoors in fear of their lives and Father Llŷr ap Cadfael, watching from an upstairs window, shouted angrily at the cavalry, demanding that they stop the violence at once for they were now in a holy place. In response, Henry ordered a group of archers to silence the abbot. In seconds, Father Llŷr's chest was pierced by five arrows. A beaker of water shattered as it fell to the floor from his nerveless fingers, seconds before he staggered and collapsed. He was dead before his body thudded on to the floor beside the shards of the beaker.

Henry encouraged his men to desecrate, steal, murder and destroy at will, and most of the remaining choir monks and lay brothers were killed or captured. Only the few who had already left the monastery to tend their flocks of sheep managed to escape. That night, many of the troops got drunk on Ystrad Fflur's stocks of wine and fell asleep in the main buildings. Most shamefully, Henry gave orders for the horses to be stabled at and around the church's high altar. The whole day of depravity was witnessed by hundreds of children the King had captured during his pillaging along the way, to serve a lifetime of slavery in England.

Before leaving on the Monday morning, Henry ordered the destruction of the church. The most important abbey and centre of learning and culture in the whole of Wales was reduced to a smoking ruin.

Rhys Ddu soon heard of the destruction of Ystrad Fflur and the murder of its abbot and most of the monks. Incandescent with rage, he quickly sent word to Rhys Gethin and Tudur before they gathered their forces and met to decide on their next moves. By now, Henry had given up hope of capturing me and, as I had guessed, after a month in the field his debts in wages alone were rapidly escalating. Food stocks were low with very little to steal from the ravaged land. To add to English misery, the weather suddenly became much worse with high winds, heavy rain and even thunderstorms. They became bogged down on slippery, muddy tracks which slowed them to half their original crawl. After several days the army was in danger of being washed away and most of the troops and even some senior officers were convinced that the weather must be an indication of God's anger after the desecration of Ystrad Fflur, or else Glyndŵr practising his dark arts in retaliation for their sins. By now the great majority of the English believed that I was a disciple of the ancient Druids, able to manipulate the weather by means of magic! Every day and most nights they were subjected to short, sharp but vicious raids by my three generals and their forces, with Henry having to withdraw the demoralised troops guarding his flanks after a week of almost constant attacks and replacing them with his personal brigade of guards.

At last – dejected, soaked, riddled with disease and starving – the grand army limped into Hereford. All they had achieved was the dispossession of Welsh gentry, many of whom had not previously given me their support, but who suddenly became ardent supporters; a small amount of gold and silver stolen from monasteries; and a thousand crying and bewildered children who now found themselves in a foreign land, unable to speak or understand the language.

The King's grand design, to defeat and capture or kill me in battle, ending the rebellion, had failed totally. They had managed to hurt me and thousands like me by their destruction of Ystrad Fflur. But their cowardly war on children and the subsequent treatment of those children turned our initial sorrow into a rock hard resolve to make them pay a heavy price for their inhumanity.

2

DESPITE IT BEING the beginning of March 1402, it was still very cold at night and closing the shutters inside the window panes helped keep some of the heat inside. I lay on my back staring at the ceiling beams while Mared rested on her side facing the window. For me the temperature mattered little. It was good to be back in our bedchamber together; one body and one soul in a way which only couples who truly love each other can ever experience or understand. There was no rush to leave it.

Suddenly she sat bolt upright.

'Owain, look at the window... there is a light outside,' she whispered apprehensively. 'Do you see the bright glow around the edges of the shutters? But how can there be so much light out there? It is still the middle of the night for goodness sake!'

I sprang out of bed and strode to the window, flinging open the shutters. The room was immediately bathed in a strange, silvery light quite unlike anything I had ever experienced before. Staring up into the sky I saw a strangely subdued moon and a few degrees to my right I noticed what seemed to be a bright new star with a glowing tail trailing behind it.

'Quickly, my love, you have to see this. It's something I have never seen the like of before...'

Mared tumbled out of bed to see the strange phenomenon. She gasped in wonder at the strange star which seemed to be falling out of the sky. She clung to me in fear and hid her face in my chest.

'Do you think it is a signal of some sort, Owain?'

'How do you mean, a signal?'

'A signal that the end of the world is nigh,' she murmured, her voice trembling.

I gripped her arms firmly. 'It is nothing of the sort. In fact, I believe it to be a portent of good things to come. In the morning I shall ask Ednyfed and Gruffudd to join us for breakfast. As you know, Ednyfed spent some years, first as a slave and then as a pupil to a famous doctor in eastern climes who was also noted for his knowledge of the moon and the stars. Who knows…? Ednyfed may be able to explain to us what this strange new light is and what it portends. And perhaps Gruffudd the bard may have some knowledge of it… and even if not, his presence always seems to have a calming effect on you.'

I was suddenly aware that we were both still naked as Mared leaned forward, her arms encircling my neck. I was very conscious of her nipples hardening against my chest and her warm furry triangle forming a small, comfortable nest against my manhood which, for its part, seemed intent on showing off again for the third time in the space of as many hours.

Instantly aware of my renewed excitement, my lady giggled mightily and hurried me back to bed, obviously impressed and delighted by my virility. This time we made love under the bright illumination of the mysterious new star. As we entered the magical wonder of a loving coupling yet again, I wondered idly whether this 'star' might be a strange new world, some of whose inhabitants might, by some magical means, be able to observe two loving humans joined together as one in happiness and ecstasy. What would they be thinking? Then our lovemaking began the inevitable, breathtakingly beautiful surge to a joint climax and soon neither of us could focus on anything other than the excruciating pleasure in our loins, the pounding in our heads and the joy in our hearts.

In the morning Ednyfed and Gruffudd gave us some strange looks when they joined us for breakfast but made no comment. We must have looked as tired as we felt. Ednyfed soon woke us up though, for he had some interesting theories as to what the bright new light might be, new ideas which we had never heard before.

Studying the stars was widely practised in the East, but for an intelligent European to have such an experience and return to tell the tale was rare; even rarer was that they should share the beliefs and ideas of the East for fear of being accused of peddling anti-Christian ideas. Heresy led only to burning at the stake.

'It was certainly a very strange feeling last night, seeing a new star in the sky above Anglesey, especially with that amazing tail attached,' Mared reflected. 'Yet it did not seem to be moving despite having that light trailing behind it. I was reminded of the story of the birth of Jesus and the bright star which guided the Wise Men to where He lay.'

'Well, my Lady,' Gruffudd murmured, 'people have always held the firmament to be a wondrous and magical thing. Any unusual light or shadow or new object is interpreted as a sign from the gods, or for Christians, from the one God. I can't help wondering whether it is sent to tell us that you, my Prince, will soon be the recipient of good fortune in your struggle to free our country.'

'Well said, Gruffudd. People all over the known world

have believed in such portents since the beginning of time.' Ednyfed smiled. 'I too feel that this new comet, for such it is, shows that the great creative force we call God is displaying his support for you, Owain. After all, your cause is just.'

'I thank you for your kind thoughts, my friends,' I responded. 'But tell me, this comet... what is it?'

Ednyfed reflected for a moment, slowly stroking his grey flecked beard. 'As you know, the common belief in this land and in all of Christendom is that the Earth is flat. Earth is also believed to be the centre of the universe, with the sun and other heavenly bodies floating around it on cushions of gossamer silk. Personally I have never believed that there are cushions in the heavens, but the rest of it is a credible theory. However, after being caught by Moorish pirates and enslaved, I had the good fortune, for several years, to be a disciple of the wisest and most knowledgeable man I have ever known, for Mustafa al-Harun was not only a brilliant physician, he was also a respected philosopher with amazing theories and beliefs about the heavens, about our world and about the future of mankind. He was not alone in these beliefs and I am convinced that many of those theories will be proved correct one day. Those truths will bring trouble with them, for we will all have to have a fundamental rethink about all sorts of subjects which we think we understand at present.'

'What sort of trouble?' I asked. 'And how far will we need to rethink our beliefs?'

'You ask pertinent questions, Owain, and I have to confess that I have very few answers for you. I do not know enough to be able to enlighten you. However, I will give you an illustration which will reveal a little of what may be to come... There are now many men in the East who believe our world is not flat but orb-shaped. Furthermore, it is not the centre of the universe. According to this theory, the sun is the centre of the universe and our world is only one of several which surround the sun at different distances from it. There is also movement; everything in the sky is constantly moving and all at different speeds. The sun, they say, is a massive centre of energy – heat and light – and much else we do not understand. Our world circles the sun once every year and spins like a top as it does so. The other worlds also travel around the sun but through different arcs and at different speeds.'

Ednyfed paused while the rest of us stared at him, dumbstruck.

Mared was the first to recover. 'That is absolutely incredible,' she gasped. 'Surely it cannot be true… I mean, everyone knows that our world is the centre…' Her voice tailed off.

'Ednyfed, listen to me.' Gruffudd's voice was shaken. 'What you have just told us is not only complete nonsense – it is highly dangerous heresy. You must promise me before we leave this room that you will never breathe a word of it again to a living soul. If a priest got to know of this belief that you harbour, he would run with the news to his bishop and you would be burnt at the stake within days.'

A slow smile spread across the doctor's face.

'Thank you, my friend. Thank you for your concern. Let me ask you something – how long have you known me? Yes, many long years. Have I ever mentioned this to you before? No, of course not. I only spoke of it now to present to three people I regard as close friends an alternative view of the night sky or, if you prefer, our universe. However, whether you believe it or not, you can imagine how upset the Christian Church would be, as well as other religions no doubt, if these beliefs were proved to be hard fact. As Christians the thought that our world is the centre of the universe fits in very nicely with the belief that God created man in his own image as the highest form of life. The new theory places our world as just one among many others. What if there is life on other worlds, and what if the life form on some of them is more advanced than mankind?'

There was a long silence as we tried to digest these preposterous but disturbing possibilities. Finally, I cleared my throat to speak, but Ednyfed beat me to it.

'I'm sorry if I have upset you but I would like to conclude with one final thought. According to Mustafa there are several great thinkers within Christendom who are secretly aware and excited by these new beliefs. It will probably take several centuries before they can be proved, if, indeed they ever will. However, I do believe it will not be long before Western thinkers start spreading these beliefs in Europe, for they are fascinating and have the potential to profoundly affect our present beliefs.'

'Thank you, Ednyfed, for sharing these new theories with us,' Mared said, at length. 'You have certainly shocked and amazed us. I would like to join Gruffudd in advising you to say nothing of these things to anyone else, for it is far too dangerous. Despite all the new thinking though, you still have not told us what a comet is.'

'The short answer, my Lady, is that I do not know. I don't think anyone does. My old teacher's belief was that a comet is probably a lump of rock which enters our universe, passes the sun and then light from the sun reaches it so that it appears to us as a new star for a while, before disappearing beyond the reach of the sun's light again. I have never heard a logical explanation for its tail though.'

The new comet remained with us for quite some time. Mared and I first saw it on the night of February 21st and it continued to be visible at night until well into April. There was even a period of twelve days when it was clearly visible during daylight. Whatever it was, its presence was very helpful to me and the cause, for Welshmen everywhere rejoiced, seeing it as a favourable portent, while English eyes stared at it with much dread, thinking that I must indeed be a powerful magician if my influence extended, not only to the weather, but even to the heavenly bodies!

Early in 1402 I resumed military action against the English boroughs and particularly the castles. Towards the end of 1401 Bolingbroke had made Lord de Grey of Ruthin one of his five lieutenants in north Wales, charged with defeating the rebels and maintaining the 'King's peace' in the area. Unfortunately for them, the King was less enthusiastic regarding supplying troops for the campaign. Grey and his fellow lieutenants found that they had to fund any action against the rebels themselves. Grey, in particular, did not have sufficient troops to be a significant threat to us and paying for extra retainers was a costly business.

I too found it a struggle to pay for large numbers of armed retainers; since we had been forced to abandon our beloved Sycharth and our lodge in Glyndyfrdwy, I had lost my means of creating wealth. We had managed to capture much of the King's tax revenues but now our increasing control of the countryside made it too dangerous for the English to attempt collection of taxes. We had also depleted Henry's grand army of much of its food, weapons and other supplies as well as considerable amounts of gold and silver, the previous autumn. Fortunately, my men were all volunteers who believed in the cause they were fighting for and not pressed men like Bolingbroke's. As long as I could provide them with food and shelter they were happy to wait weeks, months even, for their wages. Nevertheless, I needed to find new ways of raising money. I decided that the time had come to gain my revenge for Reginald Grey's predatory confiscation of much of my territory. It was now my turn to confiscate some wealth and I began planning the objectionable Marcher Lord's downfall with anticipatory pleasure.

In the first week of January I had sent Rhys Gethin with 200 men to lay siege to Ruthin castle, only to find that Grey was attending the privy council and scheming to dispossess more Welsh landowners in north Wales.

February and March were months of hard, unusually cold weather with several heavy falls of snow. At last, in early April, I resolved to send Rhys Gethin to open our military campaign season with a further siege of Ruthin castle. However, I was forestalled by the arrival of Rhys and Gwilym Tudur with a force of 500 men. Having endured a long winter of inactivity, the men of Anglesey and Gwynedd were chafing at the bit for some action. Despite the long ride to Dolbadarn in the still chilly mountain air, the brothers came bounding upstairs to my private chamber, taking the stone stairs two at a time. They rushed in through the open door with the enthusiasm of teenagers; Rhys, short, square and swarthy with already brindled locks, with the taller, leaner and younger Gwilym at his shoulder. They hastily halted, stood to attention briefly before bowing low, taking me by surprise. I never would get used to my hard-bitten cousins showing such deference to me, for our relationship, although amicable, had always been of the rough and tumble variety.

'Come on, lads.' I gave a short, embarrassed laugh. 'There is no need for that.'

'Oh, but there is, cousin, if only to show that even relatives have to show respect. After all, you are now recognised by all true Welsh people as a prince of the blood… our *Tywysog.*' Rhys regarded me with a slightly sardonic glint in his eyes but I knew that he meant it. 'We are and always will be friends, Owain, but your new position as our Prince means that we are also your subjects and that adds a certain gravitas to you which cannot be ignored or taken advantage of.'

'Very well,' I responded grudgingly. 'But now you have afforded me the honour due to my rank, perhaps we can sit down and share a tankard of ale together in the way we always have done?'

As we took our seats at the spanking new oak table, constructed by Thomas Easton, in February, Gwilym chuckled delightedly. 'There you are, brother, he is still the same old Owain… *Tywysog* or not.'

Having settled down with full tankards I outlined my plan for outwitting Reginald de Grey. I described how a siege of several weeks would drive the man to distraction. I then added some ideas on how we could increase his frustration while we waited for his nerve to break. There was virtually no hope of capturing the castle, for it was a formidable fortress, and without siege engines and cannon it would take several thousand men many months to seal the surrounding land and starve the garrison into submission. It was merely a statement showing the ordinary Welsh and English people in the town how weak their lord was and demonstrating to them, to other Marcher Lords and to King and Parliament, who was really in the ascendancy in Wales – and that we could attack English castles while their occupants cowered behind their walls.

I also encouraged Rhys to gather crowds of onlookers outside the castle and to offer several challenges every day, inviting de Grey to show some courage and come out to face me in a duel with weapons of his choice. While I did not expect him to accept, I knew he would find such public shaming extremely annoying and, day by day, it would gnaw away at his sense of pride and feelings of superiority. Eventually, he might allow his righteous indignation to get the better of his common sense and play into my hands.

Both brothers were grinning delightedly and ready for my command. We spent more time discussing my longer term strategy for the coming summer, which appeared to please them greatly and ended our session with some domestic banter.

'Tell me, cousin,' Gwilym had a twinkle in his eye, 'how is our brave carpenter, Thomas Easton, faring in your service? Is he still round-eyed and entranced by his Welsh teacher, the maid from Conwy castle?'

The maid, Gwen, had met Mared during her stay at Penmynydd, the brothers' home on Anglesey. My lady had been greatly impressed with her warmth and efficiency and, as a result, Gwen soon became Mared's personal lady-in-waiting. This, of course, was unbelievably good luck for Gwen – now that Tom was in my employ, there would be frequent opportunities for them to be together.

I grinned. 'Well, let's just say that when they are in the same room together they seem oblivious of everyone else. Seriously though, I am very pleased with Thomas.

Originally, as you know, I was suspicious of his motives but he has proved himself as courageous and sincere as any true-born Welshman. He is an excellent fletcher and has shown loyalty and bravery on the battlefield. Gruffudd Llwyd told me after Hyddgen that a shouted warning from Thomas during the battle saved his life. He has also worked hard at learning Welsh and now speaks it fluently. And Mared tells me that Gwen has rapidly become a trusted friend as well as a dedicated servant.'

'Then you are in our debt, my Prince,' Rhys chortled. 'We will accept as payment nothing less than an order to lay siege to Ruthin castle tomorrow.'

'In that case,' I responded with mock gravity, 'you give me no choice. You will attack the Lord de Ruthin in his lair tomorrow morning and the siege will continue until we have our aim!'

Both brothers bowed graciously and we left the chamber together so that I could address the troops and impress on them the importance of their task.

3

GRUFFUDD LLWYD AND I reined in our horses and dismounted behind an imposing beech tree on the edge of the wood.

'Blowing a bit eh? You are out of condition, old girl,' I murmured in Llwyd y Bacsie's ear. 'The winter has been long and cold, and you were far too cosy in your stable, weren't you?'

The faithful destrier snorted, as if in disgust, making Gruff laugh.

'I'm convinced she understands everything you say and she certainly did not approve of those remarks. I would not be at all surprised to hear a good Welsh swearword break forth from her mouth one of these days.'

'We understand each other perfectly, don't we, Llwyd? Regular exercise every day for a few weeks and we'll soon have you back in fine fettle.' I clapped her neck gently and she reciprocated by turning her great head to nuzzle my armpit.

Gruffudd tied the reins of his black gelding loosely to a tree branch. I left Llwyd untied. She would not be going anywhere until I came back. We were at the end of the heavily-wooded area which covered the lower slopes of the steep hill leading up to the castle and walled market town of Ruthin, the Red Fortress. I undid the canvas bag and slid it from the horse's back before taking out a long, flowing, black robe covered with stars, moons and various hideous, unearthly creatures. Then, covered from neck to toes, I took out a wide-brimmed, plain, black hat and placed it on my head. Gruffudd examined me, making sure that bits of the grey hairs of a wig stuck out in unkempt fashion, covering my real hair. In my youth I had always been inordinately fond of dressing in outlandish costumes to perform little plays and masques for family and friends. Now I was itching to enter Ruthin dressed as a wizard to play for the superstitious populace and the equally superstitious holders of the castle.

As I handed my sword and belt to Gruffudd for safe keeping, he tried one last time to dissuade me.

'Owain… sire… in the name of common sense and our long friendship, will you please think again and cancel this dangerous adventure. I know how good an actor you are but you will be exposed to de Grey and all his archers on the castle ramparts. It will only take one person, just one person to even suspect that you are Glyndŵr and you will be a dead man… In God's name, can you not see that?'

'I appreciate your concern, my friend, believe me. But I am confident that I can do this and it may be just enough to tip the balance and force de Grey to lose his self-control and attack us. Then the die will be well and truly cast… Come, pretend to help this old man up the hill to the town gates. Our men control the town and if I can fool them then I will certainly fool de Grey. Let us have no more dissent.'

We left the cover of the trees, weird old man and beefy helper, in full view of the town and the castle. It took quite a while, for I hobbled feebly with an occasional stagger to make Gruffudd grab my arm frequently for the benefit of any who might be studying us. When we reached the town gates I was breathing heavily, leaving my companion to explain to the two men of Gwynedd on sentry duty that he was taking me to Rhys Tudur.

'Aren't you Gruffudd Llwyd, the bard who is reputed to wield an axe with as much skill as his quill?' one of them asked, leaning on his pike.

'Yes, I am Gruffudd Llwyd,' Gruff answered civilly.

'And who might your strangely dressed companion be?'

'I am not at liberty to say anything about him until I have delivered him to Rhys Tudur,' Gruff responded, turning to move on.

The man seemed to take exception to this and stared at Gruff before stepping deliberately in front of us. The bard drew himself up to his full and considerable height. The change in his bearing did not go unnoticed by the sentry staring up at him. The sentry glanced nervously at his companion who studiously turned away to look for more visitors, though there were none in sight. There would clearly be little support from that quarter.

'Orders,' Gruff thundered. 'Now move aside… and I will not be saying that twice!'

The pikeman paled and hastened out of our way. As we started towards St Peter's Square, where the weekly market was in full swing, my friend turned to me and winked. I quickly raised the collar of my robe to my mouth to stifle a chortle.

Considering that the castle itself was under siege, Ruthin market was an island of normality. Hawkers at each corner of the square were trying to out-shout each other, persuading passing matrons that their produce was far superior to any their competitors might offer, while more established stall-holders chatted and bantered with customers. It appeared that there was little tension between the besieging troops and the townspeople. The good burghers of Ruthin were perfectly aware that this was a quarrel between besiegers and besieged. Indeed, hundreds of additional soldiers in town were good for business as long as friendly co-operation could be maintained. On market day the numbers of English burghers were also swollen by many Welsh traders and customers from the surrounding countryside.

We picked our way slowly through the noisy crowds. Despite my outlandish garb, most people's attention was on the produce. Only the children openly stared at me, faces frozen in incredulity as I passed. Eventually we reached the castle end of the square and a large open area leading to the massive outer walls of the fortress. Hundreds of our men filled the area, some standing, obviously on the alert for any significant move up on the castle ramparts, while others sat around in groups relaxing in the weak sunlight, but with weapons and bucklers close at hand. We made our way to a small canvas pavilion directly opposite and less than 200 yards away from the massive iron gate at the castle entrance with a heavy portcullis firmly in position behind it. The siege was being directed by Rhys Tudur and his senior officers from this white pavilion, at the entrance of which flew my princely standard with the four lions rampant on red and gold on one side and the red dragon standard on a field of white and green on the other.

The sentries had picked me out from a distance because the Tudur brothers were waiting to greet us long before we reached the entrance. They were both aware that I would be clothed distinctively when we arrived but they affected the same surprise and half-shock, half-amusement, as their officers at seeing this strange old man.

'*Henffych*, Rhys Tudur.'

Gruffudd shouted his greeting so that dozens of troops in the surrounding area as well as the leaders in the pavilion could hear him distinctly. Rhys returned the greeting, also in a loud voice.

'I bring you this day the famed seer and hermit, Cyndeyrn Dderwydd Du, Cyndeyrn the Black Druid. He claims to have travelled in spirit to a country beyond the grave which can only be reached by braving the eternal fires of Hell.'

The words struck home with all who heard them and dozens of the resting troops were suddenly on their feet pushing their way forward in search of advantageous positions from which to listen. Any tale involving the fires of Hell was usually worth listening to.

'This great seer claims to have met the spirits of several of Reginald de Grey's antecedents and now has messages to pass on to the Lord of Ruthin. He wishes to be allowed to pass on these messages to de Grey and his men when you, Rhys Tudur, issue the challenge today.'

There was an excited reaction at the prospect of hearing messages from beyond the grave. Rhys seemed to ponder before responding to the strange request.

'Does Prince Owain know about this?' he asked doubtfully.

'Prince Owain is fully aware of this request, Lord,' Gruffudd answered firmly. 'He also looks favourably upon it.'

'Then it shall be done as our Prince wishes. Now, bring the great seer inside so that we can offer you both some refreshment.' Then he turned to the wide-eyed troops and proclaimed, 'Let it be known throughout the borough that the great Cyndeyrn Dderwydd Du will be passing messages from beyond the grave to the cowering lord at noon today.

Let us hope that de Grey will have the courage to stand in person to listen to Cyndeyrn… if only from the safety of his battlements.'

As the excited troops turned to do Rhys's bidding, I smiled into the depths of my outrageous robe and proceeded with Gruff past Rhys and into the pavilion.

It was strange conversing with the Tudur brothers and Gruffudd while pretending to be Cyndeyrn. Of course, they must have found the discussion bothersome as well as they strove to maintain my anonymity. Conversation with others that I knew well was even more difficult. In truth, I was glad to finish the meal and leave the table to prepare for the real test.

At last it was time to issue the challenge. Rhys and I mounted the makeshift platform so that we could be seen by the populace in the square behind us as well as by our men in front of the castle. The battlements were lined with archers and men-at-arms but there was no sign of de Grey. Our own archers were positioned in rows four deep, with arrows already notched in their bowstrings. Rhys raised his hand for silence and cupped his hands around his mouth:

'Yet again I stand before you as I have done thrice each day for two whole weeks. And yet again I offer the challenge of my Prince, Owain ap Gruffudd Fychan, to Lord Reginald de Grey to single combat, with weapons of that lord's choice, to be fought to the death or until one or other submits, with possession of Ruthin castle as the winner's prize. I call on Reginald de Grey to show himself and accept this challenge to honourable combat, or to refuse, thus proving himself to be a coward without honour.'

There was silence for several moments before a short, stocky figure in full armour stepped up to the battlements.

'I am tired of you, Welshman. Every day you shout out this challenge several times. We all know it is just a stupid, rabble-rousing ploy to annoy me. I do not know who you are, but your brave champion has not shown his face in this town since the siege began which shows how enthusiastic he is for this confrontation.'

The Marcher Lord paused to allow his men to laugh.

'In any case, why should I risk life and limb to gain a prize which I already possess? You must think I am totally stupid to even think I would consider such an arrangement.'

'I am Rhys Tudur of Penmynydd and I have fought alongside you in King Richard's army against the Scots some years ago. Of course you would not remember a mere Welshman, would you? You are correct, though, in saying we must think you are stupid. We most certainly do.'

Now it was the turn of Rhys to pause for his men's laughter.

'Today, however, I have someone who has messages for you, some of which come from beyond the grave. His name is Cyndeyrn Dderwydd Du which means Cyndeyrn the Black Druid. He is a great seer who is famous for his predictions, for his spirit can travel to worlds beyond the grave.'

Lord de Grey chuckled, though his face looked more perplexed than amused.

'I can't wait to hear what the old man has to say. I've heard of these extraordinary seers but I have never met one. Let us hear what strange ramblings you have concocted for me.'

While I could speak in a quavering voice, it was well-nigh impossible to shout and so Rhys relayed my words to the listeners on the battlements.

'Heed me well, de Grey. You are to be pitied, for you are

doomed to unhappiness and torment in this world and the next,' I began. 'I would not take these words lightly, for you are already damned to burn in the fires of Hell. On the one hand you are trapped in your own castle and your downfall will be soon… very soon. On the other hand, in my spirit travels beyond the grave I have met with several of your ancestors, all of whom are so angry with you that they will ban you from the halls of the de Greys in your life after death. They say you have brought disgrace and dishonour to your family by your actions in this world. That is a horrendous sentence on your head, for anyone who is denied access to the halls of his own family in the afterlife is doomed to everlasting burning in the white hot fires of Hell.'

There was a deathly hush in the square and on the battlements. Then the crowd started whispering to each other in tones of fear and dread. There were uneasy murmurings from the castle's defenders as well, and I found it hard not to grin as I observed the soldiers nearest de Grey taking several steps backwards. I could not see de Grey's face very well, however his body movements betrayed his discomfort. He had abandoned his straight-backed stance and was leaning forward, hands on the stone wall, probably to hide the trembling in his limbs, momentarily at a loss for words.

'Know this, Reginald de Grey. You are on the brink of losing your castle and your fortune. I also bring you a message from Prince Owain. He will be here tomorrow at midday. Before he enters the square he will order all his troops, except his personal guard of sixty men, to leave Ruthin and disperse. He does not expect you to meet him in single combat, for you have displayed your cowardice already. He asks that you, at least, have the strength of character to come out and fight at the head of your men who will easily outnumber his. You may indeed possess the castle now, but of what use is that when you are forced to hide like an old woman, a prisoner behind its walls?'

De Grey had recovered much of his composure, helped no doubt by the anger our words had aroused. 'You and that old charlatan beside you will regret the threats and insults you have heaped on me this day. Do you not know who I am, damn you? Well, I am the senior Marcher Lord of this whole area and a confidant of the noble King Henry IV of England. You… you Welsh savages are a conquered people. We are your masters and your role in life is to do as we say. Let me tell you, as soon as I have disposed of your worthless sham of a prince tomorrow I shall seek you out and, like Glendower himself, you will be hanged, drawn and quartered on the very spot on which you now stand. Needless to say, your deaths will be slow and brutal.'

With these words the Lord of Ruthin turned on his heel and vanished into the gatehouse guardroom. Rhys turned to me, looking pleased with himself.

'It is my belief that between us, we have got the great lord severely rattled,' he chuckled as he helped me down the wooden stairs of the platform.

'Let us hope,' I croaked in my old man voice, 'that he will still be as rattled at noon tomorrow.'

'And what of de Grey? Do you want him dead or alive?' Rhys already knew the answer to his question. A living, breathing Reginald de Grey would be worth a fortune in ransom money.

I grinned at him. 'I think you know which, cousin. Now take me to Gruffudd Llwyd so that we can get back to our horses and I can rid myself of the limp and this infernal robe.'

That night, in our base camp in the Clwydian hills, my senior officers and I dined in style on fresh venison, thanks to the generosity of a local *uchelwr*. Everyone was eager for the fray. The long, bitter winter had given us all a chance to refresh ourselves mentally and to recover from wounds suffered in the various military confrontations of the previous summer. Also, now that I had a detailed plan to lure de Grey out of his lair, not only would a ransom for his freedom hurt the English nobles in their pockets, it would sound all sorts of alarm bells in the Marches and beyond. Most importantly, it would allow me to pay outstanding wages to my faithful retainers and to arm, feed and clothe us for a long time to come. Of significance too would be the positive effect on Welsh morale and the negative impact on that of our enemies. And not least, it would make prospective allies such as the French and Scots, sit up and take notice.

In the morning we woke up to low cloud and drizzle; not ideal conditions for waging war. The ten-mile ride to Ruthin was damp and cheerless and after only a few miles we were wet and uncomfortable in the saddle. I prayed that the weather would clear so that visibility, at least, would be good for the fray, and since we were, as usual, heavily reliant on our archers, the bowstrings would be dry when strung to our bows.

We entered Ruthin half an hour before midday and I immediately sent word to Rhys Tudur to meet me in a quiet lane behind St Peter's Square. The rain had long since cleared away and we were slowly drying out in the pleasant spring sunshine. Though not normally a market day, there were crowds of people in town and the owners of several market stalls had noted the crowds and the excitement and hurriedly opened for business. It looked like becoming an unexpectedly profitable day for them. I had only brought the sixty members of *Y Cedyrn* into town. We had left our horses under guard outside the town gates and the remaining fifty-four of my men had been instructed to mingle with the crowds in market square and to be ready for instant action. Nearly 200 men had been left in a rock-strewn clearing in the woods, ready to surprise de Grey and his force when the time came.

Rhys soon arrived in the lane on foot, accompanied by his burly captain, Gerwyn Dal, who was only an inch or so shorter than Gruffudd Llwyd. I saw the two grin good-naturedly at each other. Although each had heard of the other, they had only met a fortnight ago and Rhys and I had watched closely to see whether there might be some animosity or, at least, rivalry now that they were almost constantly in each other's company. To our surprise they quickly became good friends, a bond of mutual respect clearly present.

'You can start withdrawing your troops as soon as you like, Rhys,' I said. 'Now, you know the drill, don't you?'

'Perfectly.'

I needed no further reassurance.

By the time the church clock struck noon, the Tudur brothers and all their men had left Ruthin and I sat on Llwyd y Bacsie on the spot where Rhys's marquee had been pitched the day before. *Y Cedyrn* sat on their mounts in three rows of twenty behind me. There was movement around the guardroom above the castle gatehouse and de Grey appeared and stepped onto the battlements encased in armour. There was a new swagger in his bearing, and when he hailed us his voice sounded supremely confident.

'Good afternoon, Glendower the Traitor. Well now… it seems that, at last, you have plucked up the courage to come in to town to face me. You are either a fool or you are besotted by all the compliments of your rabble. Tell me, you Welsh peasant, do you honestly believe that you and your little force of guards can take on the most senior of all the Marcher Lords and win? If so, let me tell you that you have made a fatal miscalculation, as I am about to prove to you.'

The listening crowd shouted excitedly at his words, and one group of men shouted loudest of all, urging the great lord to charge the rebels and destroy them. I made a mental note to compliment the Tudur brothers later on their skills in mob training. The stubby figure on the battlements seemed to grow in stature with every shout of encouragement.

'Tell me, my Lord.' I stopped to snigger. 'Is it not the case that you have refused my offer of single combat three times a day every day for weeks, proving to all your good burghers and your retainers over and over that you are a coward? Perhaps you would prefer an easier challenge? What if I were to ask you to show your horse-riding skills to the people of Ruthin. Perhaps you would consider mounting my own destrier, Llwyd y Bacsie, and displaying your acrobatic skills in jumping on and off a horse without touching the ground with your feet?'

There were roars of laughter from my men and the townspeople, for de Grey's unfortunate encounter with my horse a few years before had become common knowledge throughout the Marches. Even his own men standing on the furthest battlements seemed to be chuckling.

My words had a remarkable effect. He first emitted a great wordless roar and drew his sword so that the blade flashed in the sunlight. There was a brief silence as he fought to get the words out without success. I thought he might collapse from the sheer force of his rage. Then he found his voice.

'H... ho... how dare you speak to me like that. Do you not realise who you are talking to? Do you not know that the de Grey family were Norman nobles who fought alongside William the Conqueror at Hastings when your stupid forebears were living in mud huts, jabbering away in Welsh... savages... all of you! But now you have gone too far. Now you are going to feel the heat of my wrath and when I catch you, Glendower, I am going to cut you up into little pieces... slowly... so you will die a lingering death. It will take so long that the terrible agony will drive you mad. Do you hear me?'

Then the great lord, sword still swinging dangerously close to some of his men, turned and stormed away into the guardroom.

I hurriedly turned Llwyd's head, making pretence of great worry and concern and shouted to my men in a high-pitched voice to follow me at a gallop. We left the market square in some disorder as if we had no stomach for facing de Grey's wrath. We heard the contemptuous comments of the English burghers and the even louder insults of Rhys's 'crowd' as we galloped out of town and made for the safety of the woods. Looking back on reaching the trees, I could see de Grey leading a force of some 200 at the charge. They were made up of mounted archers and men-at-arms and they were only a few hundred yards behind us. I realised that he must have had the horses saddled and ready. I also realised, with satisfaction, that he had allowed his hurt pride to stifle his better judgement.

We followed a well-worn path through the trees towards a clearing. Even so, we were forced to reduce the horses to a slow canter and even to a trot in some places. Our pursuers would be forced to do the same so I was not particularly concerned. Rhys had done his work as I knew he would. A lone spotter would have seen us 'retreating' from Ruthin and would have warned our ambush of our coming. Finally, we swept into the clearing, cantering in single file through our grinning comrades to a prearranged position where a dozen grooms waited to tether our horses. We ran back to reinforce the ambushers and waited.

The tense silence barely lasted three minutes before we heard the muffled drumming of hooves and the first horsemen swung into view. I waited until the last possible moment so that we had at least thirty horsemen totally exposed in the large clearing before giving my archers the order to shoot.

The first row of fifty archers loosed their arrows in unison and the air was filled with the low, seemingly innocuous hiss of deadly projectiles hurtling towards their doomed targets. Then it was a scene from Hell as horses reared and screamed with arrows in their breasts and men dropped silently to the ground, dead before they left the saddle. Others dropped their weapons as the force of the arrows tore into their bodies, shattering bones and destroying vital organs as a prelude to a slow and cruel death. Yet others, simply unhorsed or wounded less seriously, picked themselves up and ran away – straight into the paths of other riders rushing forward, to be trampled under iron-clad horseshoes and left – shapeless bundles amid blood, gore and voided faeces. The new arrivals were met by a volley from the second row of archers firing over the heads of the first row as they kneeled to fix their next arrows. Again the slaughter was horrific. And again the unhorsed survivors ran unheeding into the paths of a new group of horsemen and died.

At last de Grey's forces realised that they were being massacred and the remainder dismounted out of our sight and crept forward warily through the undergrowth, led by grim-faced archers with longbows at the ready. I could imagine de Grey peppering them with choice insults and colourful curses.

There was silence once again in the clearing, now the scene of bloody slaughter with mangled bodies strewn around like the enactment of a nightmare.

'Get back… find cover quickly!' Rhys Gethin shouted urgently at our archers. As they did so, a fierce volley was released from the other side of the clearing and a dozen of our men were felled by enemy arrows. Arrows do not discriminate; they have only one purpose, and that is to kill. Again we heard the shouts and screams of pain and anguish. This time, however, these men were our friends and supporters, many had been companions through good and bad times for many years. Seconds before the others could reach the comparative safety of the undergrowth, another cloud of arrows darkened the sky briefly, and at least another eight of our archers were slaughtered.

As soon as the lucky ones had reached cover, scores of our hidden archers waiting for their moment shot a huge salvo into the greenery on the other side of the clearing. Despite shooting blind, the sheer number of arrows blanketed the greenery and the howls and shouts drifting across to our positions was proof that many of the enemy had felt the bite of the harbingers of death.

A new sound, like the low rumble of distant thunder, was suddenly audible and our men roared their approval as they realised that Rhys Tudur, with his large mounted force, was closing rapidly to attack de Grey and his men from the rear. At a brief shouted command from Rhys Gethin, small groups ran forward to assist six of our wounded men who were still crawling desperately towards safety while two rows, each of forty archers, lined up to finish off any of the Ruthin men who might, in desperation, attempt to escape from Rhys Tudur's onslaught by running back through the clearing. Then there came the sound of a vicious battle among the trees. The noise of metal on metal, shouts of encouragement and howls of pain came ever nearer and it was clear that de Grey's men were being swiftly vanquished. Then they came running out of the trees, their minds fixed solely on getting away from the savage assault of the men of Gwynedd. There was a momentary hesitation as the two rows of archers held back from releasing their arrows. The enemy was being pressed so hard that any arrows fired at them would inevitably hit Rhys Tudur's men as well. Again Rhys Gethin's voice rose above the tumult.

'Drop your bows. Draw your swords and attack at will!'

Immediately the archers raced forward to seal off the enemy's escape, short swords drawn and ready to spill blood. The melée in the clearing was brutal but short-lived. The English were surrounded and being systematically cut down. Soon they had been reduced to thirty or so and a captain, looking around in despair, shouted the order to surrender. As his comrades immediately dropped their weapons, officers of both Welsh forces shouted orders to stop fighting and, though it took a few of the struggling groups several minutes before they realised that the battle was over, the surrender was eventually concluded.

Despite the jubilation on our side, I ran forward for a closer look at the English survivors, feeling sick at heart, for I could see no sign of Reginald de Grey among them. Could he have been killed or had he somehow managed to escape? Without de Grey as a living prisoner the day's events would represent a pretty hollow victory. The first blood-stained archer I came upon was my youngest son, Maredudd, who grinned broadly when he saw me. I breathed a sigh of relief at the realisation that the blood that drenched his clothing was not his own.

'Well, Father,' he called, giving me a mischievous look. 'Bad luck… looks like you somehow missed all the action. Your clothes are spotlessly clean. Mother will be pleased.'

'Enough of your sarcasm, young man. Let's be serious, Maredudd. There is no sign of de Grey and that concerns me greatly. I want you to find the English captain who ordered the surrender. Hurry, find him and bring him to me, quick as you can.'

'This is not what we anticipated, my Prince. It looks as if our bird has flown.' Rhys Gethin's tone was sour. 'The men of Gwynedd were right behind him. How could they have failed to make capturing de Grey their priority?'

I looked at the impatient young man and, not for the first time, wondered whether one day, despite his tactical brilliance and leadership, his natural impetuosity would lead him to disaster.

'Patience, Rhys, as I have often impressed on you, is a virtue, particularly in a leader of men. I have sent Maredudd to bring me the English captain who surrendered. We will question him to see if he knows his master's whereabouts.'

'Give me five minutes with him, sire, and – believe me – he will talk!'

'That will not be necessary,' I responded coldly.

I looked at him and saw the barely concealed irritation. I sighed quietly. The hill man in him would never be civilised... which was a shame, for he was highly intelligent and a naturally gifted general. He was, however, intensely loyal to his mother's people and to their age-old religious beliefs, customs and traditions. Those very traits could be his undoing some day.

I saw Maredudd returning, accompanied by a tall, tough-looking man approaching middle age. The prisoner had a mass of curly black hair, greyish at the temples. His hands were tied behind his back and he walked with a distinct limp; I could see that his breeches were stained by a large patch of wet blood. I removed my helm and, as the man recognised me, he immediately stood to attention.

'Father, this is the prisoner you asked to see.'

'At ease both of you. Now then, captain, perhaps you would be good enough to state your name.' I kept my voice and my expression neutral for the moment.

'My name is William Middleton, sire. We fought together at the Battle of Ridge back in 1387. I don't expect you remember me for I was a raw recruit back then. But you were noticed by many for your exploits that day.'

'My word, William. So we were comrades in arms...' I smiled good-naturedly for a moment. 'Unfortunately a great deal has happened since that time, so today we find ourselves fighting in opposing armies...'

'A situation I regret,' the captain conceded.

I stared directly into the prisoner's eyes, searching for

any sign of guile. He held my stare. This, I decided, was an honourable man.

'Would you happen to know the whereabouts of your Lord of Ruthin, William? And if so, would you be prepared to help me find him by sharing that information?'

William smiled sardonically. 'And why would I do that to the man who pays my wages?'

This was too much for Rhys Gethin. 'If you value your miserable life, Englishman, you will tell us all you know and quickly, unless you want me to put out your eyes with red hot coals.'

'Enough, Rhys,' I snapped. 'As you well know, nobody who serves me puts anyone to torture. You will not repeat such words again in my presence if you want to remain a general in my army.'

I turned away, for I knew I would see smouldering resentment in Rhys's eyes and I was not at all sure I could control my desire to strike him if I did. Maredudd was staring at me in amazement. I rarely allowed my temper to get the better of me in public and it was certainly not my style to give a senior officer such a dressing down in front of his subordinates. William, though, seemed to find the situation amusing, for he was grinning hugely.

'You have no cause for concern on that score, sire. I have neither love nor respect for Reginald de Grey. I am actively seeking an opportunity to serve another lord, for I have had my fill of being insulted and undervalued by that oaf. I am quite happy to tell you that, at the first sign of our being attacked from the rear, de Grey and half a dozen of his cronies vanished into the forest heading south by east. My guess is that they were making a desperate dash for Chirk castle to seek the protection of his friend, Lord Talbot.'

'Thank you very much for your cooperation, William. May you find a worthy lord who will afford you proper respect. You are free to go.' I motioned Maredudd to untie him and escort him out of our camp.

Captain Middleton looked disbelievingly at me at first. He had fully expected to be held prisoner or even killed. When it finally dawned on him that he was being unconditionally released, he bowed to me in gratitude.

'You are indeed a prince, sire. Only the finest of a royal bloodline would act so graciously towards the retainer of a defeated opponent. I thank you for my life and my freedom and pledge that should we meet again as foes on a battlefield, I shall yield my weapons at once for, from this moment, my life is forfeit to you.'

He turned and left with Maredudd, still limping but with his back straight and his head held proud. I instructed a disgruntled Rhys Gethin to take a dozen men and ride to Ruthin in case the wily de Grey might have doubled back to his lair. Then I sought out my sons, Gruffudd and Madog, and with ten of my finest guards, went in pursuit of the fleeing Marcher Lord.

One of my elite guards, Arthur ap Bleddyn Foel, was an acclaimed tracker who, as a youth, had travelled with his elder brother Cadog to France, and later to Spain in search of adventure. They had fought as mercenaries for French and later for Castilian nobility. While serving on a Spanish warship off the coast of North Africa they had been trapped by a fleet of Arab slavers and captured. Later they were sold as slaves to a potentate of Alexandria in Egypt. Cadog had later been killed in a brawl with other slaves and Arthur, along with many of his Spanish comrades, had been sold in the Alexandrian slave market. The Caliph was a keen hunter and Arthur and several of his comrades had been taught the art of the tracker, for the Caliph needed scores of expert trackers to seek out wild animals for him to hunt.

Arthur searched the only two paths which our quarry could have taken out of the woods in a south-easterly direction. On a grassy bank after leaving the trees he discovered positive evidence of de Grey's departure along that route. He, or one of his companions, must have removed his helm, for a cloth arming cap, worn under the heavy helm to make it a little less uncomfortable, had been carelessly thrown away into the long grass. Arthur pronounced it still damp with sweat, then mounted his horse and led us at a canter south-eastwards as the sun sank a little lower in the sky behind us.

Some hours later we crested a low hill, and a mile or so ahead we saw a much bigger hill with its lower slopes heavily clad with stunted thorn and mountain ash. Arthur immediately turned his horse and signalled us to follow him some way back down the hill so that we were hidden from anyone who might be sheltering in the trees ahead. It was getting dark as we dismounted to discuss the situation.

'You are thinking that the thorny undergrowth ahead would provide ideal cover for an ambush should de Grey be nervous of possible pursuers, Arthur?' I ventured.

'If I were de Grey, my Prince, and with darkness encroaching, I would have been looking for a safe resting place for the past half-hour. And after today's debacle I would also have had the man at the tail of the column charged with keeping a keen eye out for possible pursuit. That position is the first we have seen since leaving the scene of battle which would provide concealment and a handy place to pick us off without warning.'

There was a chorus of agreement from several of my men.

'It sounds as if we all agree,' I smiled grimly. 'There is, of course, a chance that we are mistaken and by stopping here for the night we may be allowing the enemy to increase his lead over us. But that is a risk we will have to take. What I propose, though, is that we wait here and rest for a few hours, then make a wide detour around that hill in darkness and find somewhere on the other side where we can surprise them in the morning. And if we have made the wrong choice at least we will be that much further along the route than we would have been if camped here.'

Again there were murmurs of agreement. Fortunately it was a mild, dry spring evening, so we settled down to two hours' rest before moving on.

When we eventually set out on a wide detour of the hill there was heavy cloud cover obscuring moon and stars. In the inky darkness we were obliged to ride our horses in single file at a careful walk, maintaining absolute silence in case our voices should carry to an alert sentry. As we passed the base of the hill in a wide arc, the going got progressively softer, eventually becoming a soggy marsh sucking the hooves of our mounts almost to their fetlocks. I whispered the order to dismount and walk, both to ease the strain on the horses and to warm ourselves, for our bodies were getting stiff and cold. Gradually we made our way to the other side of the hill, and a few stars appeared through breaks in the cloud. We headed for the higher ground and eventually we were walking on a firmer surface. This side had the same tangled growth of thorn and rowan and we forced ourselves through it, leading the horses into a small clearing and a welcome rest to while away the few remaining hours before dawn.

I gave Maredudd the task of drawing up a rota for sentry duty and sent Ifor Foel, the most experienced campaigner in *Y Cedyrn*, with a younger man to the top of the hill so that they would have a vantage point to see movement in our direction from any camp on the lower slopes of the other hillside when the new day dawned.

I awoke the following morning, with Maredudd shaking me by my shoulders.

'Father, wake up, wake up! You and Arthur were correct in thinking that de Grey would have chosen to camp on the hill. He and six mounted men-at-arms are headed this way.'

I was awake in a trice, peppering Ifor Foel with questions. I learned quickly that he and his companion had been observing the general area where we suspected the Lord of Ruthin was camped since first light. After an hour or so they had heard voices calling to each other and laughing. Upon waking, de Grey and his men were clearly pretty confident that they were not being pursued, or, at least, that any pursuers must have misjudged their route. All they had to do was ride to the safety of Chirk castle and Lord Talbot. In the meantime our two observers had come down from the top of the hill to warn us. Maredudd and I, together with our ten guardsmen, quickly armed ourselves and collected our mounts.

We left the horses under guard some twenty yards in from Ifor's position and organised the ambush carefully. We were still eleven to their seven and the ten experienced guards strung their bows and stood patiently within the tree line, hidden from the relaxed group of horsemen walking their mounts casually towards us, and waited for my order. I felt exultant and in control. At last I had my sworn enemy, de Grey, who had caused me and mine so much grief over these past years, walking innocently into my arms. There was a singing in my ears and expectation in my heart; this man might well be the instrument of our salvation, providing the money we so desperately needed to present a serious challenge to Henry Bolingbroke.

They came ever closer, harnesses jingling and the fresh horses a trifle skittish, eager to expend energy. Reginald pulled viciously on the reins and swore at his mount as it attempted to start cantering. He muttered something and his men, three to his left and three to his right, laughed dutifully. When they were a mere twelve yards from the trees. I called out the order,

'Forward five paces and challenge!'

We all emerged from hiding in a line. The ten guards holding their bows at the ready with arrows notched caused startled consternation among the English riders.

'Halt and be perfectly still,' I snapped. 'Anyone going for his weapon or attempting to ride away is a dead man.'

They all stopped in shocked silence. For a moment everyone was still. Then de Grey began to chuckle, a dry humourless sound betraying his nervousness.

'Surely you mean everyone except me, Welshman. I'll wager your archers have been given clear instructions not to kill me… I'm far too valuable alive.' He reiterated his dry, mirthless chuckle, trying to buy time.

I turned to Maredudd and ordered him to arrest the Marcher Lord but, before he could make a move, de Grey tugged at the rein and wrenched his horse's head around before digging his spurs into the animal's flanks so that it squealed in pain and began to gallop back up the hill. My sons ran for their horses and de Grey's six henchmen desperately went for their weapons in the confusion. It was a final and mortal error, for they had hardly moved before they were swept off their mounts in a hail of arrows.

I screamed at my son to stand down and leave de Grey to me. One shrill whistle and, in seconds, Llwyd y Bacsie was at my side snorting in excitement. I leapt into the saddle and we set off in pursuit. I did not force the pace, for I knew that Llwyd could outrun and outlast the other horse. As our quarry disappeared over the crest of the hill I took the precaution of guiding Llwyd well to the left. I did not want to gallop over the crest straight into the path of a well-aimed arrow. I need not have worried however, for the great lord was intent on reaching the cover of the rowan trees smothered in their mass of creamy-white, spring blooms. I called for speed and Llwyd immediately lengthened her stride and we tore down the hillside, taking a risk on the uneven slope but eager to avoid a long game of hide-and-seek if we allowed him to reach trees ahead of us. We soon caught up with them as both man and horse appeared to be blowing hard and the horse seemed a trifle lame.

'Stop, de Grey… stop in the name of God or I will have to knock you over and that will be painful.'

'Go to Hell,' the Lord of Ruthin gasped, red-faced and breathing hard.

We were only thirty yards from the trees – I would only get one chance to unseat him. I decided on a move which Llwyd and I had used several times in battle.

'Get ready, girl… we're going to ram them.' I shouted the word several times. 'Ram… ram… ram him, girl… ram him…'

As we came up level with man and horse I could feel Llwyd y Bacsie tensing and she bared her teeth.

'Now Llwyd… noooowwww!' I only needed the lightest

touch on the rein to draw her towards the other horse and I steeled myself for the impending collision. We were within less than two feet when Llwyd lunged over in a precise and perfectly-timed movement smashing her shoulder into the area just behind the other horse's shoulder, using every ounce of her weight and power. At the same time I tugged at de Grey's mailed arm, pulling him towards us at the very moment his off-balance mount staggered away in the opposite direction. For the second time in his life, Reginald de Grey suffered a painful unseating due to skilful action by Llwyd y Bacsie.

My companions had cantered over the ridge just in time to marvel at Llwyd's strength and skill and to witness the unfortunate lord's abrupt fall. I could hear their delighted laughter, but I was far more concerned for de Grey as he had not moved since hitting the ground. As I anxiously approached, he groaned loudly and struggled to a sitting position, clumsily attempting to remove his helm. I almost felt sorry for him, until I reminded myself of all the harm he had inflicted upon me and on hundreds of ordinary Welsh folk. Now it was payback time and I was going to squeeze his considerable bag of wealth as near to dry as I possibly could.

4

'ELEVEN THOUSAND MARKS? Did you say eleven...
thousand?'

My brother Tudur stared at me. A ripple of amazed gasps ran around the heavy oak table where we sat in the sumptuous dining room of John Trevor, Bishop of St Asaph. I looked at the tall, thin, scholarly form of the man seated opposite me. His real name was Ieuan Trefor but he had found it easier to be accepted by the English hierarchy of church and state as John Trevor. He had served the King and the Pope and was a highly educated and erudite man. Soon he would have to make the most important decision of his life; whether to remain an ambitious religious and political figure in the heady world of the senior English clergy or to turn his back on a successful career and become again Ieuan Trefor, cultured, patriotic Welshman, embracing the dangers of our cause. Already a respected thinker and philosopher, Bishop Trevor had a quick and ready wit that endeared him to many. He obviously found the startled gasps a source of amusement for his eyes twinkled as he struggled not to smile.

'My friends, let me assure you, the sum is not set too high.' The cleric spoke in a quiet but authoritative voice.

'Owain and I have been doing a little study of de Grey's financial circumstances. We have been helped, in confidence, by a few key individuals at Court, in Parliament, and one or two in the Royal Treasury who make it their business to know the financial state of leading individuals. We have learnt that in addition to his considerable fortune and lands as a Marcher Lord, de Grey owns extensive lands in Ireland on which he pays taxes to the Crown. He also owns an imposing manor and estate at Harleigh in Kent. I had news only this morning that the Bishop of London has been given power of attorney to sell the manorial estate in order to raise money towards de Grey's ransom. In addition, let us not forget that de Grey is a great favourite with Bolingbroke, and one of the relatively few nobles Henry can trust.'

'And as you know,' I broke in, 'Henry has had several people he suspected of supporting us, including some priests, executed without fair trial. The capture of Reginald de Grey has clearly upset him and he will be keen to ensure the safe return of one of his few friends at any price. For once he will not have to contribute much, if anything, to the ransom. No, de Grey himself will have to bear that burden and 11,000 marks is rather more than he will be able to raise. He will have to borrow a pretty daunting amount. One thing is certain, he will never be a rich man again, so he will no longer have the strength to be any kind of military threat to us. What is more, we are not yet sufficiently in control to set up and administer a fair system of taxation to replace the crippling taxes which the English, thank goodness, can no longer collect in most of Wales. Our attacks on their tax collectors have seen to that, for they do not have large numbers of troops available to defend them. This ransom, however, is essential to tide us over so we can pay and feed our retainers, buy weapons and pay informers until we are in a position to set up a new and fairer source of income.'

'What news of de Grey?' Gwilym Tudur enquired brightly. 'Has he learned to behave himself yet or is he still allowing his tongue to be his worst enemy?'

'Reginald was luckier this time than on the previous occasion we saw him fall off a horse. According to Ednyfed, despite considerable bruising in some uncomfortable places, Lord de Grey of Ruthin has suffered no broken bones. His good fortune, however, has not tempered his tongue. I left him in the tender care of Gruffudd Llwyd, confined in a small but reasonably comfortable chamber in Dolbadarn. I have since received a message from Gruffudd to say that, because of the prisoner's foul mouth, he has been removed to a small stone storehouse next to the pigsties. He will stay in that malodorous hut in the stinking summer heat until he learns some manners. He has also been reduced to half-rations until he learns his lesson.'

I looked around the table at all the smiling faces. There was little sympathy in this company.

I thought, and not for the first time, how fortunate I was to have so many leading members of the Welsh clergy supporting me, though it was essential to keep that support covert for the time being. In addition to the Bishop, the Dean of St Asaph, Hywel Gethin or Howel Kyffin as he was known within the Church, had played an official role in my proclamation ceremony, and other cultured rising stars such as Gruffudd Yonge, regarded as a future Bishop of Bangor, was a firm supporter. Some of my most hot-headed supporters were the Cistercians and the Franciscans. None was more enthusiastic than the Abbot of Llantarnam Abbey in Monmouthshire, Siôn ap Hywel.

We had realised that the capture of de Grey would ruffle feathers in London and cause alarm among the English in

Wales and beyond, as well as raising my profile in the eyes of my own countrymen. However, none of us had expected the reaction to be as dramatic as it proved to be. Almost overnight I found myself being treated with a new respect by both friend and foe. No longer was Owain Glyndŵr some guerrilla leader causing problems for the King in Wales and instilling fear in the English border counties. Overnight I had become, for many, a credible Prince of the Welsh, capable of capturing leading Marcher Lords and forcing the King of England to send representatives to discuss ransom terms as he would have done in a conflict with any other king or ruler. Psychologically it was a huge step forward in our struggle for freedom. It was also to inject substantial wealth into the empty princely coffers.

A week after the clandestine meeting in the Bishop's home, I received a message from my spymaster, Robert Puleston, warning me to expect a missive from Bolingbroke inviting me or my representatives to a meeting with a group of his knights at a place of my choosing to 'discuss' the terms of de Grey's ransom. Several of these knights were known cronies of de Grey, including Sir Hugh Hals, Sir William de Willoughby and Sir William de Zouch.

I bade the messenger wait while I had my new secretary, Dafydd ap Gruffudd ap Rhisiart, write a brief reply. Dafydd was one of scores of Welsh students from Oxford and Cambridge who had left their studies to flock to my banner after our victory at Hyddgen. I informed Bolingbroke that three of my retainers, headed by Ednyfed ap Siôn, would meet three of his at the Boar's Head, a hostelry in the small hamlet of Pwll y Wrach, or the Witch's Pool, on the road from Chester to Flint. His delegation would be informed of the terms, over which there was no room for discussion.

Half the ransom would be paid no later than a month hence when de Grey would be freed, on condition that his eldest son took his place as hostage until the monies had been paid in full.

Ednyfed and his companions, Gruffudd Llwyd and Dafydd, my secretary, trotted their horses into the stable yard of the Bull's Head at tea time on the appointed day. They were glad to have their mounts led to the stables to be cleaned and fed after travelling along muddy tracks in torrential rain for hours. The King's representatives had arrived an hour before, equally drenched. An hour or so later, after having their clothes dried, Ednyfed led my team into a small, poorly-lit room on the first floor which boasted only one small window and a solitary candle flickering uncertainly in the centre of the table. The two men sitting at the table introduced themselves as Sir William de Zouch and Sir William de Roos. The latter introduced a shadowy figure sitting by the fire as John Gaunt, their secretary. My delegation introduced themselves and took seats around the table.

Sir William de Roos, a balding, middle-aged, tough-looking man with a livid scar disfiguring most of his face, was the first to speak. His voice was surprisingly soft.

'Well now, I don't think we need indulge in polite twaddle when we are so clearly mortal enemies, so I suggest we get on with our business here at once, though I hope we can conduct it with some civility.' He stopped to stare coldly around the table for some reaction.

'That is fine by me.' Ednyfed's voice was relaxed but he felt glad of the dagger hidden in his boot, for this de Roos was clearly a dangerous man. 'Do you have any messages from Henry Bolingbroke before we state the amount of Earl de Grey's ransom and the details of its eventual transfer to Prince Owain?'

'Listen to me, Welshman, and listen well. If you value your life you will refer to our sovereign as King Henry from now on.' William de Roos's voice trembled with anger and his lips were compressed into a thin line after he had spoken. 'Now what has the rebel, Glendower, got to say to us?'

'I have listened and now, Englishman, if you value de Grey's life, you will listen well also,' Ednyfed responded. 'I shall refer to Henry as King when you stop calling Prince Owain "the rebel, Glendower".'

There was a short, tense silence, broken by a placatory laugh from the other knight, Sir William de Zouch. 'Come now, gentlemen. Let us remember that we are engaged in a weighty matter here which can in no way be resolved by quarrelling.'

The three Welshmen turned to view de Zouch with interest. They saw a man of average build in his early thirties with curly, light brown hair worn down to his shoulders. His face would have been good looking were it not for his eyes. They were a watery blue and constantly swivelling between the three Welshmen, somehow managing not to look at anyone directly. They were the shifty eyes of a crafty man who could not be trusted, Ednyfed decided. A quick glance across at Gruffudd, and Dafydd confirmed that they were of the same opinion.

'I agree,' he responded, turning back to look de Roos in the eye. 'Let us get on with the business in hand. The ransom demand is a straightforward one. Reginald de Grey will be released on payment of half the amount of the ransom. However, that will have to be paid one month from today. In order for de Grey to be released, we will firstly need his eldest son to be delivered to us. He, in turn, will be given his freedom as soon as the remainder of the ransom is paid.'

'All that sounds reasonable except, without knowing the sum you ask for, we cannot confirm that the first half can be raised in one month. So, how much is this ransom?' asked de Zouch, a contrived grin accompanying the honeyed words.

Speaking for the first time Gruffudd Llwyd's words were brief but blunt.

'Prince Owain has asked us to point out that the ransom amount is not subject to discussion or negotiation. The sum required is 11,000 marks.'

For a second there was an incredulous expression on the faces of the two knights. The shadowy John Gaunt, who had been silent, suddenly chortled, then laughed aloud and clapped his hand on his knee.

'Perhaps Glendower is a prince after all,' he gasped at last. 'Only royalty would have the gall to ask for such a sum.'

The knights were in no mood for laughter. After spluttering for several seconds, face red and eyes glaring furiously, Sir William de Roos at last found his voice.

'Good God. That is disgraceful… you are totally dishonourable men… bandits… Why, can you not see… even the King would have difficulty raising that amount? It… it would reduce Reginald to penury for life!' He banged the table in frustration.

'No one has been more of a bandit than de Grey himself.' Gruffudd's voice had taken on a dangerous edge. 'For years he has been doing his best to reduce our Prince to penury and has been responsible for scores of tenants dying of hunger. He has also brought poverty upon others which has to be seen to be believed. Do you think we care a damn if he now gets a taste of it!'

'Hmmm. So, if you live by the sword you must be prepared to die by the sword. Well, there is a certain logic to that view,' John Gaunt said quietly, as if talking more to himself than to the others.

'Believe me, we have given this ransom much thought. We have also been studying the probable value of de Grey's various holdings in Wales, England and Ireland. While we accept that he would not be able to afford the entire sum he could raise a goodly proportion of it. As for the rest, he could surely rely on his good friends, yourselves included, to provide the remainder and he, being an honourable man, would pay you back as and when he could…' Ednyfed paused with a whimsical smile on his face. 'Furthermore, ridding de Grey of his wealth would ensure that he is no longer a problem militarily, as he would be in no position to retain large numbers of armed men.'

'By the bones of my ancestors, but this is insufferable. You will not get away with this. We refuse your terms. We will talk further when you set a reasonable sum for this ransom. This meeting is closed.' Sir William de Roos was still beside himself with rage and Ednyfed could see an artery alongside the hideous scar on his face pumping furiously.

'No, de Roos, the meeting is not closed.' Gaunt had the voice of a very young man but now it reverberated around the chamber like a whiplash. 'This is a ransom which the King wants paid. He wishes his friend, de Grey, to be freed as soon as possible. Gentlemen, we accept all your terms in the name of King Henry of England. One half of the sum will be brought to your stronghold in Snowdonia under heavy guard from Chester one month from now. Reginald de Grey's eldest son, also called Reginald, will be exchanged for his father. The remainder will be paid as soon as it can be raised.'

The two English knights sat quietly, heads bowed. Neither showed the slightest desire to argue with the young man.

'I thank you, John Gaunt,' said Ednyfed respectfully as he and his companions stood up to leave. Ten minutes later they were cantering westward along the still-muddy road, although the rain had ceased and their surroundings were bathed in bright moonlight. Half an hour later they left the road and walked their horses along a winding footpath until they reached the holding of Dyfrig Ddistaw (Dyfrig the Silent), a fervent supporter of Glyndŵr whose teenage son had been killed at the battle of Hyddgen.

They left their mounts in the care of Dyfrig's eldest son and as they turned towards the small, thatched house, Gruffudd stopped and turned to the other two.

'That was a strange meeting and no mistake. Did you see how the two knights succumbed so completely to the wishes of their so-called secretary? I think I know who that cocky young fellow is and I suppose you have both guessed as well.'

Dafydd laughed softly. 'He had me wondering throughout but that last show of control proved it beyond doubt.'

'I don't wish to sound superior, gentlemen, but his identity did come to my mind as soon as we sat at that table and the young pup kept himself in the shadows by the fire.' Ednyfed allowed himself a self-congratulatory grin. 'Then, when they gave his name as John Gaunt I knew I had guessed correctly. The youngster's grandfather was none other than the first Duke of Lancaster, universally known as John of Gaunt, and, of course, father of Henry IV… in his day the wealthiest and most hated man in England. If that was so, then the young man has to be young Prince Henry, son of

Bolingbroke and regarded by the English as the Prince of Wales.'

'By all that is holy,' Dafydd breathed in wonder. 'Who would believe it? But we have just been in conference with a youngster who will one day be King of England. It is no wonder those knights deferred to him so quickly…'

5

W E WERE POSITIONED in a narrow valley in the eastern foothills of Snowdonia. I had chosen the spot with care. There were 200 archers concealed in the straggly woods on either side of the valley and another 200 heavily-armed, mounted men in full view at my back. Llwyd y Bacsie was standing stock-still with ears pointed forward. She had become aware of the sounds and smells of many horses and riders closing in on us and she was alert and ready to carry out any manoeuvre I might require. There was a slight rasping sound as I loosened my sword in its scabbard and I sensed the increased tension among the cavalry behind me.

It was six weeks since the meeting at the Boar's Head and we were waiting for Henry Hotspur and some 200 mounted soldiers from Chester bearing the first instalment of de Grey's ransom, slightly later than agreed. My officers and I had decided that allowing the English to bring the money to Dolbadarn was not a good idea. Far better to meet them several miles away in the foothills to exchange the Lord of Ruthin for the first ransom payment in a chosen spot which they would be unfamiliar with. I had also taken the precaution of leaving de Grey with a dozen of my personal guard a mile or so behind us. They had orders to take him straight back to Dolbadarn at any sign of conflict between us and Hotspur's men. I was not unduly concerned that the English might attempt to wrest de Grey from us without parting with the money. I had met Hotspur in a few clandestine meetings in the weeks before Hyddgen and found him an honourable man. In fact, we had got on well together. Of course his master, the King, was a different proposition so I had come prepared for any eventuality.

The sounds of the English cavalry were now increasing in volume as I waited for them to appear around a bend in the rocky road some 400 yards away. I turned to my mounted support and raised my arm. Then I faced forward and raised my arm, first to my left and then to my right, to ready the hidden bowmen. A lone rider appeared, leading the armed English force around the bend. As soon as he saw us he shouted a warning to his men and called a halt.

The reaction was understandable for they had not expected to be faced by armed men in this area. I raised my arm again, this time in greeting and pressed my knees into Llwyd y Bacsie's flanks so that she began walking slowly towards the Englishmen. I heard Hotspur shout to his men to relax but maintain vigilance before he began walking his horse in my direction.

As we approached each other I could see signs of irritation on his face. He was clearly not a man for surprises. I smiled broadly and offered a warm greeting using his family name.

'Greetings, my Lord Percy. For once I face you and an English force with no acrimonious intent. I came to meet you in a neutral spot thinking to shorten your journey a little.'

'That is most kind of you, Owain.' There was only a hint of sarcasm in his words. Then grinning, he added, 'Acrimonious intent or not, I would bet all my worldly goods that you have infested the woods on either side with archers to ensure we keep the peace.'

'I would not say infested,' I grinned in return. 'Let us say that there are a few in the trees to ensure fair play.'

The grin slowly vanished to be replaced by a mock-hurt expression.

'I would have thought that after our unofficial meetings last year you would have learned that I am not one to stoop to treachery.'

I felt myself flush with embarrassment, for I divined that the expression covered genuine disappointment at my actions.

'I am sorry for treating you in this way, Hotspur. I assure you I am well aware that you are an honourable man. My actions have more to do with distrust of Bolingbroke and the fact that this deal is of crucial importance to our cause. I could leave nothing to chance in dealing with a snake like the present English King.'

There was a short silence between us.

'I thank you for your kind words. Believe me, I would have done exactly the same in your shoes, now that I think of it.' He was smiling again. 'I would imagine that de Grey is some distance from this place at present. I see from your face that I guess correctly. Very well, I'll have my men bring the sacks containing the ransom here so that your people can count the contents to ensure that I have brought the correct amount... In the meantime, perhaps you would be good enough to send for de Grey while I hand over his son to your safe keeping.'

In little more than an hour the various transactions had been concluded to our mutual satisfaction. The only unhappy people were de Grey and his son. The latter was mortified at having to volunteer for incarceration so that his father could be free. The father was still angry at having suffered the ignominy of capture and devastated by the huge ransom I had insisted upon. As he was led past me on horseback but with his hands still tied in front of him, he glared at me, spat on the ground and growled.

'You have used me very badly, Glendower. Be warned, for I intend to pay you back in kind one day. I shall capture you in battle and put you through far worse treatment before you die an agonising death.'

I smiled at him.

'Don't be so tedious, de Grey. There is nothing more pathetic than an impotent lord trying to make threats which he is in no position to deliver. I have made certain that it will take you the rest of your life to pay off your debts. You will never have the means to raise a credible armed force again. You will be forever weak and ineffectual. I have destroyed you and you have only your own avarice to blame for that.'

I motioned the young guard leading de Grey's horse to hurry him over to the English and the last I heard were more spluttered threats being spat out at me, but I turned to Hotspur and ignored him.

Hotspur seemed to be enjoying the little confrontation.

'Poor old Reginald... You have certainly ended his influence and his usefulness to the King. He can splutter all he likes, for he will no longer cut any kind of figure other than that of a foolish old man.'

'Is it true that you have had to carry out your duties in north Wales at your own expense, Hotspur?'

'So far, yes. Despite many letters entreating Henry to send me monies to pay my men's wages and other costs, he has not sent me a penny. In truth, I am getting very disillusioned and if he does not pay up soon I will have to return to Northumberland and leave the onerous and expensive business of keeping order in north Wales to others.'

'It sounds to me as if the man does not deserve your loyalty,' I said sympathetically. 'Though I cannot deny that I am the cause of most of your costly endeavours,' I grinned wickedly.

He laughed easily.

'At least you are an adversary I have learned to respect… a word which does not feature in my relations with Bolingbroke.'

'Well, who knows…? The day may come when our stars will coincide.'

I paused before looking him straight in the eye, 'And we could, perhaps, operate as allies rather than as foes.'

Hotspur's eyes locked on mine and he gave an almost imperceptible nod of the head. I leant over Llwyd's neck and reached out. He clasped my hand in his and we shook hands firmly. Then, without another word, he turned his destrier and trotted back to his column, shouting out a string of orders. He rode away around the bend, head held high, the muscled shoulders full square, followed gradually in disciplined formation by his men.

As I mulled over the possibilities which would open up for us if we could form an alliance with the redoubtable House of Percy, I was blissfully unaware that this was the last time I would ever meet him.

6

I KNELT AT the holy well on the northern side of the church of St Mary on a hill called Brynglas near Pilleth. This ancient church, mentioned in the Doomsday Book, was originally dedicated to the Welsh St Cynllo as early as the fifth century, when England and the rest of Europe had yet to be converted to Christianity. Like hundreds of similar churches, it had been rededicated by the Normans to saints such as Mary, John or Michael.

On a stifling hot afternoon, 21st June 1402, I knelt, like hundreds of pilgrims before me, in reverence at the well, famous for its powers to heal all manner of eye ailments, and drank deeply of its ice-cold, pure waters. I would need all my faculties highly tuned on the morrow when we would almost certainly be facing a formidable army led by young Edmund Mortimer.

Following the release of de Grey on payment of half his ransom, I had gathered a sizeable army and spent several active weeks in Maelienydd, which the English call Radnorshire, attacking the lands and castles of the Mortimers. Until now I had steered clear of antagonising them, for the Mortimers owned more land on both sides of the Welsh-English border than any of the other Marcher Lords. Moreover, they were of royal blood and Edmund Mortimer had a stronger claim to the English throne than Henry IV himself. His nephew, another Edmund, and still a child, had an even stronger claim to that throne, which is why Bolingbroke had taken the little boy into his charge, the better, no doubt, to act as guardian and therefore nip in the bud any rebellion in favour of the young Earl of March by nobility who favoured the Mortimers.

Now, however, with nearly 2,000 trained soldiers to back me, and the wherewithal to pay them regular wages, I felt confident enough to show even the powerful Mortimers that I was prepared to take them on in pursuit of an independent Wales where everyone would have the same rights before the law. In fact, their Marcher castles were far easier targets than the ring of mainly coastal royal castles which were immensely strong and mostly capable of being reinforced and supplied from the sea. Indeed several of the Marcher castles were in a rather neglected state. Their owners had never had to defend them and had seen little point in spending large amounts of money ensuring they were adequately preserved. The whole area had been firmly under their control for more than a century.

Our advance into Maelienydd had been swift and successful. Descending on a series of castles like ravenous wolves on sheep in winter, we had taken and pillaged a string of Mortimer fortresses including Cwm Aran, Cnwclas, Bleddfa and Cefnllys. Churches paying tithes to the English were also sacked. By the time we reached the Knighton area morale was sky-high, for we had concluded a series of outstandingly successful attacks and were well blessed with booty, several senior Mortimer officers who would be ransomed, a plentiful supply of food and enough cattle, sheep and victuals to keep us fed for weeks. We had suffered very little injury and no deaths.

We were enjoying the beef of Maelienydd at supper in our camp a few miles west of Knighton one evening when my spymaster and brother-in-law, Robert Puleston, rode in with a small escort bringing important news.

I instructed my seneschal, Iwan Goch, to arrange a good meal for the members of Robert's escort and invited the spymaster to join me and a small group of senior officers at my table to share in a jar of good French wine and a generous plateful of succulent roast beef straight from the spit.

I was familiar with Robert's penchant for good food, and waited patiently before opening the formal conversation until he had eaten his fill and offered an appreciative belch or two in between hearty draughts of red wine.

'It has been a month of victories and the sharing of much spoil, Robert. We are all extremely content but my instincts tell me that you are carrying news which I have been awaiting for the past week or two…'

'As ever, your instincts serve you well, brother-in-law. Edmund Mortimer is furious about the damage you have inflicted upon his lands, castles, churches and tenants. For the past two weeks he has been in urgent conference with the great and the good of Herefordshire. He now has an army of more than 3,000 at his back and is on the point of making a determined attempt to search you out and destroy you.' Robert belched again.

'And this army you speak of. What sort of army is it? Are we speaking of yokels with scythes and pitchforks or is it a body of professionals who need to be given respect?'

'Believe me, my Prince, this is an army which needs to be given the utmost respect. Not only is it a professional force but it includes many of the best military leaders in England. It is led by the Sheriff of Herefordshire, Sir Kinard de la Bere. Several other leading knights such as Sir Walter Devereux of Weobley and Lyonshall castles, Sir Robert Whitney of Whitney-on-Wye castle, Lord Kinnersley and Sir Thomas Clanvowe are present and have supplied troops. They have all been joined at Ludlow by Mortimer's archers.'

'Then we have some serious thinking to do.' Ednyfed ap Siôn's voice was tinged with concern. 'We are considerably outnumbered by professional troops led by a number of experienced, battle-hardened knights, unlike the very ordinary and under-strength garrisons we have disposed of recently.'

I glanced around the table. My three sons, Gruffudd, Madog and Maredudd were all looking expectantly at me. Ednyfed was wearing a concerned frown, while Gruffudd Llwyd and Rhys Ddu were looking at each other as if the news of the enemy army's competence had surprised them. Only Rhys Gethin was wearing a slight but unconcerned smile as he waited for guidance as to whether to speak or defer to me.

'Before I comment on this situation I would like to hear Rhys Gethin's views. What say you, Rhys?' I smiled in Rhys's direction.

The usually volatile Rhys seemed to have taken the news surprisingly calmly. He grinned at everyone.

'There is no doubt that we face a serious challenge here. But then, it was always so. When have we ever challenged an English army which did not outnumber us heavily? And whatever else we may think of the English, it has to be said that their competence in military matters is second to none. Their armies, at their best, really are well-organised, professional and brave. You will rarely encounter a tougher lot. Having said all that, there is no need to feel overawed. We are from a different tradition. We have different strengths.

We need not fear comparison in terms of bravery, for we are also renowned for that. We are best known for the speed of our lightly-armed cavalry and archers. We rely on the accuracy of the longbow, the speed of our attacks and a deep well of cunning which is as important as any other attribute in battle, if not more so. Nevertheless, we need to find ways of evening out the odds. The first necessity is to find a favourable position to meet them… a location which will slow them down and, preferably, force them to attack us uphill. If, as I would expect, they march up the wide valley of the Lugg, then I think I know a place which could give us the advantages I mentioned. Perhaps, sire, you would allow me to take you there so that you can form your own opinion of its suitability?'

Before responding I turned to Robert. 'Do you think the valley of the river Lugg is a likely route for Mortimer to use?'

'It would be the obvious and easiest for him. I have no hard evidence that it will be his chosen path into Wales, of course. However, I have spotters looking out for his movements and once he starts marching from Ludlow we will soon know his intentions. But there are other dangers I have to bring to your attention. As you are aware, the siege of Harlech castle is ongoing and Hotspur has been instructed by the King to send a force of 500 archers and 200 pikemen from Chester to relieve it. Further, he has ordered Hotspur to provide whatever support he can to Mortimer's forces. We know that even after sending 500 archers to Harlech he has at least another 1,000 at his command in Chester, together with several hundred light cavalry. It is not clear whether these forces are to join up with Mortimer before he finds you Owain, or whether they are to act independently. I have men in Chester as well on the lookout for any developments.'

These disclosures evoked murmurs of concern around the table, mingled with plaudits for Robert's thorough information as well as his competent response to each situation.

I decided that it was a moment for strong leadership and a show of quiet confidence in our ability to deal with the various threats.

'Gentlemen, first may I compliment you all on your actions these past weeks. Apart from the considerable material damage and havoc we have caused, it would seem that we have also hurt English pride. And now, not surprisingly, they are making considerable efforts in their search for revenge. They are also under pressure from a frightened populace, particularly in the English border counties, as they hear how we are roaming the Marches waging war at will, with the English authorities having no apparent means of stopping us. What will the Welsh do next? If nothing is done to stop them they will invade the fruitful plains of England in search of more and richer spoil… that is the cry!'

I paused to gauge the reaction to my words around the table and was pleased to see nodding heads and smiling faces. Encouraged, I continued in the same vein.

'Rhys Gethin is absolutely correct in saying that we need to find means of evening out the odds as we are clearly outnumbered. Rhys, you and I will travel to inspect your favoured site in the morning. We do have another card to play against Mortimer too. The vast majority of his archers are also his tenants. And they include hundreds of longbowmen from lands on the Welsh side of the border. I believe they could be tempted to change sides if we could find a way to appeal to their Welsh lineage, the pride in their rich and ancient heritage, and loyalty to their native Prince.'

There were several exclamations of support. I held up my hand and said, 'Yes, I shall have to think on that and see what we can dream up as a practical plan to try and win over the Welsh members of the enemy's company of archers. Turning to the siege of Cricieth, there is not much we can do to help Rhys Tudur and our Gwynedd friends who are attempting to capture that redoubtable fortress. They will hear of the impending English relief force in plenty of time to retire into the mountains. The Chester archers will only be able to stay for a few weeks before the costs of maintaining them will force Bolingbroke to signal a return to base. Once they are gone we can besiege the castle once more. As for the suggestion that Hotspur is to lead another strong force from Chester in support of Mortimer… I am convinced that Percy will do no such thing.'

I smiled as they all vied with each other to question my statement. Once more I raised my hand for silence.

'Believe me, my friends, Hotspur is sure to find good reason not to do that at present.'

'Are you sure about that, brother-in-law?' Robert sounded extremely sceptical. 'After all, Hotspur is married to Mortimer's sister, Elizabeth, and failing to give military support to Mortimer will not serve Hotspur well in such a circumstance.'

'Well, of course I cannot be absolutely certain that a force from Chester will not join Mortimer's attack. I can only say that Percy and I have had a few secret meetings recently. Those discussions lead me to think that it may yet be in his interests in the longer term to avoid attacking us at present.'

I let my eyes rove around the table, looking levelly at each individual in turn, leaving them in no doubt of my confidence in my own assertion.

Rhys Gethin and I left camp at dawn and rode to Pilleth, arriving at Brynglas before the powerful late June sun had reached its full potential on that still, oppressive day. After circling the base of the hill we walked our horses up to the church of St Mary on the crest and slaked our own and our horses' thirst at the famous well. During our inspections we noticed that on the northern side of the hill there was a wide depression in the land behind the church where hundreds of men could easily be hidden from an enemy travelling up the Lugg valley from the south or south-west. We spent some time on and around Brynglas working on a battle plan. Then, in mid-afternoon, a messenger from Robert Puleston came galloping towards us with news of Mortimer's departure from Ludlow at dawn that morning. His army was marching in a direction which would bring it straight up the wide Lugg valley directly towards Brynglas.

I began to plan my strategy for the coming battle. I felt the strange, queasy feeling in the pit of my stomach. It always hit me in the hours before the conflict. It would not leave me now until the fight was over but would gradually increase, bringing with it nervousness and the odd twinge of fear. This, in turn, would slowly develop into a steely resolve. My mind would blank out everything other than thoughts of battle. It would channel my thoughts to our strategy, tactical planning, our responses to any and all eventualities, and these would be run through again and again until my responsibility as supreme leader took over my whole being. After that I would switch my mind to my personal contribution to the struggle. There was no room for fear now – I was a fiend drawn from the depths of Hell… a machine of war. And when battle was joined I would flex my muscles, grip my sword, harden all my finer feelings and transform myself into a cold-blooded killer, something less than human. Then, with Llwyd y Bacsie carrying me with skill and pride, I would charge into the melée, the blade of my sword whispering chilling promises of death to the enemy as I waved it above my head.

It had been dark a good hour when Gruffudd Llwyd and I entered the camp of Mortimer's archers on the left flank of the greater army's base for the night. No one paid any attention to us as we trudged wearily among the makeshift tents and cooking fires. We were both dressed as archers in the coarse clothing of poor farmers. Our bows were stout but showing signs of long use and our arrows were packed into worn and frayed quivers. For all the world we looked like two latecomers catching up with their comrades. I had called for Gruffudd Llwyd as soon as our army arrived at Brynglas. I also ensured that our camp was established on the northern slopes of the hill, safely hidden from anyone travelling up the valley. I placed sentries at the church who duly reported an hour before dusk that a large army had marched along the banks of the Lugg to a position some three miles from the foot of Brynglas hill, and were now setting up camp for the night. A little before dusk Gruffudd and I, disguised as archers, had slipped around the base of the hill and made our way there.

A thin man stood by one of the fires, his back to us. He was obviously an officer. I walked up to him.

''Scuse me sir, sorry for bein' late gettin' here like, but

could you show me and my friend where the Welsh lot are camped?'

The officer turned. He was obviously aware of his audience seated around the fire in fine humour, eating freshly-cooked meat, and of his own authority as an officer. He was of average height but wished to be taller, for his feet were encased in built-up boots. His main characteristics seemed to be a thin aquiline nose, and a protruding forehead which did little to enhance his appearance. He was a foot shorter than me, while Gruffudd loomed over him. This too seemed to displease him, for his answer to my query was given in a raised, waspish voice which attracted the attention of several of his men.

'How can I possibly excuse you when I do not even know who you are?'

'Please forgive me, sir.' I made a pretence at a nervous shuffle. 'I am Elwyn ap Dafydd Fugail and my companion is Gruffudd Bleddfa. We are sheep farmers when not doing duty as longbowmen for our lord. We were up in the hills and did not hear of the muster until yesterday afternoon, but we have come here as fast as we could.'

'Humph ! You bloody Welsh tell so many bloody lies in that weird accent of yours, it is difficult to know when to believe you and when not to.' Several of his men guffawed in agreement.

'On my life sir, I am…' I began to stutter but he was suddenly bored with the situation.

'All right, all right,' he interrupted, raising his hand wearily. 'What do I care anyway. You will find your uncouth comrades on the extreme left of the archers' encampment. Now get out of my sight before I decide to discipline you for dereliction of duty.'

Gruff and I dutifully moved quickly on and we were soon in friendlier surroundings where the men sat around their fires eating hungrily and conversing in Welsh. It was a relief to be surrounded by the comforting sounds of our own people. We were immediately offered meat and small beer. We sat beneath a venerable oak, resting our backs against its gnarled old trunk to have our supper, a short distance from a group of archers. They looked over in our direction raising their hands and calling out in greeting.

After a while a burly fellow got up and walked confidently over to us. We guessed he must be the leader of the group. He introduced himself as Llŷr Fychan, and I quickly assessed him as a seasoned warrior but had clearly not been well briefed about the current campaign, a fact which irked him. Llŷr, clearly hoping we might have information about the campaign, started plying us with questions.

'Well lads, late you may be but I dare say you know more about this campaign than I do, like as not.' He glanced quickly from Gruff to me then back again, eager for information.

'I'd have thought it pretty straightforward,' Gruff said, tucking into a chunk of hot roast beef. 'I mean, we all know that Owain Glyndŵr has been creating mayhem in Maelienydd for weeks. You don't need to be a great scholar to realise that Edmund Mortimer has had enough and wants to sort out Glyndŵr's rebellion once and for all.'

'Humph! He also knows that the King and Prince Hal, not to mention Hotspur, have all had a go at Glyndŵr and he has outwitted and out-manoeuvred them every time. Owain uses the terrain to his advantage, though he will never be able to match the English military's strength in numbers or in funds to wage war, yet Mortimer seems not to have learned any lessons from the struggle. Here we are with a large, experienced army boasting heavy cavalry which the Welsh have never had, lumbering along the Lugg valley as if he fully expects his enemies to meet him in a pitched battle. No, no. Whatever else he may be, our kinsman is no fool. He is an experienced soldier who knows the limitations of his smaller army and its strength which is the longbow, speed and the element of surprise. Why, therefore would anyone imagine that he will play his weakest hand by facing us in open battle?'

'Everything you say makes sense,' I agreed. 'Yet how will Glyndŵr ever win this war unless he stands and fights in pitched battles?'

Llŷr scratched his head and pondered.

'Well, that is the whole point you see. That is his major problem for which, I am afraid, there is no solution.'

He paused a moment, a strange, wistful look in his eye. He seemed to be weighing me up, wondering how far he could trust me.

'I'll tell you one thing, though. If he ever did manage to gain a resounding victory over a powerful English army in a pitched battle, he would gain hundreds, no, thousands of extra supporters to the cause. We…' Llŷr paused, anxious to control his emotional outburst which would not have been appreciated if overheard by his English comrades. His reference to 'the cause' rather than 'his cause' or 'their cause' was a revealing one.

'Don't you think that Owain might be tempted, following his recent Maelienydd successes, to do the unexpected and surprise us by facing us in a set-piece battle this time, Llŷr?' I offered unconvincingly.

'No, I don't,' he responded emphatically. 'I see no reason

for him to change tactics which have been so successful when a pitched battle against this experienced army would be, at best, a dangerous gamble. Why, we are not even sure that Glyndŵr is with his army. After all, he is not a young man any more and he may leave the fighting to younger warriors whom he trusts to stick with tried and tested tactics.'

'You may well be correct in your assessment, captain,' I said. Then, lifting my hand and pointing my finger at him for emphasis I added, 'But what if you are not? What if the Welshman who has dared to declare himself Prince of Wales, and that means prince of all the Welsh…all of… us…'

I paused dramatically spreading my arms wide as if to encompass all the men sitting around us.

'What if Prince Owain has decided to lead this army in person, making the age-old appeal to kith and kin, urging them to give their all in support of freedom? What would these brave Welsh warriors seated around us do if, as battle commenced, you, and they, were to see the ancient and magical standard of old… yes, I am talking of the golden dragon on a pure white background which has evoked reverence and loyalty from your fathers, grandfathers and thousands of brave Welshmen since the beginning of time. What if our *Tywysog* were to ride his fabled war horse, Llwyd y Bacsie, back and fore in full view of both armies tomorrow, parading the historic war standard which has evinced a mixture of dread, awe and fierce pride and uniting the Welsh since time immemorial… what… would… you… do?'

Llŷr took a step backward, startled by my sudden challenge to his Welshness. He looked around hurriedly, his eyes flicking quickly across dozens of his companions who had been listening intently to my intentionally loud comments. Such words were downright treason in an English army camp and Llŷr was decidedly nervous in case the words had been overheard. I had taken a calculated gamble and, looking at the faces of those who had heard me, I saw a few registering various degrees of shock, others grinning broadly, but all sympathetic to my standpoint.

Having gained a reaction I decided to switch the conversation to less dangerous topics. 'All right, Llŷr. Enough of such foolish chatter. Let us talk of music and singing. This seems an awfully quiet camp considering the hundreds of Welshmen present. Do you not sing to entertain each other and help gather courage to face the carnage ahead?'

'Singing is normally a common feature of our camp, my friends. It is just that tonight, with only a sketchy idea of what to expect tomorrow, nobody seems to be in the mood,' Llŷr answered wearily.

'That is no way to prepare for battle, captain. We cannot have the lads hanging their heads on the eve of conflict! Now, my friend here, Gruffudd, when he is not waging war... is an accomplished singer. Perhaps you would allow him to sing one or two of our traditional songs of valiant deeds against enemies of the Welsh through the ages. I can assure you, my friend will raise their spirits in no time.'

Llŷr turned to the nearest archers. 'What say you, lads? Shall we listen to some of the big fellow's songs?'

Several gave shouts of approval. News that a Welsh troubadour was on hand spread quickly, and by the time Gruffudd had finished his meal and risen to sing there were close on 200 eager listeners gathered around us, with scores more hurrying to join the audience.

It soon became a night to remember as Gruff appealed to

the full range of his listeners' emotions, singing of bravery and vengeance, of massacres and poverty, of valour and honour, of defeat and glorious victories, of cruelty and struggles for freedom from the yoke of foreign tyrants. And all his songs raised the ghosts of one Welsh hero after another gaining immortality by leading their warriors into battle under the sacred banner of a golden dragon on a field of white.

Two hours later, when the final haunting notes of the rich baritone voice had faded away, Llŷr came over and spoke quietly in my ear.

'It is my belief, your Highness, that tomorrow I too will see the dragon of gold on a field of white. I shall ensure that all true Welshmen are on the extreme left of the massed ranks of archers. I shall wait for a suitable moment before I issue the command to switch our support to our true Prince, Owain IV of Wales.'

He went down on one knee and I hastily ordered him to stand up, for I had no wish for my true identity to become common knowledge, else I would be a dead leader, for I would never escape alive.

'You are a good man, captain. I look forward to supping with you in celebration tomorrow night.' I squeezed his arm and turned to go.

'You too, my Prince, are a good and brave man. I look forward to celebrating with you tomorrow night,' he whispered, as Gruffudd and I began our stealthy withdrawal from Mortimer's camp.

7

I STOOD ON the northern side of the church of St Mary looking down into the wide dell where more than half of my army of 1,800 men was hidden from curious eyes in the Lugg river valley to the south of Brynglas. It was too dark for anyone to see the hundreds of lightly-armed cavalrymen mounting their fleet-footed Welsh mountain ponies in any case, for they were getting ready to move out in the pitch darkness just before dawn. The quiet talk of soldiers readying for action was kept to a minimum and the only other sounds were the slight rustle and rattle of harnesses, the occasional muffled metallic clang of a sword being thrust into or loosened in its scabbard, and the nervous neighing of ponies. I was accompanied by Gruffudd Llwyd, my son Maredudd and Thomas Easton who, on the current campaign, was sharing a tent with Maredudd.

'Father, I have to tell you that I do not understand the logic of your battle plan.' He sounded exasperated and worried. 'In the past you have always chosen to avoid battles where the opposing army is so clearly too strong for us to face. But not this time. And not only are you going to stand and face them but you are splitting your already much smaller army which, I have to say, seems a suicidal move.'

I turned and looked with pride at my second son. Maredudd had now grown to full manhood and, though several inches shorter than me at just under six feet, he was strong, his movements light and well-balanced. He had already been involved in several violent encounters, including the battle of Hyddgen and the fighting which led to the capture of the Earl of Ruthin, and was skilled in the use of longbow and sword. A thoughtful individual blessed with an equable temperament – Maredudd was a good man to have at your side in a fight. I watched dawn break as the first of the sun's summer rays pierced the eastern horizon with effortless beauty, before responding.

'You are absolutely correct that splitting your forces is always a risky ploy, particularly when you are outnumbered. In this case, however, I believe that the risk is minimal and could make the difference between winning and losing.' I paused, looking around at the unconvinced expressions of Maredudd and Tom Eaton. Gruff returned my glance with an unconcerned grin.

'Gruffudd and I paid a secret visit to Mortimer's camp last night dressed as a couple of archers arriving late.'

'You did what?' Tom's voice was shocked, while Maredudd simply stared at me, dumbfounded.

I smiled before continuing. 'Yes I know it was risky but – nothing ventured nothing gained is what your grandfather, David Hanmer, used to tell me as a youngster. In fact we learned several useful things in that camp. Most of the army has little idea of when they may expect to meet us and I'm pretty sure that they have no idea we are here at Brynglas. That gives us one huge advantage – surprise. We also got the feeling that, as far as the archers at least are concerned, there is a deal of dissatisfaction at the lack of information on objectives, on the legitimacy of what they are about and their leaders' failure to foster feelings of unity, loyalty to a cause or comradeship within the army. Basically, morale seems to be pretty low. They number 3,000, of whom I would estimate at least 1,500 are archers. Of those, at least 500 are drawn from Mortimer's holdings in Wales. We even got to test their pride as Welshmen and their views on our rebellion. Indeed, Gruffudd ended up regaling them with patriotic songs describing the mighty deeds of our past heroes fighting foreign invasion and domination. Both Gruff and I feel that when battle is joined, any sign that we are gaining the upper hand will cause those archers to switch allegiance and could provide the final impetus for victory. So, if you add those things together, the odds are evened up a little. I also intend to have at least half our army hidden from sight initially. This, I hope, will encourage them to ignore caution and launch an uphill attack which will further disadvantage them. Our cavalry has been split in two, with 400 making their way in a wide arc to the trees on the eastern side of the approach to Brynglas while the other 300 take up a similar position in woods on the opposite side. When the time is right I will reinforce the smaller company on the western side with my sixty personal guards. The 250 pikemen and axemen will remain hidden in the dell behind the church to await orders. Finally, I have asked Rhys Gethin to station 200 archers in full view at the southern base of the hill, with the remaining 600 hidden in the low bushes and bracken halfway up the hill. How does all that sound to you, Maredudd… and to you, Tom?'

The two doubters looked at each other.

'Yes, it might just work…' they said in hesitant unison. Then they shared a rather more confident chuckle as we all left for our appointed positions.

Some time later I knelt in a thick outcrop of bracken close to the church of St Mary gazing expectantly at the valley below. I was sweating profusely, for I was dressed in full armour apart from my helm lying close beside me on the grassy slope. The Lugg was a mere sliver of silver, snaking its way weakly through the dry valley before disappearing into the distant haze. I was conscious of the chirruping of grasshoppers all around me, broken occasionally by the joyous warbling of a skylark hovering somewhere out of sight to my left. The full complement of *Y Cedyrn* was close at hand, all sixty hand-picked, experienced warriors – the cream of my army. They lay or sat amid the undergrowth, well used to long waits. Llwyd y Bacsie and the guards' horses were tethered in the shade of some stunted trees in the dell a short distance behind and below us. Yet again I looked at the backs of the bulk of our archers hiding in more bracken and scrub halfway down the southern slopes of Brynglas and the 200 totally exposed longbowmen way down at the base of the hill who would be first to face the enemy. They were seated in small groups chatting, but keeping a wary eye southward.

I saw a buzzard circling lazily high in the sky, gradually losing height as he came to take a closer look at the unusual human movements on the hill. Eventually, he was chased away by two crows, insulted by his appearance in their territory. The buzzard offered no resistance but slowly flapped his broad wings and retreated gracefully down the valley, more from a lofty boredom than fear of the crows. Suddenly I was aware of a smell of burning somewhere behind me. I stood up quickly and stared back up the hill. The church of St Mary was well alight and, even as I stared in astonishment, clouds of noxious smoke rose straight up into the still air, though the sharp smell of burning wood was already filling my nostrils as I saw the first flames licking the lower sections of roof.

Llwyd y Bacsie was the first to hear a sound that made the hairs stand up on the back of my neck. I heard her characteristic snort, followed by a warning neigh. I spun around thinking there might be some threat to our rear, but all was still. I picked out Llwyd among the other horses still grazing, oblivious to any danger. She was looking up at me shaking her head, her powerful neck arching gracefully. Then I heard it too – a distant drum beating in steady marching tempo. My guards had seen my agitation and immediately readied themselves for action. The band of archers at the base of the hill still seemed unaware of the sound. I stared into the distant heat haze but there was nothing visible other than the ethereal shimmering of the air above the hot ground.

Then I saw what I had been waiting for, the gradual, awesome revelation of more than 3,000 armed men marching to destroy an enemy – and that enemy was me. There was an ominous, threat-laden inevitability about the approach of Mortimer's army but, as I looked about me at the hundreds of faithful followers who were putting their trust completely in me that day, I felt a new confidence and pride. They were the Cymry and I was their *Tywysog* and there was no way we would be denied victory as long as I had breath in my body. Outnumbered maybe, but we had thrived over the centuries battling against the odds.

Gradually we could see that Mortimer and his powerful fellow knights were leading a large section of heavy cavalry with companies of light cavalry on each wing, perhaps 1,200 in total. Behind them marched 1,500 archers, followed by several hundred pikemen with a host of camp followers some distance to the rear. A multitude of Mortimer banners in the form of a shield emblazoned in alternate yellow and azure stripes were prominently displayed. Ahead of this impressive array rode a number of mounted point-men, scouring the land for any sign of the enemy.

My forward company of archers had seen Mortimer's host by now and were calmly stringing their longbows in readiness. Tudur was the officer in charge and he was walking up and down the rows of archers, no doubt giving words of encouragement as he went.

Mortimer's two forward point-men were walking their horses straight towards Brynglas, presumably to investigate the fire at the church. It was incredible that they had not yet noticed the company of archers directly in their path making no attempt at concealment, albeit still a mile or so away. The two must have been deep in conversation, having made no connection between the fire and the possibility of Welsh rebels in the area. They were only marginally outside bowshot when, inevitably, they realised what was in front of them. Tudur had already set up a team of a dozen archers, poised and aiming their arrows at the two scouts, waiting for them to come within range. Both riders appeared to see the Welsh bowmen in the same instant, for they both shouted in alarm, wheeled their horses about and retreated towards their own army. The main body of the English force was still a good two miles away and, after a few minutes, came to a sudden stop as their leaders saw the point-men galloping urgently back towards them.

My heart skipped a beat as I realised that we were now irrevocably committed to this battle. So much depended on how the English would react. The worst scenario for us would be a decision by Mortimer to stand his ground and wait for us to attack him. Outnumbered by more than three to two and without heavy cavalry, we would only do so as a last resort, for defeat would be almost certain. He had a number of experienced leaders to advise him such as Sir Robert Whitney and his renowned son-in-law, Sir Thomas Clanvoe, as well as other uncompromising warriors such as the current Sheriff of Herefordshire, Sir Kinard de la Bere, and Lord Kinnersly. I had staked a great deal on hiding most of my men to make the English think that they had only a minor force to reckon with. After the initial surprise, his forces would be eager to get to grips with us, for many of the men of Maelienydd would have lost kinsmen, farm animals and property thanks to our raids over the past weeks. Young Edmund Mortimer would be seething also, having been humiliated by us in his own domain and eager to return the favour.

My breathing was shallow as I waited and watched for the enemy's next move. My commanders, Rhys Gethin, my general-in-chief with the main body of archers; Tudur, in charge of the 200 bowmen acting as bait at the foot of the hill; Rhys Ddu of Deheubarth, with the largest section of cavalry in the woods to my left; and my eldest son, Gruffudd, with the 300 cavalrymen hidden to my right, all waited for me to join them at the head of *Y Cedyrn* and were all, like me, nervously willing the English to an all-out assault. If they did, attacking uphill in this heat was sure to drain even the toughest troops of their strength.

The English army began to move forward, fully armed and armoured, ready for action. I sincerely hoped that the heavy armour was as sweaty and stifling as it looked from a distance. When they were a mere mile away I decided it was time to add a little to the spice of the moment. I mounted Llwyd y Bacsie and summoned my secretary Dafydd, now designated standard bearer, to my side. There was no breeze, so I ordered Gwynfor Gleddyf, renowned as much as a maker of swords as for his skill in using the weapon in battle, to ride a few yards to Dafydd's right so that they could both present the most inspirational banner in the history of the Welsh people in its full glory to enemy and kinsman alike. As the golden dragon spread its arrogant presence on its field of white I heard the age-old chant of the hundreds of archers halfway down the hill, its ancient, blood-curdling bass uttering the druidic phrases chanted by the Welsh in battle through the ages but barely understood any longer. The effect on all of us was incredible.

We were 1,800 individuals, yet all at once we were one, itching to get into the fight for our kin and fatherland. At my signal the hollow booming of our war horn sent shivers down our backs, and the English army stopped once more. I rode at the head of my company of guards back and forth in front of the church, giving friend and foe plenty of opportunity to observe the golden dragon. Then their drums started, the simple yet chilling marching tempo echoing around the valley below, and we saw hundreds of their cavalrymen setting themselves up for the charge. Tudur was shouting at his archers to hold their ground until he gave the order to retreat.

'Save your arrows till later,' I heard him roar. 'Nobody to move until I give the order, but when I do, you will run like startled rabbits back up to your comrades on the hill. They will already be loosing their arrows at the English cavalry and, as soon as you have your breath back, you will join in the carnage… Is that clear?'

The response was an enthusiastic roar of understanding and then there was no more time to think. The English heavy cavalry charged.

I felt for my brother and the lads at the foot of the hill. The English destriers drummed a heavy beat of their own on the hard turf and their riders in their outlandish armour with swords drawn, clanked and clattered along like Hell's own demons. Even from my vantage point high above, they were a truly frightening sight.

Tudur held his nerve, waiting until the charging horsemen were little more than 250 yards away before he shouted the order to retreat. The archers needed no bidding and all ran up the steep gradient like mountain hares. For a while it looked as if they would be caught and slaughtered by the cavalry. However, the entire hillside was scattered with boulders hidden by the luxuriant bracken. Several of the horses fell, some screaming in pain, dislodging their metal-clad riders who struggled to get to their feet in the confining armour. The remainder, already beginning to labour in the heat, had their strength sapped even more by the sharp gradient so that even the leaders slowed to almost walking pace. They were now well within range of the main archer force who began firing volleys of arrows at them over the heads of their fleeing comrades. This proved catastrophic for the cavalry. Many were killed outright, while others had their mounts killed beneath them so that they were sent sprawling. The few survivors could see that their cause was lost and hurriedly retreated down the hill out of bowshot, cutting a sorry sight as they walked their mounts dejectedly back to their shocked comrades. Meanwhile, the Welsh archers raced down among the fallen knights, capturing those who looked as if they might command a ransom and dispatching the others swiftly with their short swords.

There appeared to be considerable confusion in the

English camp. A stream of messages was being interchanged on horseback and on foot. After the first realisation that, somehow, their large and much-vaunted force of heavy cavalry had been practically obliterated in the space of twenty minutes, the leaders were reacting furiously. I wondered how much of that fury was directed at me and how much at each other.

Then, their entire company of archers was moved to the front and assembled in battle order. It was an interesting formation, with a company of 500 archers in the centre and another two companies of 500, one on either flank. And, as I had suspected, the company on their left was the one made up of Welshmen from Maelienydd, all proudly wearing leeks in their caps. Yet again our archers would be outnumbered by almost two to one… unless Llŷr Fychan's archers on that left flank decided to defect. But would they? First we would have to fight what was in front of us, without relying on help from anyone. And again that steep incline should give us some sort of advantage.

I saw Rhys Gethin standing among his archers gesticulating and issuing his orders. Then he looked up at me and drew his hand across in front of his throat. Did I want a fight with no quarter given? I quickly emulated his gesture. He raised his hand in acknowledgement and, as I raised mine in return, I could sense the satisfaction which my decision would have given this untamed warrior. If anyone could inspire my 800 bowmen it was he. But it was time to lead my guards down to join Gruffudd and his cavalry hidden in the trees and explain our plan.

The English drums rolled once more and the three companies of archers moved forward at a trot. They halted just out of longbow range and the lead company in the centre prepared to attack. In the unnatural silence before the order was given, our war horn was sounded again and reverberated around the valley. Dafydd and Gwilym, who had stayed hidden near the church with our pikemen and axemen, again emerged on horseback displaying the evocative golden dragon and our archers gave voice to their chilling, unearthly war chant. We were by now in the trees a short distance from our cavalry unit. I peered over at the opposing archers on the left flank readying themselves for action, leeks prominently displayed in their caps. As the sound of the ancient chant reached them, they bunched a fist and held it to their hearts. My heart skipped a beat. Surely there was no way those lads could take offensive action against the chanters, was there…? I had to get to Gruffudd quickly, for if Mortimer's Welsh bowmen switched sides his two companies of light cavalry still in reserve would be ordered to charge them from the rear and we would have to be there with our own cavalry to defend them.

A shouted English order, and the lead company of archers raced towards the base of the hill seeking some form of shelter as the Welsh bowmen sent a thick cloud of arrows raining down on them. The deadly volley cut swathes in the English ranks but they still raced onward only to be struck by a second cloud of arrows momentarily darkening the sky, then killing and maiming dozens more before they could reach cover. The open ground at the bottom of the hill was littered with the bodies of dead and injured. The screams of the injured was an inhuman sound while the blood flowed freely on the dusty ground, quickly congealing into sticky black stains on the hot earth. With nearly half their number killed or disabled, the remainder of the centre company bravely stood their ground and returned a volley of their own. The distance, however, was too great and most of their arrows fell well short of the Welsh archers halfway up the hill. Rhys Gethin's men released a third volley and, favoured by their elevated position, it was incredibly accurate, mowing down scores more.

The archers on Mortimer's right flank now came hurrying over to reinforce their comrades, but as soon as they were within range the Welsh contingent on the left flank suddenly turned and fired a totally unexpected volley of arrows into their midst causing heavy casualties. The survivors were beside themselves with rage at being fired on by their own men. They lost their discipline completely and launched a disorganised, shambling attack upon them, oblivious to the danger of exposing themselves to the massed Welsh archers on the hillside. Rhys Gethin immediately ordered his men to fire at will and the English archers were cut to ribbons, leaving Gethin's men and the defecting Welsh archers in the valley staring aghast at the carnage they had wrought.

In the momentary lull there was a pounding of galloping hooves as the two companies of English light cavalry bore down on Welsh defectors. They, in turn, quickly formed themselves into battle order and faced about to deliver more of their deadly missiles at the closing riders. Suddenly they became aware of more galloping hooves on either side, and for a few seconds were filled with dread knowing they could not deal with cavalry attacking them from three sides at once. There was huge relief as Llŷr's men realised the newcomers were Welsh cavalry who had materialised from the woods on either side and were launching themselves at the English horsemen in a pincer movement. Yet again Edmund Mortimer, who was personally leading this attack, found himself outmanoeuvred. But by now he was fully committed and there could be no turning back.

The English riders were met by a hail of arrows, but managed to keep their formation despite suffering heavy casualties, with several riderless and frightened horses breaking in all directions. Then they collided with the Welsh cavalry units, cutting them off from either side. The archers were forced to hold their fire as horses and men whirled around each other in a wild melée, cutting and slashing with swords and fending off blows with their bucklers. It was a fascinating and gruesome contest between two sets of cavalry with very different fighting styles. Though called light cavalry, the English were on bigger, heavier mounts and wore more protective armour. Their tactic was to batter their way through opponents wearing far less armour and some with no protective clothing at all. For their part, the Welsh, on their smaller but much more adroit mountain ponies, sought to use speed and unorthodox moves to unsettle their opponents. I was the only Welshman riding a destrier and I urged Llwyd y Bacsie directly at Mortimer. I saw that he had been unsettled by the death of his standard bearer, stabbed in the throat moments before by a Welsh sword, his corpse and the proud Mortimer banner trampled over by countless hooves.

English confidence had been severely shaken and now the Welsh cavalry, confident and desperate to emulate the success of their archers, executed their audacious and unconventional moves with courage and precision. They quickly began to gain the upper hand and the enemy had no answer to their swift, cavalier attacks. I kept losing young Mortimer in the ebb and flow of the action, but at last I saw that he had been isolated and surrounded by three of Rhys

Ddu's south Walians who were hell-bent on his destruction. Desperately, I shouted at them not to kill him, that I needed him alive. As I shouted, one of the attackers used his nimble pony to sidestep the English leader's horse and deliver a terrific blow which dislodged Mortimer's sword from his grasp, leaving him with only his great shield sporting the family crest to fend off further blows. Fortunately, one of the attackers heard me at and ordered the others to stop… not an easy task, for all three were possessed with the bloodlust of intense conflict. My unexpected appearance in full armour finally cleared their heads and they closed in on Mortimer so that he was hemmed in, unarmed and with no way of escape.

'Well, my Lord Mortimer, will you order the survivors of your army to surrender or do we have to kill them all?'

Edmund Mortimer stared at me, his eyes glittering with rage under his visor. He seemed on the point of defying me when his shoulders suddenly slumped. He threw his great shield to the ground and wearily removed his helm. Thick, light brown hair fell almost to his shoulders. Though sweating profusely, his face was pale and tired, his spirit broken by the day's fateful events. I guessed him to be about twenty-five, his blue eyes, normally so distinctive I imagined, looked listless and drained.

At last he said resignedly, 'It would seem I have little choice. It would help if you instructed your men to withdraw for a short while so that I can make myself heard when I tell my lads to lay down their arms.'

I sent one of Rhys Ddu's men to find a trumpeter to give the withdrawal signal, and gradually the two sets of cavalry disengaged so that Mortimer could order the battered remnants of his own cavalry to surrender.

Fighting on the hill had already ended. Rhys Gethin had not offered the English archers an opportunity to surrender, nor had such a request been made. The great majority had been slaughtered and a few lucky ones had managed to escape back down the valley. Seeing that their entire army had been utterly defeated, the few hundred pikemen and non-combatant element of Mortimer's forces had hurriedly taken flight. I decided to stop my men from following them since there was nothing to be gained from further killing. After handing Mortimer into Rhys Gethin's custody for the time being, I rode back up to the church, talking gently to the loyal Llwyd, praising her and patting her great neck. She swished her tail appreciatively and whinnied softly in response.

It was some time later, as I wearily discarded my armour in my tent, that the significance of the day's events began to dawn on me. The victory was greater than any I could have imagined even in my dreams. Not only had we won the day but we had practically annihilated the enemy at low cost to ourselves. This was our most resounding victory over the English for centuries, a victory which would cause fear and consternation in royal circles and in Parliament, as well as panic and dread in the Marcher counties of Herefordshire, Cheshire, Shropshire and even Gloucestershire. Not only had we proved that we could take on a numerically superior English army in a set-piece battle and defeat them comprehensively, but we had done so only a few miles from the English border with the rich plains of England now lying close at hand, defenceless and ripe for plundering. I fully expected emissaries from the major towns and cities of those counties to visit me within days to offer considerable sums of money in return for my protection.

The general mood in the camp that night was not one of great joy and unbounded celebration. It was rarely so in the immediate aftermath of battle, even for the victors. That would gradually surface in the days and weeks to come. We were all rather subdued, though relieved and quietly proud of our unexpectedly complete victory. Feelings, however, were raw. Though our losses were comparatively light, many of us had either lost a dear friend or had friends injured during the battle. Few of us had escaped any injury at all, from bruises and cuts to broken bones. Our celebration was therefore muted. We had recovered huge amounts of arms and armour from the enemy dead as well as from their camp, along with considerable amounts of money and valuables and, perhaps more importantly, large quantities of food and other supplies, invaluable to an army in the field. Early in the morning we would be rounding up hundreds of horses which had run away when their riders had been downed but which would, by now, have spent the evening grazing not too far away.

Of my officers and close advisers only my dear friend Gruffudd Llwyd had been injured. The huge axeman had been felled by a glancing blow from the sword of a cavalryman who, fortunately for Gruff, had been killed by an arrow moments later. But the big man was soon on his feet again, slaying about him with his axe like a demon from beyond the grave, with blood streaming down his face. The injury was a nasty one, for he had a deep cut from ear to chin which Ednyfed ap Siôn had to treat with a poultice of herbs known to prevent infection. Ednyfed expected the skin to heal but warned that Gruff would have a livid scar on the left side of his face for life. Gruffudd accepted the prognosis with characteristic stoicism and an attempt at a grin which swiftly became a grimace of pain.

'It's nothing,' he murmured. 'After all, I could have been killed. At least I am still here. My looks were never my strong point anyway,' he added ruefully. He had never managed to come to terms with his totally hairless body.

I walked over to him and laid my hand on his heavily-muscled shoulder. 'As I have told you many times before, my friend, your singing and your poetry have won you friends and admirers all over the country. You are one of the greatest of Wales's living poets and a redoubtable warrior too. Believe me, your name will be remembered by Welsh people for centuries to come. Nobody will care whether you had hair on your body or not, just as nobody today bothers to ask whether the revered poet Aneirin was bald or had a long nose.'

Everyone within earshot laughed good-naturedly at this and, after a second or two, Gruffudd Llwyd's eyes twinkled too.

Exhaustion set in early that night and the tented area behind the burnt-out church was silent by midnight apart from the hooting of a distant owl and the occasional crackling of a glowing ember in one of the rapidly-dying cooking fires. I lay in my blanket outside my tent. The air was still and warm, and I wanted to enjoy the magic of the bright, starlit night after all the burning and killing of the day. Sentries had been posted as usual, though I could not imagine who in the area would wish to, or be capable of, attacking us. The vast canvas of the heavens held me spellbound for a while but then my eyelids grew heavy and I slid into a deep sleep.

Sometime later I was aware of a cowled figure standing

over me. I went to grab the dagger which was always strapped to my waist when sleeping in the open, but the figure whispered an urgent, 'Hush… there is no danger…' I paused, more in shock than conviction, for my visitor was a woman! I had not heard that voice for twenty years but I recognised it instantly. It was Modlen, Rhys Gethin's mother…

'Modlen,' I gasped. 'In the name of God what are you doing here? Don't you realise that you might have been killed by one of the sentries?'

She giggled quietly and seated herself beside me, throwing back the hood which had hidden her features.

'Oh Owain, do not say that you are worried about me… surely that cannot be, for I have heard naught from you these past twenty years.'

Though the words were uttered light-heartedly I felt uncomfortable, for there was pain in those words which her smile could not hide. She leaned towards me so that our faces were very close. 'You will be telling me next that you have missed me…' Her breathing was a little uneven and I glanced down to see that the top of her loose gown had slipped open. Despite the passage of time, this woman who had captivated me so long ago had lost none of her ability to excite me.

'Do you like what you see?' she murmured huskily.

Then, before I could react, her open mouth closed on mine and I was lost. My mind went blank and soon we were both oblivious to the world around us and it seemed as if we had never been apart.

Later, when I made to move away she held me tight.

'No, no my love, stay. I want to remember us as one under this blanket. God knows what you will think of me tomorrow, for you will not want to see me after this night...'

I did not understand her meaning but she would say no more on the subject. Instead, she caressed me and kissed me tenderly, holding me tight all the while. Before drifting off to sleep I fancied I felt a tear or two on my forehead as she kissed it very gently... but then sleep overtook me once more.

I awoke to find Rhys Ddu shaking my shoulder. It was still dark – in fact it was pitch-dark, for now the stars were obscured by clouds. There was no sign of Modlen.

'Owain, come quickly. A sentry has just woken me. He was genuinely scared stiff. He claims there are evil spirits interfering with the corpses of the English dead on the southern side of the hill.'

I rubbed my eyes and stared speculatively at Rhys. 'Oh come on, Rhys. Don't tell me that a tough old boot like you is frightened by talk of evil spirits?'

Rhys coughed to cover his embarrassment. 'It... it is simply that I heard some weird wailing followed by high-pitched voices chanting one of those ancient chants the Druids used to use in worship of Mother Earth.'

'And?'

'And... well... I just thought you might wish to come with me to... er... investigate.'

'That is very thoughtful of you, Rhys, thank you.' I tried to lighten the sarcastic tone of my words, for the warrior had clearly been unsettled by thoughts of the supernatural.

Together, we made our way up to the remains of the church where the few remaining blackened roof beams pointed like accusing fingers up into the only marginally lighter sky. Then I became aware of the ghostly chanting Rhys had referred to, but the hillside was too dark – we could make out movement among the dead bodies but little else.

Then, quite unexpectedly, the moon emerged from behind a cloud, bathing the hillside in an ethereal glow. There were a score or more women clothed in cowled cloaks such as I had seen Modlen wearing earlier. They moved slowly but inexorably across the slopes chanting, with some occasionally cackling with glee, while they bent to their horrible task; for they all carried knives with which they were systematically castrating the corpses of the English dead.

I swallowed the bile rising in my throat and instructed Rhys Ddu to go back to find reinforcements, for we would have been very foolish to challenge these deranged creatures with their long knives on our own. I averted my gaze so as not to see the evil deeds being enacted in front of me. After what seemed an age, Rhys reappeared, followed silently by a party of archers with longbows strung at the ready. I signalled them to surround the women and await my orders. This was accomplished with stealth so that, when I eventually challenged the cowled figures and called upon them to stop, there was no means of escape; wherever they looked there was a bow notched with an arrow trained on them.

Unconcerned, the women paused and stared at us in silence. Then their leader, a tall figure, limped casually towards me, removing her cowl to dislodge long, snow-white hair reaching halfway down her back. Her age was difficult to determine but she appeared ancient, especially when she opened her mouth to reveal only a few stained stumps. She stopped a few feet away from me and curtsied stiffly, her arthritic joints obviously hampering her.

'*Henffych Dywysog*,' she greeted me. 'I am sorry if I and my sisters awoke you from your rest. I would like to congratulate you and your men on your glorious victory and wish you many more in the years ahead.'

'I thank you for your congratulations,' I responded evenly, 'but what you and your sisters do this night does not please me at all. There are some rules, even in war, and as Prince of a civilised people, one thing I do not do is defile the helpless corpses of enemy dead. They, after all, are brave warriors who have fallen in battle. That is no reason to despise them, or indeed to mutilate their corpses.'

The woman stood her ground, apparently unmoved by my admonition.

'Prince Owain, we are of the hill people and though we recognise you as *Y Mab Darogan* and our lawful Prince, we do not follow your Christian religion. We cling to the old ways, to the old religion. The English have performed most cruel and unacceptable acts against us. You only have to think back to last year when their King ravished the land, raping and enslaving more than 1,000 Welsh children. The spirits tell us to strike back. One of our beliefs is that warriors who die in battle have their bodies reformed in the next life. By castrating them this night we have ensured that when their bodies are reformed they will all be eunuchs, unable to procreate or enjoy the pleasures of a woman's body. That is our revenge for their treatment of all those poor, dear children…'

For a long moment I stared at the old woman in silence. I knew that nothing I said could change her beliefs or those of her people.

'As you say, your beliefs and mine are very different. We will not argue but I cannot allow you to complete this… this… desecration of the dead. I therefore command you and your sisters to leave this place immediately and return to your homes. Anyone who does not comply will be put to death.'

She nodded her head vigorously. 'Your orders will be obeyed, my Prince. As you say, your religious beliefs and mine are very different. Our work here is almost complete in any case. You are a great man, Owain, and your name will reverberate through the centuries among the Welsh and beyond. Unfortunately, you are a man ahead of your time. Still, your hopes and dreams for the Welsh people will be realised… eventually…'

Without another word she turned and limped away, followed in a long line by her companions, many with bloodied hands and blood-smeared cloaks. I looked carefully trying to see a face I knew, but they all had their cowls pulled well forward. The last to pass me paused fleetingly and whispered,

'Goodbye, Prince Owain, may your struggle for freedom meet with success and bring you much honour.'

I drew a sharp breath but before I could respond she had hurried away to catch up with her companions. I hesitated, wanting to stop her and talk to her. Then I considered what my close companions and others would think if they saw their *Tywysog* scuttling after one of the crazy women who had committed such desecration on the dead bodies of the enemy. No, it would be a grave mistake. I tried to convince myself that I had been deluded in thinking I recognised the voice. Indeed, my earlier encounter with Modlen could have been nothing more than a dream. However, I could not explain away the fact that the voice of the last female who had whispered her good wishes was the same voice that had moaned in pleasure and showered me with words of love in my 'dream'!

By now the whole camp had been disturbed and most of the men were getting up to prepare for the day ahead, even though they would have to wait another hour for the break of dawn. The only officer still apparently asleep under his blanket was Rhys Gethin. Out of curiosity I sauntered over to him.

'Still asleep, Rhys?'

'No.' His voice was muffled under the blanket. 'I have been awake for some time, and yes, I did hear the night's disturbance.'

I bridled a little at his tone. 'So you heard the disturbance and, despite being my second in command, you thought it not worthy of your attention!'

Rhys threw his blanket to one side and rose slowly, at last giving me the deference I was due.

'You do not understand, sire. I knew my people would come to seek vengeance. Don't forget, some of the children taken away into slavery by Bolingbroke were ours. I guessed my mother would be among them and I also knew they would be no danger to us. I saw no reason to stop them.'

I stared hard at the young man for a while. We would never rid Rhys Gethin of his wild and ancient heritage.

Without another word I turned and walked away. As I went he added quietly, but loudly enough for me to hear,

'You forget, Father – I am one of them…'

I paused in shock. The only time he had ever claimed to be my son was on the day he first walked into our lives as a young boy dressed in animal skins. Now, all these years later, he had chosen this time to remind me of his connection to the hill people and called me Father. For once, I did not know what to say. Instead, I walked on in bewilderment. I wondered whether he and his mother had spoken to each other during the night. Then I felt a surge of embarrassment at the thought that he might also be aware of his mother's visit to me.

8

W E RESTED AT Brynglas for several days, giving ourselves, and particularly the wounded, time to recover. We calculated our losses to be forty-seven killed, ten badly wounded, three of whom died during our stay on the hill, and a further eighty or so wounded in varying degrees but who should be restored to full health eventually. It was not possible to know the full extent of enemy losses but there were several hundred dead on the hill and its environs. We discovered more than thirty badly wounded who all died within days despite Ednyfed's best efforts to save them. We guessed that the remainder of Mortimer's army, after fleeing the field, would have dispersed to their homes for they had been left leaderless. We had also gained 500 trained archers, swelling our numbers to close on 2,300 men. We rounded up more than 300 enemy horses, most of which were in prime condition, and twenty or more with broken limbs which we had to be put down. Other material gains were large amounts of food, wine and ale, as well as an impressive array of weapons and armour.

More important though was the fact that we had beaten a professional English army so completely and that the King had lost several of his leading knights, killed in the battle. These included Sir Kinard de la Bere, Sir Walter Devereux and Sir Robert de Whitney. To add to Bolingbroke's woes we had captured young Edmund Mortimer, whose family could legitimately claim the right to the English throne, and yet another of his ablest knights, Sir Thomas Clanvowe. Both would command ransoms which the King could ill afford. We were soon to discover that while Clanvowe would readily be ransomed, Henry was determined not to pay a penny to gain the release of Mortimer. It was not difficult to see why. Henry already had Edmund's young nephew, another Edmund and the true heir to the English throne, directly under his control. Now with the older Edmund, and next in line of succession, a prisoner of the Welsh rebels, he could rest a little more securely at night.

However, for Sir Henry 'Hotspur' Percy, the King's Commander in north Wales, this was the last straw, for Hotspur was married to Mortimer's sister. Also, he had been forced to fund the King's military activities in north Wales for two years, the monarch having failed to meet his monetary obligations. Bolingbroke's refusal to pay for Mortimer's release was seen as a personal insult to the Percys. Hotspur appealed to Parliament for support on the issue and received none. Annoyed and disillusioned, he left London without the King's permission and rode home to Northumberland determined to do no more to quell the Welsh rebels. Instead, he urged his father, Henry Percy, Earl of Northumberland, and his uncle, Thomas Percy, Earl of Worcester, to commit the Percy family to leading a rebellion to depose Henry IV.

All this, however, was yet to come about when I led my successful and enlarged army away from Pilleth and marched south. My intention was to attack English-held boroughs and castles in the east and south-east of Wales, areas which had been under English dominance for a century and more. I was determined to prove to my English enemies, and to those of my fellow countrymen who still needed convincing, that I was rapidly gaining control of more of Wales than even Prince Llewelyn the Great or his illustrious grandson, Prince Llewelyn ap Gruffudd, had achieved. I left behind a guard of 100 men under the command of my eldest son, Gruffudd, to take the prisoners being held for ransom back to Dolbadarn where they would be confined until my return.

My men, jubilant, rested and well-fed, were in high spirits as we headed down along the border from Pilleth. We destroyed the castle of the recently-killed Sir Robert Whitney at Whitney-on-Wye in Herefordshire, before advancing on Monmouthshire attacking and burning the castles of Abergavenny, Usk and Caerleon, then headed west and took the castles of Cardiff and Newport, causing considerable damage to both.

Earlier that summer my spymaster, Robert Puleston, had made contact with our Celtic cousins in Brittany, and Breton pirates were now operating in the waters between France and England. In August one of my influential followers in Tenby, David Perrot, landed Bretons and followers of Owain Lawgoch there, and they made their way to Llandybie where they buried Lawgoch's heart before joining my rampant forces as we made our way to the Vale of Glamorgan where we demolished several castles including Penlline, Llandough, Flemingston, Dunraven, Tal-y-Fan, Llanbleddian, Llancaian, Malefant at Llanmaes, and Penmarc. By now the army had gained many more men and camp followers, and we were reduced to a lumbering pace as we headed west. During the journey westward I managed to hand over many of the additional numbers, including the Bretons, to local commanders such as Henry Dwn of Cydweli and William Gwyn ap Rhys Llwyd of Llansteffan. Later, after we had laid siege to Aberystwyth castle, Rhys Ddu of Ceredigion took most of the remaining camp followers when he and his forces went home for a well-earned respite.

The ring of royal castles built by Edward I was far more difficult to attack than the castles we had attacked so successfully in the border country and the south. The latter were mostly poorly-maintained fortresses of Marcher Lords, often defended by under-strength garrisons with low morale. The royal castles were massive edifices, many situated on the coast so that they could be reinforced and provisioned directly from the sea. They were considered practically impregnable and could be defended with ease by relatively small garrisons of experienced soldiers. Anyone hoping to mount a successful siege would need large forces deployed around such a castle for many months and at huge cost. I had neither the numbers nor the wealth to contemplate that kind of siege. Still, I or one of my commanders would often lay siege to these castles, knowing that such action caused concern in London and enhanced our reputation as a serious threat to the King so that we were taken seriously at home, in England and in countries with whom we would soon be seeking alliances, such as Scotland and France.

Such was the reasoning behind the siege of Aberystwyth castle in the early autumn of 1402 where we camped for several weeks before releasing Rhys Ddu and his men. I was left with an army of almost 2,000 which I now split in two. I made Rhys Gethin my senior commander in the south and gave him 1,000 men to continue attacking English castles and boroughs and the right to call up local commanders and their forces when necessary. Accompanied by my brother Tudur, my sons and my other close advisers and officers, I led the remainder north to join the brothers Rhys and

Gwilym Tudur whose forces were already besieging Harlech castle in the north-west.

In September the King launched his third invasion of Wales. In a three-pronged attack his teenage son, Prince Hal, led a large army into north Wales from Chester, while Henry marched another powerful force from Shrewsbury into mid Wales. The earls of Stafford, Arundel and Warwick were detailed to attack south Wales from Hereford. Their combined forces numbered 30,000 troops. They soon created havoc as I had nowhere near enough men to take them on in head-to-head battles. The Welsh countryside was already desperately impoverished after previous vicious invasions which had simply added to the misery caused by the Black Death just a few decades earlier. Unopposed initially, Bolingbroke and his son scoured the land, burning, killing and raping but found plunder hard to come by. Eventually their forces met near the town of Llanrwst. They killed all the inhabitants they could find – men, women and children – before destroying the town completely. Fortunately, some Llanrwst folk managed to escape into the hills before the English attacked but were left homeless and with no means of support. Even now, nearly three years later, the town is a collection of blackened, uninhabited ruins with grass growing in the streets.

The news made my blood boil and I was mortified some weeks later when I learned that the King had paid people to spread a rumour that it was Owain Glyndŵr, and not he, who had massacred the people of Llanrwst and destroyed the town. I have burned many towns in Wales during this struggle but they were always towns where there were English castles garrisoned by English soldiers and the burghers of such towns were overwhelmingly English. Why would I destroy a Welsh town with no English castle and massacre its inhabitants when there were no English burghers? How could I possibly gain anything from such a senseless act? In any case, there are plenty of former townspeople of Llanrwst still living in caves in the hills who can say precisely who murdered their families and friends.

God, according to his adherents, never sleeps – as the two Henrys soon discovered. The winter of 1402 was the coldest in living memory and it started early. No sooner had the English entered Wales than they were subjected to uncommonly severe storms of rain, sleet and snow rarely experienced in autumn. Several soldiers were killed by armour-piercing thunderbolts and the King himself was injured, only narrowly escaping death, when a gale-force wind snapped the main pole of his tent which then fell on top of him while he slept. Had he not been wearing armour, the jagged end of the pole would have pierced his chest. Each storm was usually followed by flash floods as huge quantities of water poured down the mountainsides into the valleys where the hapless English sought shelter in vain. They struggled to overcome the cold and the wet but when they thought that life might once again be bearable, my men would carry out swift but deadly surprise attacks, shattering their morale once more. It was no surprise when, after little more than a fortnight, we heard that the King and his armies were short of victuals and in full retreat, making for the border with unseemly haste. We, of course, did our very best to increase the speed of their departure, sending in groups of a few hundred mounted archers to attack them in relays in daylight and during the hours of darkness. It was little wonder, I suppose, when stories filtered through from beyond the border that Owain Glyndŵr was possessed of superhuman powers. He was undoubtedly a master of the black arts and could control the wind and the rain and all aspects of the weather. How else could you explain why the English encountered such dreadful weather every time they ventured into Wales in strength? Why, he had almost succeeded in murdering the King by sending a devil wind to shatter the royal tent pole! I, of course, did nothing to quash these beliefs in any way.

Passing through Machynlleth and on to Dolgellau, I heard some news which caused me to alter my plans. After spending two nights in Dolgellau at the home of an old friend, Rhun ap Gwynfor, I conferred with my advisers and captains and decided to send the army, apart from Gruffudd Llwyd and the sixty members of *Y Cedyrn*, my troop of personal guards, on to the siege of Harlech castle while we attended to some business which I should have sorted out years earlier.

My cousin, Hywel Selyf, had always been a thorn in my flesh. He had recently been openly convening meetings in the Dolgellau area to persuade my loyal followers there to join him in seeking ways to rid the world of 'my traitorous cousin, Owain ap Gruffudd', as he described me, who had 'been the cause of good King Henry's animosity towards Wales and the Welsh'.

Many had told me over the years that it was high time I did much more than alter the shape of my kinsman's nose, or I would eventually live to regret my familial restraint. It was obvious that I could not allow Hywel to preach rebellion against me to followers in the very heartlands of my support. The following morning, Tudur led the bulk of my force out of Dolgellau to join the siege of Harlech castle.

I ordered *Y Cedyrn* to saddle up – we were going to Nannau to pay my errant cousin a visit. Rhun ap Gwynfor felt that it would be wise to take a larger force, as we were headed for an area where Hywel held much influence. He insisted on accompanying us with fifty of his own mounted and armed followers. As we rode out of Dolgellau I had no idea how grateful I would soon be for Rhun's help and forethought.

9

I RODE UP to the gates of Nannau accompanied only by a dozen guards, carrying no banner since I wanted to gain access before Hywel became suspicious of my purpose. The others stayed concealed in a wood half a mile from the fortified house. They were to follow within half an hour.

'Who calls upon my Lord Hywel Selyf unannounced?' The guardhouse challenge was delivered in a neutral voice tinged with only the slightest curiosity.

'He is Owain ap Gruffudd, your Prince and your Lord,' Gruffudd Llwyd responded on my behalf. 'He wishes to speak with his cousin and is in some haste.'

There was a babble of concerned voices, followed by the sound of boots hurrying briskly over cobbles. My arrival had obviously triggered surprise and some alarm. We waited several minutes before Gruffudd informed the guard that Prince Owain did not appreciate being kept waiting.

'I… I have sent for my Lord. I am sure he will be here to greet you very soon, my Prince.'

After several more minutes I was beginning to feel some irritation when I heard the loathsome voice of my cousin shouting to the guard to open the gates as he came marching across the courtyard.

We had not met for some years. Shorter than me but with a chunky, powerful body, his whole demeanour signalled only faintly-disguised dislike. I stared at his misshapen nose, remembering the guilty satisfaction I had felt all those years ago when I delivered the blow that caused the disfigurement. Now his grey eyes showed some concern and considerable displeasure.

'Welcome to Nannau, Owain,' he said loudly in an unconvincing tone, adding after a short pause: 'It is so good to see you, even though you have ignored good manners by coming here with no prior warning.'

I could sense the grins of delight on the faces of his guards and the annoyed intakes of breath of my own men at his pointed lack of deference.

I forced a smile. 'Ah well, some of us have wars to fight and do not have time to observe the niceties afforded to those who stay at home, openly colluding with the enemy. Indeed it is a discussion of that situation which forces me to visit you, for we need to come to some sort of understanding on the issue. I would be grateful if we could go somewhere a little more comfortable than this gateway so that we can have a civil discussion.'

For a moment I thought he would defy me and insist on continuing the conversation in public. With slow deliberation I moved my hand to the hilt of my sword and I heard the reassuring clicks from behind me as my escort followed suit. Gruffudd's hand slid along his horse's neck to flip open the leather cover of his battle axe, his still fresh scar turning a bluish colour as his heart rate increased. I could tell by the slightly startled look on Hywel's face that this little pantomime had not gone unnoticed. He took a step back and bowed stiffly.

'Of course, of course. I am forgetting my own manners.' His tone did not match the servility of his words however and, as he called to his head ostler to stable our horses, I saw him smirk at his guards, making little attempt to hide the gesture.

'Let us continue our discussion in my private quarters. My servants will provide hospitality for your men in the great hall.'

'Very well,' I said, adding, 'I would have my friends Gruffudd Llwyd and Rhun ap Gwynfor accompany me.'

'As you wish, Owain. They are most welcome,' he responded, but I sensed a certain resentment which again did not sit easily with his words.

We entered a large room which I remembered well from the time when Hywel's father had whipped me, leaving me unconscious with the skin of my back torn and bloody. I remembered too the kindly ministrations of Hywel's mother who did her best to aid the healing process in this very chamber. It looked exactly as it had done thirty-five years before except that, due to the early onset of the cold weather, there was a blazing log fire crackling away in the huge fireplace.

I examined Hywel as he took a seat at the long table and gestured the three of us to do likewise. He was now fifty-one years old and he looked it with his white beard and fast greying hair surrounding a deeply-lined face. There were heavy pouches under his eyes and I wondered how much he supped of the area's strong ale in a week. Before sitting down I took a quick glance at myself in the mirror above the fireplace to check on the progress of the grey in my beard, and was shocked to discover that I also had streaks of grey in my hair. When I had left Mared at Dolbadarn in late May my golden mane had been intact. Now, in late September, I was returning to my wife an old, grey-haired man. I found the realisation thoroughly depressing but hid my feelings as we all sat down.

'So, cousin, what is the subject which you thought so

important that you hastened to Nannau without a thought for princely protocol?'

'I was not aware that you were a prince, Hywel, and if you are starting to see yourself as such then, let me warn you, you are playing a dangerous game.'

'Well, if one of us in the family calls himself a prince we must be of royal blood and it follows that royal families often have more than one prince.' Hywel smirked, knowing that he was irritating me.

We all jumped as Gruffudd Llwyd banged the table hard with his fist. His face was white with barely controlled rage. 'It seems to me that it is you who have lost sight of good manners, sire. Let me remind you that Owain ap Gruffudd is not only a prince, he is the Prince of Wales, proclaimed as such by the people. He now fights to drive our enemies out of Wales and he can do without family members who still side openly with the English. You seem to have lost sight of reality as well, for your whole attitude towards our Prince is rude and ignorant. If you think that you will be allowed to continue to address him in such an insulting manner, then you will have painful lessons to learn.'

'Are you threatening me, bard?' Hywel blustered, but there was a worried look in his eye.

I decided to cut in before Gruff could respond. 'I have called with you, cousin, because I am tired of your constant scheming to get my loyal followers in this area to change their allegiance. I have tried to persuade you many times to give me your support but you insist on carrying on with our feud even to the extent of publicly supporting Bolingbroke. This, in the current situation, is treason and being my cousin will not save you from the consequences.'

I spoke in a restrained voice which made my message all

the more effective, for Hywel Selyf was now staring at me in disbelief. He tried to interrupt but I continued in the same tone.

'I will now ask you for the last time to support me. If you refuse then I will arrest you on a charge of conspiracy to commit treason and you will be taken from this place in chains.'

'You would not dare…' He sprang to his feet, his eyes taking on a fanatical light as he stared at me with unconcealed hatred.

I turned to Gruffudd and nodded towards the door. The big man stood and left the room. I turned back to Hywel.

'Oh yes I would. At any moment now a large troop of men will ride up to your gates. Any attempt to oppose me and Nannau will be burnt to the ground.'

As I spoke we heard a commotion at the gate as the guards challenged new visitors.

'You had better order them to open the gates, unless you want to see your home go up in flames,' I said tersely.

Hywel Selyf sat open-mouthed for a second or two. Then he tore himself away from the table, tipping a chair over in his haste to reach the door. I heard him bellow for a servant as he rushed down the corridor. I watched from a window as he spoke urgently to the servant, before striding towards the gates while his servant ran towards the stables. For a moment I thought he was going to attempt resistance but then he motioned his guards to open the gates and the rest of our force rode unopposed into the courtyard.

Rhun ap Gwynfor and I made our way down to the courtyard to join Gruff and our men. There was quite a din, for the open area had not been designed to take 100 men and their horses. While we were organising half the men to ride out of the gates to wait for us, a lone horseman emerged from the stables and, jostling past the disorganised riders in the courtyard, he headed urgently for the open gates and galloped away. For a moment I thought of sending a few of my men to bring him back but decided not to; after all it was just one servant and all I wanted was to take a captive Hywel Selyf with me.

Rhun had also seen the rider. 'I think you should know that the rider was Hefin, Selyf's head ostler, and I wouldn't mind betting that Hywel has sent him to his son-in-law, Gruffudd ap Gwyn of Ardudwy. Gruffudd has some influence in these parts and is the one man who could quickly raise a force to try and prevent us from imprisoning Selyf.'

'Damn! I should have followed my first instinct and hauled him back here. But it is too late, for he must be a good few miles away by now,' I groaned. 'Still, let us hope that we will get back to Dolgellau unopposed. If we are challenged we will simply have to take them on, come what may. I am certainly glad that I have your support, old friend.'

Rhun grinned. 'Well, I did warn you that your plan might not be as straightforward as you first thought.'

Then Hywel was at my shoulder with a wry smirk on his face.

'Is there a problem?' He had obviously heard my conversation with Rhun.

I smiled at him grimly. 'Nothing we cannot deal with.'

'I would not be so sure of that if I were you…'

'Your concern is touching, cousin. All you have to worry about is yourself. Come what may, you are now my captive and you are going to remain my captive until you recover some of your common sense. Now where is your wife,

Catherine, and young Meurig, your son? Find them quickly. I will give you ten minutes to say your goodbyes.'

'That will not be possible, for they are away visiting my daughter and her husband in Ardudwy.' He paused before murmuring archly, 'Unless of course you wish to take me there first?'

I ignored the jibe and instructed Gruff to tie Hywel's hands behind his back, put him on a horse and secure him to his mount. That horse was then to be secured to Gruff's own horse. Having overseen these precautions, which had the prisoner protesting and swearing loudly, I ordered the whole column to mount and we left Nannau at a brisk trot heading back to Dolgellau along a path which took us north of Moel Cynwch and down the Ganllwyd valley. As a precaution, I sent one of Rhun's men, who had good local knowledge, to scout the route ahead.

We had been riding for some time when I saw the scout galloping back to meet us. I raised my arm to signal a halt and waited for the horseman to arrive.

'There are armed men ahead, sire. I counted 200. They crossed Llanelltyd bridge which spans the river Mawddach and formed up as if to defend the bridge. I believe it is Gruffudd ap Gwyn of Ardudwy and his followers. He has obviously heard that you have captured his father-in-law and knows full well that you will have to cross the bridge for the river is in flood after the rain of the last few weeks. You would have to travel many miles to find another crossing.'

'How far are we from the bridge?'

'Some two miles, sire.'

'What we need first is to find a vantage point where we can observe ap Gwyn's strength and his defensive preparations,' I pondered.

Rhun cut in. 'In less than a mile we will enter a large copse of trees. A few of us could go ahead, sneak through the trees and then we should have a clear view down the mile-long hillside which slopes down to the bridge. Siôn here could lead us back there.'

'Fine,' I agreed. 'We will have to take great care though. If I were in this Gruffudd's situation I would now be sending one or more of my men up to that wood to act as lookouts, and we don't want to be seen until we are ready to take them on. We are outnumbered almost two to one. Rhun – you and I will accompany Siôn and we will take four members of *Y Cedyrn* with us to take care of any lookouts we may come across.'

All of my guards were experienced professionals and I chose four who were renowned for their tracking and close combat skills. Before we got in sight of the trees I instructed my guards to split into two pairs, one pair going east and the other westward along circuitous routes to try and enter the wood unseen. We gave them a fifteen-minute start before Rhun, Siôn and I continued along the direct path which would expose us to any watchers in the trees.

Though there had been nothing to indicate we were being watched, the three of us were tense as we entered the trees in single file. I prayed that our four protectors had already searched the copse and were now ready for any eventuality. We continued on our way in silence until, at last, we reached the far side without seeing a soul. There was a clear view of the hillside and the path meandering down through low outcrops of rock and bracken to the swollen waters of the Mawddach and the solitary stone bridge spanning it. There were armed men spread over the area on both sides of the bridge, with a large contingent of archers on the near side already in position to repel attack. And Siôn was correct, for the defenders of Llanelltyd bridge outnumbered us two to one.

I heard the alarmed croak of a startled raven and the flapping of wings as the bird swept out of the nearest tree, vacating its perch and rapidly gaining height. We spun around to see two men, bowstrings taught, aiming arrows at us from a distance of only a few yards. They both looked nervous and there is nothing more lethal than a skittish archer. For a second I contemplated making a grab for my dagger, but instantly rejected a move which would have been suicidal in the circumstances. Seeing us transfixed by their presence, both seemed to relax a little. The ginger-haired eldest of the two even took on an attitude of bravado.

'No, no, good sirs.' He forced a little chortle. 'Even *Y Mab Darogan* would drop any thoughts of resistance with an arrow trained on him from this distance.'

They were the last words he would ever utter, for we heard the familiar, deadly whisper of an arrow speeding to its target. The ginger-haired man knew nothing of what happened, for the arrow pierced his back, its lethal tip emerging from his chest. His eyes widened and there was a sharp exhalation of breath as he slumped to the ground. His companion spun around to face the new danger but a long knife, as if by magic, suddenly appeared embedded in his throat. He made a horrible gurgling sound as the blood welled up in his throat, choking him before pouring out of his mouth in long spurts. Then he, too, lay lifeless on the muddy ground.

Our rescuers came running out of their hiding places and our relief was so palpable that we flung our arms around them in an instinctive display of gratitude. One of the four was their recently-appointed leader, Gerwyn Dal. I learnt afterwards that the knife which killed the second archer was his. Gerwyn had impressed me immensely during the capture of Reginald de Grey. I had approached his lord, Rhys Tudur, for permission to ask the big, experienced warrior if he would consider being leader of *Y Cedyrn*. To my surprise, and Rhys's obvious regret, Gerwyn had accepted as soon as Rhys had assured him that, though it was not a development he welcomed, he would not stand in his captain's way if he really wanted to accept the honour. In a few short months he had proved an excellent and popular commander of my elite guards. Now he had saved my life. The whole of the little drama had been enacted in minutes and we all turned back to study the scene around the bridge, looking for possible weaknesses in ap Gwyn's defensive formation. But the man was obviously a capable leader and I could discern no weaknesses in the disposition of his troops.

'I must say it does not look good,' Rhun said pensively. 'An all-out attack on that bridge by an under-strength force would be suicidal. There is one ploy you could try, but it would be, at best, a gamble.'

'What do you have in mind?' I asked eagerly.

'Four or five miles upstream there is small group of rowan trees spanning both banks of the river. In the shade of those trees is Pwll y Diafol (the Devil's Pool). For some thirty feet the banks of the river are considerably wider and the pool is up to eight feet deep in places. It is very popular with fishermen, for it is an ideal spot for trout. What is not generally known is that it was created more than a century ago by partially damming the stream with a causeway of large boulders. By now that causeway has sunk a little into the bed of the stream and, at times of flood, the boulders are a foot or more below the flow of water. Few people know of its existence but it may be possible to ford the stream on horseback at that end of the pool.'

'It would be excellent if we could,' I interrupted enthusiastically. 'But carry on. What would be your plan?'

'Well, this would be my suggestion.' Rhun paused with the five of us hanging on his words. He grinned, for we must have made a comical-looking audience.

'Give me twenty of your guards to add to my own force of fifty and we will advance on foot to the bottom of the hill to a position just within bowshot of the enemy. We will use the cover provided by the rock outcrops and low bushes to encourage them to expend their arrows while we shelter holding our bucklers over our heads but returning fire occasionally to show serious intent. You take your remaining forty guards on horseback to Pwll y Diafol, cross the river and sneak up behind ap Gwyn to attack him from behind, cavalry-style. As soon as you arrive we will use the moment to send a few deadly volleys of arrows into them before charging them with swords drawn. The rest would be in the hands of the gods!'

'And what if we fail to ford the river... what happens then?'

'If that happens then we will not be able to take the bridge.' Rhun frowned. 'You would have to return here to cover our retreat from our forward position before we all withdrew.'

'I think your plan is an excellent one, Rhun. We will ford that damned river, I promise you,' I said grimly as we set off back to our waiting companions.

I decided to leave Hywel in the care of two of Rhun's men, ignoring his sarcastic chuckle as he asked whether we were having 'a little problem'. An hour later I rode Llwyd y Bacsie into the little cluster of rowan trees Rhun had described and stopped on the bank. I watched the raging torrent cascading into the Devil's Pool and exploding out of it downstream in powerful waves, looking as dangerous as any stretch of flooded river I had ever seen. I was filled with serious misgivings. There was no sign of the sunken causeway. It would take a brave rider and a very trusting horse to risk entering this maelstrom. My allocation of forty guards moved up to assess the situation. They had proved themselves a tough, hardened bunch many times but all their faces registered shock and varying degrees of trepidation on seeing what was involved if we were to ford the swollen river. The only face which looked calm was that of Rhun's retainer, who had been brought along to witness the crossing and report back to his lord so that his section could start its offensive against Gruffudd ap Gwyn's men.

I was still deep in thought when Gerwyn Dal rode up. 'Would you allow me the honour of being the first to attempt the crossing, my Prince?'

He spoke through gritted teeth but his voice was steady as a rock. Nothing ever seemed to overawe this man. I looked at him gratefully.

'You are either very brave or very foolhardy,' I said, softening my words with a broad grin. 'But, before you do, I want you to tie a strong rope around your waist which we will tether to one of these trees. I don't want my best soldier to throw his life away without some means of rescue.'

'That is not a compliment I deserve, my Lord,' he said quietly.

'It is most certainly deserved,' I responded warmly. 'I rarely say anything I don't mean.'

With a stout rope tied to his waist and anchored to a suitable rowan trunk, Gerwyn nudged his horse forward but, as the animal neared the water's edge, it shied violently away. The big man made soothing noises and tried to coax his mount into the water but it refused each time. Frustrated, he called on everyone to move back and took his horse back twenty paces before kicking his heels into the animal's side to take it at a run. The horse, still obviously terrified, skidded to a halt at the last moment, wild-eyed, neighing and all but unseating its rider. Its fear seemed to be spreading to the others, many of whom became agitated. I had to do something quickly, for our venture was looking less possible by the minute.

I called on Gerwyn to take his animal away from the torrent. I whispered quietly in Llwyd's ear.

'*Wel, fy merch i – mae hi i fyny i ti a mi.* It is up to you and me, my girl… like it has been so often in the past.'

Llwyd was not so young any more to be taking on life-threatening action of this kind, but I calculated that she was still a big, strong destrier unencumbered by armour, and she had always had a big heart. She had never refused me anything in her whole life, but I had never asked her to tackle a raging flow of water such as this before. As I walked her slowly up to the river bank I could sense the others holding their breath. Gerwyn had insisted on tying the rope around my waist. And, all the while, I chatted to her quietly and calmly, telling her how proud I was of her. She gave no inclination of how she was reacting to the challenge. She just looked straight ahead and paced slowly to the water's edge. Just as she entered the surging flow she gave a low whinny, though whether as a gentle protest or as a calm indication of intent I do not know. For a moment her feet scrabbled as she tried to swim but to her surprise and mine, found solid footing only some two feet below the surface. It was still not easy, for she had to maintain a kind of wading gait, pushing hard against the flow, which she managed superbly. As we reached halfway across, the current became suddenly stronger and the causeway fell away another foot, but I shouted my encouragement and again she responded strongly. The depth of water quickly decreased again and then we were safe on the other side to loud cheering from our comrades. I dismounted quickly and flung am arm around the brave horse's neck in gratitude. She simply shook her head up and down, snorting her disgust at my public show of emotion, making me laugh.

Our troubles were far from over, for all the other horses baulked at making the crossing. In the end Llwyd and I had to recross the river so that we could rope Llwyd to another horse. In fact we had enough rope to tie six other horses together. Again, Llwyd entered the torrent with confidence and, after some hesitation and forceful pulling, the second horse too scrabbled in, then found a firm footing. This seemed to energise the other horses and, as we reached the far bank, I could hear my men encouraging their mounts to follow the others. In a surprisingly short time we were all safely over and I could signal Rhun's man to go back to inform his master of our successful fording of the Mawddach.

After a short break we began our return journey to the bridge at a canter for the first three miles, then reduced the pace to a walk to give our horses time to recover. At length we reached the outcrop of large rocks we had noticed when we were passing by along the other bank of the river. Dismounting, I ordered two men to climb the rocks to examine the scene at the bridge where we could hear sporadic shouting. They came back quickly to report that the defenders of the bridge had Rhun and his outnumbered force pinned down under intense volleys of arrows. They were probably hoping to soften up the attackers before launching an all-out attack with pikes and swords, confident that they had the numbers to prevail.

We held a hurried conference. I stressed that we would need to launch a ferocious charge into the backs of the unsuspecting enemy. There were only forty of us, but we were all mounted and could create havoc when we surprised the foot soldiers from the rear. Our first task, though, would be to walk our horses up to the bridge and form two ranks to fire heavy volleys of arrows into their backs as they began their own attack on Rhun and his seventy stalwarts. The first rank would fire three rounds of arrows, before moving their mounts smartly to one side to allow the second rank to release three more volleys. It might even be possible to repeat the manoeuvre before charging them. All we needed was a little luck so that our targets were unaware of us until the last possible moment, for a good archer could be relied upon to get three arrows per minute away in accurate volleys. Our chance of achieving complete surprise was quite high, for the enemy had no reason to believe they might be vulnerable from the rear. After all, the Mawddach was in flood and impossible to ford.

I ordered the royal standard of the house of Gwynedd to be unfurled with its four lions rampant on a field of gold to remind the enemy that they had taken up arms against their rightful Prince. It was lodged between two rocks on full view of the bridge, for it would also alert Rhun and his men that we had arrived and were ready for battle. None of the enemy saw it, for they were concentrating on loosing arrows at their opponents. It was not an occasion to display the fabled golden dragon, for these were merely rebel subjects who were not worthy of its wrath.

Then Rhun's forces stood clear of their defences and started an offensive of their own, firing heavy volleys of arrows which created huge gaps in their ranks. I saw Gruffudd ap Gwyn. He was easy to spot, for he was dressed in a blue surcoat and shouting desperately to his men to take cover.

I swung myself on to Llwyd y Bacsie. 'Now is the time to surprise them,' I called. 'Let us show this rabble how real warriors make war!'

Rhun ordered his men to cease firing and to run at the enemy with pikes and swords at the ready. The much smaller attacking force rushing to engage them in hand-to-hand fighting seemed to paralyse ap Gwyn's men for a minute or two. Then I heard their leader swearing at them to get into a defensive formation. With Rhun's company only some fifty yards away, some of the bridge's defenders heard galloping hooves behind them and turned to stare in disbelief at a large troupe of cavalry attacking them from their own side of the river. I had instructed my men to space themselves further apart than normal for such a charge and to shout and scream, making as much noise as possible.

There is nothing more devastating in battle than to be faced with the unexpected. To face a force you outnumber two to one can also breed over-confidence. Gruffudd ap Gwyn and his men were both surprised and over-confident on Llanelltyd bridge that day. In addition, they soon discovered that they were facing, in my sixty guards, warriors they simply could not match in power, skill or experience. I rode directly for ap Gwyn, bludgeoning his small group of personal guards out of my way. He stood still, sword drawn, his balanced stance telling me that this was a man who had been trained to fight. I brought Llwyd to a halt a few yards away and dismounted, taking my time, trying to weigh up this young man who faced me so confidently. I drew my sword and walked purposefully towards him.

He proffered me a sardonic smile. He must have been in his mid-twenties, almost as tall as me, broad-shouldered and powerful – almost certainly skilled in the use of the sword. I was surprised at my unease. I had been a champion jouster and never had I considered that my next opponent might beat me. I had been in many battles in King Richard's armies and I had never been bested by another swordsman. Come to that, I had never been beaten in a fist-fight either. Suddenly I was uncomfortably aware of something which I had steadfastly ignored; the encroaching years. I was now beyond the age when a man went willingly to war. Oh, I had kept myself fit. I rode every day and practised with the sword and the bow several times a week but, in that moment, by Llanelltyd bridge I suddenly thought of those mornings when I got out of bed aware of a stiffness, a pain, sometimes in my knees, more often in my back; of the aching of an injured finger or shoulder which seemed to be taking much longer to heal than it used to. In short, I was not a young man any more.

It struck me like a body blow that my struggle for independence for my own people had come to me at the wrong time in my life. I should have seized the moment when I was young and strong. But life is not like that. The struggle began when a set of circumstances had made the call almost impossible to ignore. That is how the fates treat us humans, and laugh at our hopes and dreams.

Suddenly Gruffudd ap Gwyn bowed low.

'Ah, my Prince, I am forgetting my manners. How are you, your Highness? Forgive me for spoiling your day, but you have my father-in-law tied up, and a prisoner. How can any man bear the wrath of his wife if he does nothing to defend her father from imprisonment… even by a prince?'

'It is indeed a predicament, Dafydd ap Gwyn. But surely, I do not need to inform you, or your good wife, that if your father-in-law preaches sedition against his lawful ruler then he is guilty of treason and is, in consequence, subject to the full rigours of the law.'

'That is correct, Owain ap Gruffudd Fychan. But what if that prince is not his lawful prince but is simply a deluded old man who sees himself as the *Mab Darogan*, but in reality, is himself guilty of treason against his lawful King?'

I struggled to control my anger, which of course was the intended result of his jibe.

'So, the son-in-law is just as seditious as the father-in-law,' I said severely. He returned my stare with a confident smirk. 'Ah well, in that case, the deluded old man must teach the deluded young pup a lesson. Unfortunately, he will not live long enough to learn from it, which is a shame.'

Gruffudd ap Gwyn gave a short, mirthless laugh. 'If half of what I have heard of you is true, there was a time when you would certainly have been a man to avoid crossing swords with. But you still have not caught up with reality, have you? You are no longer the young lion who could beat anyone foolish enough to challenge you. You are now an old man… you have the reflexes of an old man, the stamina of an old man, the strength of an old man and the skills of an old man. I shall go down in history as the warrior who killed Owain Glyndŵr.'

'In that case,' I said, with an easy confidence which I did not feel, 'you had better get on with that task.'

As we circled each other, swords drawn, I knew the young upstart was correct. For once I had miscalculated. I probably was too old to take on this young lion. I was in with a chance if I could find a means of ending the bout in a few short minutes. I could probably keep up with him, be better than him even, for five to ten minutes. If the struggle went on for longer than that, then my life would be over.

Suddenly he came at me attacking fast and hard, putting power into his flashing sword so that I had to concentrate entirely on fending off his blows. I did so comfortably enough, eventually coming back at him with a vicious attack of my own which made his eyes widen as he desperately fended me off. The pace continued, fast and furious, and I began to lessen the firmness of my blows and affected some breathlessness. Gruffudd soon noticed the signs of weakening and his frown of concentration changed to a knowing half-smile as he redoubled his efforts to pierce my guard. Then he stepped back gloating as I made pretence of losing my grip on my sword for a brief moment.

'I knew it,' he jeered. 'You have miscalculated in taking me on. You are a spent force… old and feeble. Prepare to die, fool!'

With that he leapt at me, swept my weak parry to one side and raised his weapon to deliver the mortal blow. For a moment his chest was totally exposed and, using my reflexes to the full, I thrust forward hard. My sword sank deep into his body with a bone-jarring shock which raced through my wrist and up to my shoulder. His face, for a moment close to mine, registered surprise and disbelief. Then it turned grey, blood pouring out of his mouth. He fell backwards and my sword dislodged itself from his chest as he fell causing another fountain of blood to appear. He tried to say something. I knelt beside him, for he was clearly dying.

He gasped, wordlessly.

'You said I only have the strength, stamina and skills of an old man… all true, of course,' I offered. 'What you failed to realise was that I also have the experience and the cunning of an old man.'

He smiled faintly, then I heard a horrible gurgling noise in his throat and his eyes glazed over. Gruffudd ap Gwyn was dead. I was dimly aware of jubilant shouts all around me, for the day was ours and the enemy survivors were fleeing in all directions. Yet I felt no jubilation. I took no joy in defeating a force of fellow Welshmen. We badly needed men like Gruffudd ap Gwyn to help us in our struggle against the real enemy. I looked at the corpse at my feet; a young man in his prime, killed long before his time. Somehow, he seemed even younger in death, his face boyish and with an innocence which, in life, had been hidden behind his bravado. The numbness I had felt since delivering the fatal thrust now faded to be replaced by a painful mix of emotions, including guilt, despair, sadness and a deep regret.

I became aware that I was surrounded by silent warriors whose noisy jubilation had been cut short on seeing me kneeling there. Then I felt a large hand on my shoulder.

'It is over, Owain. Come, let us ride back to where our prisoner is being held. We could still make Dolgellau by dark.'

My old friend Gruffudd Llwyd's voice was matter-of-fact, but somehow comforting. I stood up and managed a restrained, 'Well done, lads. You were magnificent.'

As they turned away to mount I could see concern on several faces. They were good men but I doubted whether they understood my torment. The exception, as always, was Gruff.

10

M Y COUSIN TOOK the news of Gruffudd ap Gwyn's
death very badly. For the first time ever, I saw genuine
anguish on Hywel's face. He was mortified by the demise of
his son-in-law and his grief was, not unnaturally, very much
for his daughter who, though she did not know it yet, had
been made a widow just days before the birth of their first
child. I offered my sincere regret for having caused such a
calamity, even though responsibility lay as much at his door
as it did at mine.

He spat in my face and railed at me. 'Why is it that
you, Owain, always bring me unpleasantness and disaster
whenever you appear? Whatever I do you always seem to
come out on top... What can I do to halt your hateful use
of me...?'

He was on the verge of tears. I carefully wiped his spittle
from my cheek with my glove, choosing not to react to
the insult. He was clearly close to hysteria and incapable
of rational discussion. I ordered that he be tied up again
for the remainder of the journey to Dolgellau. In truth, I
actually felt sorry for him in his grief – but he was still my
prisoner, and sedition and treachery are matters which no
ruler can ignore.

When, at last, we reached Rhun's impressive hall near
Dolgellau it was night; our surroundings bathed in the
magical glow of a bright full moon. A line of large sycamores
grew majestically beside the road to my friend's home.

They cast long shadows, with their overhanging branches partly bared due to the early leaf fall. The interplay of light and shadow as the moonlight shone through the trees' gnarled limbs created a peaceful and harmonious picture far removed from the savage killing fields surrounding Llanelltyd bridge.

Rhun wanted to incarcerate Hywel in one of his pigsties but I prevailed on him to afford the prisoner a comfortable bed and a decent supper. He was, however, to be chained to his bed and at least one of Rhun's servants was to sit in the room at all times to guard him, because I feared he might attempt to take his own life in his disturbed state.

Later, at supper, I was pleasantly surprised to see Seisyll, Abbot of Cymmer, an old acquaintance and, as a Cistercian, a strong supporter of mine. He had heard the tale that I had gone to Nannau to arrest Hywel Selyf, a piece of news which had spread through the whole district like wildfire. He knew of the long-standing quarrel which divided us and had tried to reconcile us without success. He had made his way to Rhun's hall immediately, intent once again, on attempting to smooth out our family differences.

As soon as the meal was over Rhun – prompted earlier no doubt by the Abbot – suggested the three of us retire to his private quarters where Siân, his plump, pretty wife had prepared chairs for us around a welcoming fire. As soon as she had been assured that we were comfortable she brought in some hot, mulled wine in large, pewter goblets, then placed an earthenware bowl of generous proportions on the hearth, filled with more wine and sporting a wooden ladle, before leaving us to our own devices.

Abbot Seisyll sipped the sweet liquid experimentally, frowning slightly, for it was far too hot to drink except in tiny sips. He was known for his love of good food and fine wine and Rhun and I grinned at each other as the cleric glared at Siân's potion, willing it to cool with ill-concealed impatience. At length he shrugged his shoulders and patted his rounded paunch as he turned to us, no doubt hoping that conversation would hasten the cooling process.

'So, Prince Owain, you have finally given up on converting your cousin to the cause and decided to imprison him.' He paused, slowly raising one bushy eyebrow to emphasise his regret at my decision. 'I can understand you losing patience with Lord Nannau, for he is a source of danger to you in your own backyard. On the other hand, making him a prisoner does not necessarily solve the issue.'

'It is far from an ideal solution, I agree,' I responded evenly. 'But at least he will be where I can see him and will not be able to go around spreading his poison.'

'Yeeees,' Seisyll exhaled as he spoke, drawing out the word so that he sounded totally unconvinced. 'Yet there is an old saying which suggests that if you make a man a martyr you will treble his support. Those who were not convinced by his views previously may find his imprisonment rather harsh. They may, perhaps, begin to feel some sympathy with him. It is only a short journey, you know, for sympathy for the man to become sympathy for his views… have you considered that?'

'Believe me, old friend, I have spent many years pondering on the future of Hywel Selyf. I do understand that imprisoning him is not a complete solution to the problem. Indeed, I agree with your perception of the dangers in taking this action. Unfortunately, this is the only course open to me, for he is becoming far too dangerous to be left at large.'

The Abbot seemed on the point of making further comment when Rhun cut in brusquely, 'Enough of this topic. I think we have exhausted the subject for this evening. Come, let us enjoy the mulled wine and relax a while. Don't forget, Owain and I have fought and killed this day. We are too exhausted to discuss weighty matters till we have had some sleep.'

'Of course, of course. It was remiss of me not to have taken account of your weariness and the numbness of your spirits after such a harrowing day.'

Even as he spoke he was reaching for the wooden ladle to replenish his goblet. Rhun and I could do nothing but smile before following suit.

I slept late the following morning and was spoilt rotten by Marged the chamber maid, a slim, worldly-wise young lady given to smothering a guest with wicked smiles with bodice partly undone, who brought me a delicious breakfast of bacon and eggs washed down with small beer. Long, languid looks and slim fingers softly trailing along the bed blanket made it plain that she would be happy to serve her prince in other ways if he so desired… Having endured months of abstinence I found it a very tempting prospect. I quickly convinced myself that this was not the time or the place and regretfully ushered the disappointed young temptress out of the chamber so that I could get dressed.

Making my way to Rhun's private quarters, I found him in conversation with the good Abbot and cousin Hywel and, within minutes, I had forgotten all about Marged the maid. It seemed that Abbot Seisyll had performed a minor miracle already that morning. He had persuaded Hywel to make his peace with me in return for his freedom. After the well-meaning cleric had given a long report on his earlier conversation with the Lord of Nannau, liberally laced with self-praise, the object of his attention turned to me and made an announcement with which he was less than comfortable.

'It seems I have little choice but to agree to refrain from fermenting opposition to you and your rebellion or to say anything, publicly or privately, which would appear to challenge your position as *Tywysog* of Wales. In return, I expect you to allow me my freedom to return to Nannau to live my life and to see how I can help my dearest daughter whom you have sorely wronged by making her a widow and depriving her infant son of his father. For this you have Abbot Seisyll to thank. However, I will not accede to his further request that I actively support you in your campaigns against King Henry IV of England.'

I stared at him in amazement. 'To say that I am shocked by your agreeing to stop spreading poisonous sedition throughout this area does not begin to describe my reaction. Frankly, it beggars belief and forgive me if I have real doubts about your conversion. But I am not at all surprised that you will not support me against Bolingbroke, for you have spent so many years licking English backsides that you have forgotten our proud family history and that you have the blood of Welsh princes flowing through your veins.'

I paused to watch my cousin struggling to control his temper after my deliberate insult, for he was no longer chained. I really hoped that he would seek to attack me so that I could end his miserable life in defending myself. His face was turning purple as he fought to swallow his pride and his anger.

The Abbot wrung his hands nervously, trying to

dissipate the tension. 'My Prince, my Lord… perhaps we can all attempt to converse in a calmer manner. It… it would be a great shame if such a historic understanding to heal a long-standing rift in the royal house of Powys Fadog should break down at the point of agreement, don't you think?'

'It would indeed be a great shame.' Hywel was now in control of himself. 'To clarify my position. I honestly believe that your rebellion, Owain, is doomed. I know you are doing well at present and you may achieve many more successes but sooner or later, English strength in numbers, English money and English control of the seas will prevail. I am as proud of being Welsh and a member of the ancient house of Powys Fadog as anyone. But I am also a realist. When it is all over I want to be one Welsh nobleman the English will feel they can trust. They may even make me their representative in these parts, rewarding me with wealth and power.'

'And the words you have just uttered paint a clearer picture of you and what you are than I ever could. I need say no more,' I said, more in sorrow than in anger, for it saddened me that this self-seeking man would never understand the meaning of loyalty to his neighbours, society or indeed his heritage, however humble or illustrious.

At lunchtime I was about to announce that I would be leading *Y Cedyrn* north to join my army besieging Harlech castle the following morning when Hywel surprised me by requesting that I join him on his journey back to Nannau, for it was time we clarified the changed situation between us. I was keen to find out how far he was prepared to alter his previous opposition to me and the struggle for freedom. One more day before setting off for Harlech would make little difference, for laying siege to castles was never a quick process.

After a hearty breakfast the following morning we said our farewells to Rhun and Siân and I thanked Rhun warmly for his steadfast military, political and personal support. Then, with my errant cousin by my side, I led *Y Cedyrn* back towards Nannau, and engaged him in serious discussion, exploring the detail of how he would have to act if he wanted to keep his freedom and secure his future. I had to accept that he would never change his view that appeasement of the English was the only sensible approach but I insisted that he must, from now on, refrain from taking any part, overt or covert, in any oral or written criticism of me and the cause. I left him in no doubt that reports of any failure to comply with that edict would result in immediate and long imprisonment.

Surprisingly, Hywel barely raised an objection. He seemed almost relaxed and nodded from time to time. He was more concerned with telling me of the large area of parkland he had developed close to his home and how he had introduced a small herd of deer which, over the past decade or so, had multiplied so that they required regular culling. This allowed him and a few friends some fine sport. As we approached Nannau he turned in the saddle and smiled at me. At least I believe it was an attempt at a smile. In truth, it was a kind of grimace, for he had to force his facial muscles into a smiling posture and there was no humour in his eyes. Still, it was a brave attempt given the flattened and bent state of his nose.

'Tell me, cousin, are all the tales I have been told of your love of hunting true? If so, why don't we have lunch and then ride in search of some deer?'

'Well, I will not be setting off for Harlech until tomorrow and the guards could do with some rest for the remainder of today. Yes, let us have some lunch first, for this ride has sharpened my appetite. Then we will ride into your park for some hunting.'

I had not been looking forward to hours of small talk in Hywel's company, and at least the hunt would be a way of passing the time.

After a pleasant lunch we mounted our horses and, having crossed two meadows, we entered some trees which marked the beginning of Hywel's parkland. As we walked the horses through the well spaced-out rowans, I noticed that the ground ahead was becoming evermore densely covered with shrubs and small trees through which the narrowing path meandered. At first I relaxed, enjoying the birdsong and the occasional rustling of some small animal scuttling away from us through the undergrowth. Hywel had gone quiet, ostensibly so as not to alert the deer to our presence. He seemed somewhat preoccupied. I became aware as well that Llwyd y Bacsie was behaving rather oddly, nervously tossing her head and occasionally whinnying softly as if all was not well. I had never seen her behave like that before and was at a loss to know what was concerning her.

Suddenly, the Lord of Nannau leaned over and touched my arm. He pointed silently ahead, indicating that we were approaching a clearing. We reined in the horses and dismounted quietly. He tethered his mount and I, in my usual way, slipped the reins loosely over the saddle. Llwyd did not need tethering, for she knew when she was expected to wait patiently for me. I followed Hywel as he tiptoed towards the clearing. Suddenly I was shocked to hear the muted clip-clop of hooves. I turned to see Llwyd, ignoring all her training, following quietly but determinedly. I turned back towards her and raised both hands above my head, palms towards her. That was the definitive sign that she was to wait for me. She tossed her head up and down registering serious displeasure then stopped, head low. I was confused by her behaviour, for I had no idea of what was concerning her so much. Then, for a moment, Llwyd was forgotten as Hywel stopped, turned and placed his finger to his mouth. I moved up silently alongside him and saw the clearing properly for the first time. Standing nose to the wind, trying to establish whether it was safe to be standing there in the open, was a magnificent stag, his head adorned with an impressive set of antlers.

My cousin was visibly trembling with excitement, his eyes glittering as he reached for an arrow to notch to his bowstring. I moved a yard or two to his right to give him plenty of room to gauge his shot. Archers have differing methods of setting up a target. Some simply aim at the target and send the arrow on its way. This is the method all longbowmen employ in the danger and excitement of battle. For the hunt there are archers who aim well to one side of the target and move back in a smooth arc towards it letting the arrow go smoothly at the right moment. Hywel Selyf was recognised as a champion archer and now he too set his sights some way to the left of the skittish stag before slowly moving in an arc to his right to pick up his quarry.

Then my brain and my instincts kicked in and several warning thoughts flashed through my mind in a split second: Llwyd's inexplicable nervousness and attempt to follow me against my wishes; my cousin's invitation to hunt which was quite out of character in our relationship; and of course, his bout of trembling while preparing to take aim – not the action of a seasoned hunter… and that arc, if it should continue past the stag would bring me into direct, unmissable range. Reacting purely on instinct I dived violently sideways and, before my body touched the ground, the arrow whistled past me slicing through the loose material of my surcoat at shoulder level leaving a small nick which, I discovered later, bled quite heavily. Turning my head as I landed, I saw Selyf hurriedly grabbing another arrow from his quiver. Desperately I lunged to my feet, my heart sinking as I realised that I was going to die, for I would never get to him before the second arrow pierced my heart at point-blank range. Then something large and powerful brushed past me knocking me to the ground. I heard a scream as Llwyd y Bacsie powered into my assailant, knocking him flying and trampling the longbow, leaving it as several useless bits of wood in her wake. Again I scrambled to my feet, my relief at being alive quickly overtaken by a wave of rage at having been tricked so easily. I half-expected to be looking at a corpse but to my amazement Hywel was also scrambling to his feet, badly shaken but not mortally wounded. I threw myself at him and for several minutes we wrestled desperately in the undergrowth. He was very strong despite having been knocked flying by a destrier and, at one point, he gained the upper hand, getting on top of me and drawing a long dagger.

'Now I've got you. How does it feel knowing you are about to be killed, and by me of all people? It seems there is justice in this world after all.' He leered at me and raised his dagger to cut my throat.

Summoning all my remaining strength, I brought my knee up viciously into his groin. He yelped and, overwhelmed by pain, he momentarily slackened his grip. That was all I needed to roll him over. I twisted his right arm into an impossible angle so that any movement would be agonising for him and drew my own dagger. His eyes widened as he realised his predicament.

'You speak truly,' I gasped. 'There is indeed some justice in this world. But then, you always were a loser. Now die, you treacherous devil.'

I thrust my dagger upwards slicing through his rib cage and piercing his heart. I heard the long sigh as his breath left his body. The Lord of Nannau was dead.

11

THE DOLBADARN MOUNTAIN fortress was enjoying exceptionally warm late summer heat and even at three o'clock in the morning the bedchamber felt close and oppressive despite the open window. Unusually for Snowdonia, there was no breeze to give us any respite. We talked for a long time, for we had been apart for months.

Mared ran her fingers through my greying locks and whispered, 'Mmm, I have missed you so much, my love. And I've been frantic with worry, for I knew you were almost constantly involved in fighting battles and sieges. I prayed to God to bring you home safely to me and now I give thanks, for those prayers have been fully answered.'

'And as usual, I have missed you badly, Mared. I left you in the spring with only a few strands of grey in my beard. I return to you with a much greyer beard and grey hair to boot. Waging war at my age is a trying business. I have realised that I am no longer the young lion I used to be nor am I any longer strong enough or fit enough to take on long, protracted campaigns.'

Mared sat up quickly, looking concerned. 'Why, Owain, I have never heard you speak like that before. Are you all right… I mean, you have not been badly wounded and not told me? Are you losing heart and the appetite for this struggle perhaps?'

'The answer is no on both counts. I am as eager as ever to ensure our freedom from foreign occupation, but I have to face up to the situation as it is, and to the physical shortcomings which befall all of us as we grow older.'

'I, for one, would be very relieved if you decided to reduce your commitment to personally lead every long campaign. Besides, as the territories you control increase and your power grows, so will your duties as a ruler. You are close to the day when you will need your secretary and your senior officers of state far more than your sword.'

'Yes, that is certainly true. I intend to turn my mind to appointing my council of advisors in the next few weeks. In fact…'

I grinned at her, for she could see me clearly in the moonlight streaming in through the open window. 'It was my intention to discuss suitable candidates for various key posts with you. I know that you are interested and knowledgeable too in politics and diplomacy.'

Her face, now fully turned towards me, broke into a wide smile of pleasure, then she bowed her head in mock humility.

'I am honoured, sire.'

'I would be delighted and proud to have my wife at my side to advise me. Your counsel has served me well in the past, I shall need it more than ever in the future.'

The next morning at breakfast we were joined by Gruffudd Llwyd, my secretary, Dafydd, and Ednyfed ap Siôn. They had accompanied me, together with a dozen of my guards, when we left the army besieging Harlech castle to return to Dolbadarn. Both Dafydd and Ednyfed were highly animated by the hostage situation, having heard rather inaccurate and contradictory stories. Gruff and I, on the other hand, had been kept closely informed of all developments by Robert's spies on a regular basis throughout the summer campaign.

Sir Thomas Clanvowe and a few other lesser knights had all been ransomed within eight weeks of their capture and, eventually, Lord de Grey had managed to raise the second part of his ransom to obtain the release of his son. However, the King had flatly refused to ransom young Lord Mortimer.

Not unnaturally, Edmund was furious when he heard that the King had not only refused to ransom him but had forbidden anyone else from doing so. After kicking his heels in his small locked chamber for a week, he had asked for an audience. Mared readily agreed, for she sympathised with his situation. Despite misgivings voiced by both guards, she insisted that the prisoner be released from his chains and also ordered them both to stand outside the door. They argued that she would not be safe on her own with such a high-ranking English prisoner, but she was adamant and they left the room.

'Please be seated, my Lord Mortimer. I hardly think a man of your quality would debase himself by attacking a defenceless woman.' Mared smiled. 'And it would be a very silly thing to do anyway as you are obviously coming to ask me for some kind of favour.'

'I can assure you, your Highness, I have never physically abused a lady in my life.' His face was almost comical in its earnestness. 'And, as you rightly say, it would take a remarkably stupid individual to even think of doing so in my present circumstances.'

'I believe you, sire. I like to think I can read a person's character pretty quickly and I knew I would be safe in your company. Now, do you think we could dispense with formal titles and call each other by our Christian names, at least in private?'

'Why, of course. Then, I am Edmund.'

'And I am Margaret, though everybody calls me by the Welsh version – Mared. So, feel free to call me whichever you prefer.'

'Marrred.' Edmund rolled the 'r' experimentally. It was obviously a sound which was outside his normal range. 'Yes, I will call you Marrred.'

Mared laughed delightedly. 'Very well. I think I'm going to like you… Edmund! Now tell me, why have you asked to see me?'

'I have a feeling that you will not believe I am sincere in my request but I want you to send word to your husband that I am totally disillusioned with Bolingbroke. He has now shown his true nature by ignoring the loyalty I have shown him and refusing to ransom me. What is more, he has even forbidden anyone else from doing so. He is obviously afraid that I, or one of the Mortimers, will eventually challenge his legitimacy as King. The oaf is too stupid to see that, by his action, he has alienated me and driven me into the camp of his enemies. Madam, I wish you to inform Prince Owain that his former enemy, Edmund Mortimer, now wants to be his ally and to serve in his forces in the struggle against Henry IV. What is more, Henry will have alienated the Percys as well, for his failure to ransom me will be seen by Hotspur, his father the Earl of Northumberland, and his uncle, the Earl of Worcester, as a slight upon the Percy family. You see, Henry Hotspur is married to my sister.'

When Mortimer's intentions were relayed to me we were almost at the end of my campaign against the English-held castles of south Wales. I welcomed his new-found enthusiasm for making war on Henry IV, since his family still enjoyed considerable influence and prestige among the English aristocracy. His personal support, even in his weakened situation, would help strengthen my position.

However, I was totally unprepared for another request of Mortimer's which reached me a few weeks later. He had obviously made good use of his new freedom as an ally of mine and had successfully wooed my eldest daughter, and had even secured another audience with her mother to request Catrin's hand in marriage! Fortunately, I was already on my way north when this request reached me and it was as good a reason as any to cut short my visit to the siege of Harlech castle and hurry home to Dolbadarn. I felt it was high time I exerted some authority, as events were progressing a little too fast for my liking.

Now, at breakfast on my first full day back at Dolbadarn, I realised that even Ednyfed was not immune to the influence of some of the wild tales that seemed to be circulating.

I waited until Ednyfed had finished speaking and cut in just as Dafydd was opening his mouth to join in.

'Much of what I've heard so far bears little resemblance to the facts as I know them, so I see no virtue in continuing to listen. Now, as you know, we arrived last night as darkness fell, so we have had very little time to establish the facts out of all the wild rumours which are being repeated in this place. However, I have spoken to Princess Mared, who docs know the true state of affairs. I can state categorically that there is no truth in the assertion that Edmund Mortimer has seduced my daughter Catrin and made her pregnant in order to pressurise me into agreeing to their marriage. Similarly, there is not a shred of evidence that Mortimer's conversion to our cause is a ploy to enable him to become an informer to Bolingbroke.'

I paused and looked at the others in turn. 'Will there be anything else, gentlemen?'

All had noticed my irritation at the rumours and had obviously decided that silence would now be their best course of action. As they all shook their heads, Dafydd and Ednyfed in particular looked decidedly sheepish.

Later I visited Catrin in her chamber. Her mother was already there and gave me a warning look. Catrin got up and ran towards me hugging me delightedly, for she had missed my homecoming the night before. I decided there and then that I would not embarrass her by making any reference to rumours of her pregnancy. From childhood Catrin had always been straightforward and open, and had she been with child she would certainly not have welcomed me with such joyous abandon. Tall like her mother, but with light brown hair and attractive grey eyes, she turned away and there was a happy bounce to her gait as she returned to her chair.

'Well, Mared, I understand that Lord Mortimer has decided to join forces with us. Do you think he is to be trusted?'

'Oh, undoubtedly, my Lord. He is a fine, upstanding young man. He has firm views and a ready smile and, from what I know of him, I believe him to be completely trustworthy.'

I glanced across at Catrin as I continued, 'Would you also be comfortable with having him as a son-in-law?'

My daughter sat demurely, hands clasped in her lap, eyes lowered. I grinned at Mared who smiled back at me.

'Well, he is English… and of royal blood, which means

we would have to take account of the political consequences. That aside, he is a very personable young man and I would have no objection.'

'My love, you know that I value your judgement highly but I should not really be asking you such a question without discussing the situation with someone else first.'

I turned to my daughter and smiled at her gently. She looked up and returned my smile awkwardly, her cheeks flaming a pretty pink.

'You know that Lord Mortimer has sent me a formal request to grant him your hand in marriage, I suppose.'

Catrin nodded, staring at her lap.

'And I can assume that he has not done this without first asking you if you would be prepared to be his wife?'

'Yes, Father.'

Despite her nervousness her voice was clear and steady.

'Yes, he has asked you or yes, you have agreed to be his wife?'

'Yes, Edmund has asked me if I would be his wife. And I have agreed, subject to your approval, that I would be happy to be his wife.'

Her cool candour filled me with love and pride. I glanced at Mared and saw that she, too, had a tear in her eye.

Suddenly, Catrin got up and ran to me, flinging her arms around my neck and sobbing, her whole body shaking.

'Oh, Father, I have never felt like this about any man before. I love him so much and I know that he loves me in the same way. Please say that you will agree to the marriage… you will make us both so happy.'

'It is not quite as simple as that, young lady. Do not forget, you are the daughter of the Prince of Wales and this young man is an Englishman of royal blood. And we are at war with the English. I first need to consider, as your mother has already mentioned, the political implications of the union. Also, I have only met him once, briefly, on a battlefield and I will need to have lengthy discussions with him on all sorts of topics. Now, now, don't look so crestfallen. In fact I have an open mind on the matter and nothing would please me more than to make you happy. Just be patient for a few days is all I ask.'

Catrin slowly disengaged herself, and after quietly excusing herself, squared her shoulders and walked stiffly out of the chamber.

I looked helplessly at Mared who smiled and said, 'Don't worry, Owain. Catrin will be fine. You had to spell out the realities of the situation and, of course, it was not what she wanted to hear. She will go away and think about it and will come to understand the wisdom of your words. After all, she is her father's daughter, you know.'

That night, Edmund Mortimer and I had a quiet supper together in my private quarters. Mared had personally cooked us a fine meal, starting with bowls of *cawl* followed by rabbit stew and vegetables washed down with our best ale. Finally, we enjoyed the sweetness of muffins liberally coated with honey.

I quickly discovered that Edmund was pleasant company with a keen interest in a wide range of topics. He was surprisingly knowledgeable about the history and traditions of the Welsh, a topic which many Englishmen dismissed as a catalogue of blood and barbarism. Young Mortimer, however, knew much of the importance of the country during the Age of Saints and I could only assume that he had enjoyed considerable education at the feet of some enlightened monk. He was also a student of warfare and had seen action under Bolingbroke and the young Prince Hal. He confirmed my view that, though still a young lad, Hal was already a far better battlefield tactician than his father. He even suggested that the young prince would eventually become the best English war leader since Richard the Lionheart. This was not good news for me. We were doing very well in our war of independence against Bolingbroke. It would appear that his son would be able to deploy superior strength in numbers, English wealth and economic superiority as well as English sea power much more effectively against us in years to come. However, it all gave me the chance to sample Edmund's considerable intellect and wide knowledge and to see in him a most acceptable ally and, indeed, son-in-law.

If I could find a means of forging an alliance with the powerful Percys as well as the Mortimers, then I foresaw a wider rebellion to overthrow Henry IV and rule England, leaving me with Wales. I might even acquire all of the March, annexing even the English Marches into a greater Wales. At present that would have to remain a dream, and a fanciful one at that. But in one or maybe two years both Henrys, father and son, could well be forced into facing a very real threat.

As soon as I gave my blessing, a happy and delighted Catrin and her equally happy suitor set about planning their wedding with all the enthusiasm of young lovers throughout the ages. And, all the while, Mared fussed around them making suggestions like a broody hen, though she was wise enough to stop short of trying to impose her will on the preparations when her suggestions did not meet with the couple's approval.

Eventually the marriage took place in the ancient

church of Llandanwg, reputedly founded by St Tanwg in the fifth century, making it one of the oldest Christian establishments in the land. Though strangely located among the sand dunes behind a fine beach on the coast between Harlech and Llanbedr, it is a simple but attractive church which was renovated and extended almost a century ago. It draws visitors from miles around to view the large traceried windows set in the relatively new east gable and the ornate rood screen separating the chancel from the nave of the church. The walls inside are liberally sprinkled with an array of texts printed in the Gothic style and the windows are glazed with coloured glass. The whole building is a welcoming and peaceful haven and we could think of nowhere more fitting for Catrin and Edmund to be united in holy matrimony.

The event was an opportunity to invite influential supporters old and new, to renew old acquaintances and establish new ones as well as to mingle and exchange views on all kinds of topics. It also proved a good sounding board for planning our campaigns for the coming year. All invitations were eagerly accepted for, apart from the chance to gather and exchange views, many were anxious to meet Sir Edmund Mortimer and to decide for themselves what kind of man he was and whether he could be trusted as an ally. I was very much in favour as I was convinced that he would make a good impression on all who met him.

The marriage ceremony eventually took place on 30th November 1402 with hesitant sunshine vying unsuccessfully with a waspish breeze coming in off the sea and spreading its cold fingers through the sand dunes of Llandanwg.

The ceremony and the later celebrations warmed all our hearts. The large company assembled from all over Wales had a most enjoyable time, entertained by the polished musical verse of Gruffudd Llwyd and by the presence of the happy couple, with both Catrin and Edmund winning over even the most hardened sceptics with their beauty, elegance and ready wit.

The wedding celebrations were hardly over before we were immersed in preparations for celebrating Christmas. On 13th December, young Edmund came to see me brandishing a document on which the ink had scarcely dried. I was getting to know my new son-in-law better every day and I had no reason to regret having given him my eldest daughter for a wife.

'Owain, would you be good enough to read this draft letter. If there is anything in it of which you disapprove I will gladly alter it or dispense with it completely.'

I quickly scanned the letter. It made me smile, for I recognised the early fruits of my decision to welcome the English nobleman as a trusted ally and as a close family member.

'I could not have written it better if you had asked me to pen it,' I chuckled delightedly.

I stood and shook his hand warmly. He flushed with pleasure at my praise and left with a spring in his step.

When Mared entered the chamber a few minutes later I was sitting by the fire, still smiling and savouring a goblet of good French red wine.

'Someone or something has pleased you greatly, my Lord. Am I allowed to enquire what has made you so happy?'

'Come and sit beside me and share a drop of this excellent wine while I tell you.'

Sir Edmund's missive was an open letter aimed at his most powerful friends, relatives, wider circle of supporters and most senior tenants. He declared himself to be a rebel whose sole ambition was to remove Henry IV from the English throne, to be replaced by his imprisoned nephew and namesake, Edmund Mortimer, the true heir and rightful monarch. He had pledged to support 'Oweyn Glendŵr' to bring this about and instructed all his loyal friends, followers and tenants to join in this crusade. Mared readily understood my satisfaction with the letter for, together with his marriage to Catrin, it ensured the consolidation of my own influence in Radnorshire and large sections of the March.

This year had been our most significant and successful period yet and now 1402 was ending on a higher note than we could ever have expected. My name was on everyone's lips in Wales and everywhere that mattered in England while Bolingbroke, by not ransoming Edmund Mortimer, had brought unexpected additional problems on himself.

12

IT WAS A week before Christmas. We were sitting in the large dining room of the Bishop of St Asaph's impressive residence. Bishop Ieuan Trefor, known to the English as John Trevor, had insisted that I take the host's chair at the head of the aged, dark-stained and polished dining table. We had consumed a hearty, delicious and elegantly presented venison dinner and, now that the plates and accompanying debris had been cleared, we were chatting informally. Then the servants brought in what I knew from past visits to be an excellent French wine from the vineyards of Burgundy.

Sitting on my right, Ieuan Trefor leaned over and murmured, 'As soon as the wine is poured I would be honoured if you would play host and chair the discussion, *eich Mawrhydi*.'

I smiled at him in some surprise, for I had never heard him address me as 'your Majesty' before. It was obvious that he could not continue to support our cause without sacrificing his career, and addressing me in this fashion was a clear message that sometime in the near future he would be declaring his hand and resigning from his post for, in English eyes, his public association with our cause would instantly brand him a traitor to Church and state.

I rapped my knuckles on the table and the rumble of private conversations subsided. On my left sat Robert, my spymaster, then Ednyfed, while Gruffudd Llwyd and my brother-in-law John Hanmer completed the row on my left.

Next to Ieuan Trefor, on my right, sat the bulky figure of Gruffudd Yonge, a current prebendary in the bishopric of Bangor. Next to him sat my old friend Hywel Gethin, Dean of St Asaph, known to the English as Hywel Kyffin, who had orchestrated my declaration as *Tywysog* at Glyndyfrdwy in the autumn of 1400. He was flanked by another of my brothers-in-law, Philip Hanmer.

'Our true host this evening has generously vacated his chair at the head of his own table in my honour and wishes me to chair the meeting. I'm sure you would therefore wish me to express our warmest thanks to Bishop Ieuan Trefor for his generosity of spirit and his excellent hospitality,' I began.

I waited for the hearty acclaim to die away. 'Well now, we have important affairs to discuss tonight so we will begin without further delay. You are all sharp-witted men around this table. Indeed, if you were not, you would not be present.' I paused as the smiles broke into chuckles.

'You will, I feel sure, have noticed that apart from myself, none of our military commanders are represented. And that is deliberate. It is not, I hasten to add, that I believe all military commanders are dullards…'

I paused again for chuckles to subside. 'In fact, were it not for the abilities and devotion to duty of my commanders, we would not be in the happy position to claim the ascendancy in this war at present.' This elicited a generous rumble of agreement all around the table.

'However, what I am now looking for is some cool, clear thinking regarding the way ahead. The problem with military men is that they tend to believe in the supreme ascendancy of the sword and longbow in any struggle between warring peoples and countries. Sometimes that is, sadly, the only obvious recourse but we, around the table tonight, also realise that governance of a country and diplomatic engagement between nations requires a far broader array of weapons. We know that clear thinking, words – both spoken and written – can often be far more persuasive than military threats. We are no longer simply rebels to be caught and executed. The English now realise that we have the support of the vast majority of the Welsh people and that is why they can no longer collect their taxes from large areas of Wales and why they and their frightened burghers are hiding in castellated boroughs, not daring to wander far from their defensive walls. It is why the commanders of dozens of their castles are furiously writing to Bolingbroke, entreating him to instigate another invasion of Wales and to send reinforcements to the castles so as to save them from being overrun.'

'I am sorry if I sound less than convinced, my Prince, but I am honour-bound to say that the vicious attacks inflicted by the King's men based in Chester on the poor people of Flintshire over a period of some two weeks recently, seem to indicate that we are not yet in full control of the country.'

I frowned and raised my hand for silence as several tried to speak at once. I looked across at the large, rotund and normally jovial Gruffudd Yonge. He held my gaze without flinching. This was the man I had pencilled in as my Chancellor when we eventually came to set up the great offices of state. Like Ieuan Trefor, here was a very well-educated, well-travelled and astute individual destined for high ecclesiastical office. I could also visualise him as a gifted diplomat, equally at ease discussing commerce and economics as he was interpreting church doctrine. Most importantly, his opinion was always based on fact and he feared no one when giving others the benefit of his views.

'Your point is well made, Gruffudd. We do, indeed, need to be careful not to overstate our dominance. Also, you are right in that we were caught flat-footed by the suddenness of the attacks you speak of. I would, however, make the point that in launching these raids the English broke completely with tradition, for it has always been understood that military activity is suspended during winter and, of course, we were not expecting them. I, too, have been thinking of extending our own military activities for the whole year. You must also remember that it is because we have disrupted and foiled all their attempts to collect taxes in the area this year that the English wish to break the morale of the people of Flintshire.'

'My Prince, may I make a point here.' I smiled as my great friend Gruffudd Llwyd asked for permission to speak. No one would be allowed to voice dissent to me when the bard was present. 'The fact that the English have seen fit to break with the traditional winter pause in military engagement is significant, and their action makes it perfectly reasonable for us to follow suit. From now on we have to be prepared for enemy attacks at any time. However, so will they, and I feel we should grasp any opportunity to respond in kind. Their actions, of course, do no more than confirm your assessment of our present strength for they are being forced to take desperate measures to try to reassert their previous dominance. But they may live to regret their cowardly attacks on the ordinary people of Flintshire.' His words went down well. Even Gruffudd Yonge nodded his agreement.

I turned to my spymaster, Robert, and indicated that his moment to address us had arrived. In his youth, he had been a redoubtable warrior but had long eschewed the sword for the pen at my request, proving that despite his rough exterior he was possessed of a fine mind.

'Prince Owain, my Lords, friends… I have matters of some importance to share with you tonight. It is not generally known, except by our Prince and one other in this gathering, but I was instructed by Owain last year to set up a network of people with sharp eyes and ears to gather information about current and planned enemy activities. We have had some success with this and I now have dozens of agents, or spies if you like, all over Wales. The great majority of them are men, but you may be surprised to hear that a few are women, every bit as brave and skilled at worming information out of unsuspecting targets as the men. We also have similar agents in Chester, throughout the English Marcher counties of Shropshire, Herefordshire and Gloucestershire, as well as in London, where we have many friends and patriots mingling with Members of Parliament and courtiers and servants at Court. Needless to say, when these friends move within those exalted circles they do so with their ears trained to pick up the slightest of whispers.'

Robert paused with a mirthful glint in his eyes. Those for whom this revelation was a surprise quickly got over it and clapped delightedly. Even Gruffudd Yonge was smiling broadly.

'Inevitably we have had a few failures and I am pretty sure the sudden and untimely deaths of two of my key men in Chester, just before the vicious attacks on the people of Flintshire, was no accident. You will be pleased to know that the dead agents have already been replaced by others who reported to me only this morning a rumour which, if correct, will be of significance to us. At present it is only a rumour and I will now need to appraise our London friends and instruct them to find out whether the tale has any basis in fact.'

'And what tale is that, Robert?' Ieuan Trefor was leaning forward in his chair, clearly fascinated.

'The rumour is that Bolingbroke will soon appoint Prince Hal the new military commander in north Wales in succession to the disillusioned Hotspur. As you know, the noble Percy has left the post and gone back to Northumberland in high dudgeon having failed to get the King to pay a penny towards his heavy personal costs in that post. More on that rumour soon, I hope! We have also discovered that, if we attack the great coastal castles in the new year, Bolingbroke, despite currently suffering from a serious shortage of funds, will be forced to reinforce the garrisons of Aberystwyth, Harlech, Beaumaris and Caernarfon castles. This will involve sending more men and supplies of food and arms by land and sea. I'm sure we are all unhappy at the way in which the English navy can deliver to these fortresses directly at will. However, any supply trains travelling overland will be sitting targets for you, my Prince, as long as I can discover their routes and travel dates in advance.'

Robert Puleston sat down to considerable acclaim and I got up to draw the meeting to a close.

'Thank you, brother-in-law, for your report and for your unflagging efforts in seeking out sensitive information from the enemy. It is not easy to carry on the normal life of a major landowner, ostensibly loyal to King Henry, while engaging in undercover activities. It is also a heavy responsibility to interpret the flow of information crossing your desk every day.'

I paused and looked around the table before continuing.

'I have no doubt that Robert's success is, in some

measure at least, due to the fact that so few are aware of this organisation. However, I now feel that everyone around the table should know about it as I hope and believe that every one of you will be taking on ever more important roles in the responsibilities of state in the months and years ahead. I must ask you to honour the highly secret nature of *Y Cysgodion*. It is imperative that no one, other than those present this evening, should know of it. Therefore, I ask you to guard your words, for a careless slip of the tongue could endanger the lives of many and do irreparable harm to our struggle for freedom.'

I paused, looking around to ensure I had their undivided attention before continuing.

'My next disclosure will surprise all of you and I hope it is a course of action which meets with your universal agreement. Some of you will have heard me stress the importance of making an alliance with another power to achieve the complete success we require. That is nothing less than the removal of Bolingbroke and his heirs from the English throne. And now we may be on the verge of achieving such an alliance. We all know that the Percys, one of the most powerful families in England, who ironically played a major part in Henry's struggle for the monarchy, have been growing increasingly disillusioned with him. I have spoken with my friend Hotspur several times and, the final straw which made him give up his role as Bolingbroke's military commander here in north Wales, was the King's refusal to allow the ransom of Edmund Mortimer who is, of course, his brother-in-law. A week ago I received a verbal message from Hotspur, delivered by one of his most trusted retainers. The gist of it was that the whole Percy clan, including his father, the Earl of Northumberland, and his uncle Thomas,

Earl of Worcester, are planning an English rebellion and are looking to us for support… He wishes me to send a senior representative to Northumberland to discuss plans of action in the new year. He promises to provide my emissary with a strong escort from Chester northwards.'

For a few seconds there was stunned silence, soon broken as everyone tried to speak at once. I lifted my hand for silence before allowing each in turn to express his reaction to this exciting news. They were, to a man, in full agreement that this was a golden opportunity for us, and that we should grasp it and give the Percys our full support. The ensuing discussion lasted long into the night. When I called a halt in the early hours of the following morning, they were all still greatly excited, but I cautioned them to observe absolute secrecy.

Christmas proved to be a short, broody lull before the storm. We all felt oddly deflated as the implications of the English winter attacks on our people in the north-east sank in. It seemed as if our world had suddenly been turned upside down and the ancient practice of resting from the toil of military action for a few months in winter had been destroyed forever. But, equally, we were determined to show the enemy how it felt to be attacked and made homeless in the depths of winter, as soon as possible. We celebrated Christmas and the New Year, and after just two short weeks of respite we resumed our guerrilla attacks on targets all over north Wales causing mayhem, destruction and suffering to many of the English boroughs. Then, in February 1403, we resumed our assaults on the great castles of Aberystwyth, Harlech, Caernarfon and Beaumaris. I was determined to turn the screw on Bolingbroke and force him to spend money on vital reinforcements and provisions, money which he could ill-afford. As predicted by Robert Puleston, the English King moved quickly to try and reinforce the castles from land and sea. Now, however, we were in the depths of winter which made such deliveries a deal more problematic, particularly to Aberystwyth and Harlech which afforded precious little shelter from high seas and winter storms to ships trying to negotiate rocky coasts.

It came as no surprise when Robert began to provide us with details of planned overland reinforcements in higher numbers than originally estimated. The sheer size of such baggage trains would make them easy to spot and, when strung out in long lines of men and animals, extremely difficult to defend in woods and on narrow, often frozen mountain paths. I split our forces under four commanders. Rhys Tudur was charged with preventing reinforcements and supplies from reaching Beaumaris while his brother Gwilym was given the same responsibility for Caernarfon. Rhys Gethin was given charge in like manner for Harlech and Rhys Ddu for Aberystwyth. Most of the baggage trains headed for Harlech and Aberystwyth and we had several spectacular successes. Several were ambushed and their guards massacred, resulting in significant new supplies of food and weapons for us and damaging losses of reinforcing troops for the castles. Soon Henry was forced into sending all his supplies to Caernarfon and Beaumaris by sea. He also had to commit much larger forces to guard his overland supply trains and, even though they eventually managed to reach their destinations, they were subject to further crippling losses as we harried them remorselessly. With the advent of spring the weather improved and they were able to use calmer seas to complete the reinforcement of

Aberystwyth and Harlech with relative ease. It had been a very costly exercise for Henry but again he had eventually succeeded in securing a high level of security for the strategically important coastal fortresses.

Then, with the English concentrating on the northern castles, I began planning our most ambitious assault yet, intended to defeat and capture English strongholds throughout mid, west and south Wales. I primed my spymaster to concentrate his efforts on secretly preparing powerful existing and new supporters to be ready for my summer arrival. I needed them to provide a significant boost to my forces when required, to gain control of all the important inland English castles in their regions.

Unfortunately, we were so intent on these preparations that we failed to foresee another vindictive enemy assault intended to damage our morale and score a painful psychological blow against us. We first heard of it on the eve of its execution when it was too late to form any kind of defence, let alone an effective one. Prince Hal, or Henry of Monmouth as he was often called, was just sixteen years old. Despite his youth he had already been leader of his father's forces in some notable actions and had shown clearly that he was a far better leader and military strategist than his father. In early March, as Robert had predicted, Henry Bolingbroke appointed his son Royal Lieutenant in Wales.

Unlike Hotspur, who had been forced to fund his campaigns out of his own pocket, Prince Hal was given a new army largely composed of veterans of the Scottish, French and Welsh wars. These, combined with his existing force based in Chester, meant that he now had 3,800 archers, 1,100 men-at-arms as well as twenty knights and four barons, together with their personal forces, at his command. Towards the end of the month the eager young Royal Lieutenant marched to Shrewsbury and mustered the majority of this powerful army for yet another invasion of Wales. His aim was to kill or capture me in battle or, failing that, to cause as much pain, suffering and destruction to my people, my old homes and lands as he possibly could. He firmly believed that a razed-earth policy would break Welsh hearts and kill off the revolt once and for all.

With all the shrewdness of a much older and more experienced military leader, he realised that the main weakness of a large army lay in the interminable supply trains slowing it down. He instructed the mounted sections of his archers and the men-at-arms to carry what food they could in their saddlebags, and his foot soldiers to be inventive and carry their sustenance however they might.

This experienced and mobile army left Shrewsbury at the beginning of May and marched directly to my beloved Sycharth where Mared and I had spent so many idyllic years together and where my children had been brought up. Sycharth and all of my lands had been forfeit since my proclamation as Prince of Wales in 1400 and ceded to the Earl of Beaufort. Beaufort had made no effort to establish himself in his new domain. No doubt the noble lord did not wish to place himself in danger and wanted the rebellion put down before venturing to claim this new bounty. I had left a force of eighty men to defend Sycharth from brigands and thieves as well as English raiders.

However, they were under strict orders to evacuate should a large army appear, for attempting to defend the property against such odds would be nothing short of suicide. Another force of fifty was stationed at my lodge in Glyndyfrdwy under similar orders. One of Robert Puleston's men reached Sycharth a few hours ahead of the English army to warn of the danger. The garrison heeded the warning and dispersed into the Berwyn hills. Unfortunately, many of the servants decided to stay, for most had lived there for many years and, in some instances, all their lives.

Meanwhile the Prince's army was on the march, killing, raping and destroying farms and holdings along the way, while known supporters of the rebellion were tortured and butchered. By the time they reached Sycharth the blood lust was upon them and, despite the fact that they were only facing unarmed civilians, they tortured and killed the men and raped and killed the women. Even the few children who witnessed these horrors were also murdered before they fired and razed what had been the most gracious and admired home in north Wales.

Next, they hunted and butchered my prized herd of deer in the adjoining woodland park, and feasted for two days before carrying as much venison as they could manage with them en route to Glyndyfrdwy. Their savage attacks continued along the way. Our servants at the lodge and tenants in the surrounding areas, having heard of the terrible deeds inflicted at Sycharth, made good their escape leaving my second home empty of food and deserted. It was duly torched and destroyed and a herd of precious cattle was driven behind the army as it continued along its bloody trail to the Vale of Edeirnion where it continued the rape and pillage of people and property.

Finally, realising that they would only face me at a moment of my choosing, they returned to Shrewsbury with the Prince roundly condemning my 'cowardice' along the way and outlawing any bards travelling around the country singing heroic nonsense to the Welsh. Henry of Monmouth's chevauchées, which destroyed my homes and many of my most faithful servants, left us numb and despairing. For once the enemy's proposed action had been kept secret, despite the constant probing of *Y Cysgodion*, until the last moment.

We had been concentrating on attacking the north-west coastal castles and ambushing supply trains in the mountains, so there had been no time to organise a large army to oppose the butchers of Sycharth in the north-east. For the first time in my life I saw Mared's spirit completely broken. Sycharth had been the one home from our previous happy existence still intact and to which she had eventually hoped to return. Now it was a smouldering ruin and, like the much-loved servants, gone forever. It brought home to her and, indeed, to all of us how the fortunes of war can change drastically overnight.

For several days Mared and I hardly left our quarters as we struggled to come to terms with the savage destruction wreaked by the Prince and his army. My daughter Catrin, Gruffudd Llwyd and many others within the walls of Dolbadarn were devastated by the news, and our sons Gruffudd, Madog and Maredudd serving with my forces attacking the coastal castles were reported to be greatly troubled.

One morning I was breakfasting with Mared and Gruffudd when, for the first time, my anguish was overtaken by a growing anger. We all sat in silence, the others hardly eating anything while I found myself suddenly assailed by pangs of hunger which seemed to increase in step with my burgeoning temper. I began tucking into a fresh loaf of bread, surprising my listless companions. As I munched, the hot flush of anger was gradually transformed into a cold, controlled but powerful rage. I wondered at the wasted days we had spent moping in our despair. I banged the flat of my hand hard on the table, making plates and cutlery jump and clatter.

'Enough!' I roared. 'Let us have no more of this infantile self-pity! Are we so weak that we cannot take a setback and fight on? Come, let us harden our resolve and remember that Prince Hal's actions are proof of his frustration at the way the war is going in our favour. Butchering our servants and destroying Sycharth have all the hallmarks of childish spite, and we should not be surprised at that for he is still little more than a child himself. Come, you two, we must spend our day reviving the morale in this place and getting our fighting men in the mood to remind the enemy that we are made of pretty stern stuff and are not prepared to bow to anything they can throw at us!'

'Spoken like a true *Tywysog*, Owain.' The bard eased his huge bulk from behind the table and I could see the great battle scar which dominated one side of his face stand out white against the flush of fighting spirit flowing back into his veins. 'There is only one way we can go… and that is forward. Leave this with me. By lunchtime I shall have the entire garrison baying for blood; then we can send riders to all our forces laying siege to the castles to remind them of their duty and inform them how their Prince is consumed by a great rage which will soon see them fighting another crusade to throw the oppressors out of Wales and end their savagery against innocent people and children.'

After the door had closed behind Gruffudd, I turned to Mared with some concern, for the words which had fired up our great friend seemed to have had little effect on her.

'I… I know that the loss of our old homes and our

faithful servants has been a huge blow to you, my love. But we must be strong, and show everyone that we will not be beaten by such savagery…'

'Oh, Owain!' Mared's voice was shrill, accusatory. In all our years together I had never heard that tone before. I stared at her in astonishment as the floodgates opened.

'I am not strong like you. I am not the strong man, the tough warrior who gets hurt, shakes his head and charges the enemy again and again… I am not even the strong wife… When… when I married you I was to be the wife of a Welsh nobleman, well thought-of by the English as well as his Welsh peers. Yes, you had to go to war in an English King's armies, but each muster was only for a period of months and, although I worried about you when you were away, I never thought you would come to any real harm. I was young, star-struck… and you were my knight in shining armour who was invincible. War was something completely outside my experience and I had no proper understanding of what battles were like. I never expected to become a princess, let alone the consort of the Prince of Wales. We are now in the fourth year of the war, and there is still no end in sight. Oh yes, we are doing well, but at what price. Owain? At what price?'

'Mared, my love, stop and listen to…'

'No, Owain. For once you listen to me! We have had to live for most of the time as homeless outlaws constantly on the move, our beautiful homes, Sycharth and Glyndyfrdwy, and all our lands given to an English lord. But that meant nothing to that heartless boy, Henry of Monmouth, for now he has destroyed them and killed all our dear servants and I… have to… have to ask… is even this just cause worth all the terrible destruction and callous murder of so many innocents?'

Her voice trembled as she laid her head down onto her arms on the breakfast table and her shoulders convulsed as the bitter tears flowed. Her outburst had shocked me. I wondered at how brave she had been, managing to keep her fears and distress so carefully concealed, knowing that I needed her wholehearted support in order to concentrate completely on conducting our campaigns. I had been blind to her anguish and I silently cursed myself for my selfishness. I sat beside her, put my arms around her and held her. She lifted her face to me and I gently kissed her tear-streaked cheek. She fumbled for a small napkin from inside her sleeve and stifled her sobs as she dried her eyes.

'I'm so sorry,' she said quietly, the earlier shrillness gone completely.

'You have nothing to be sorry for, my love…'

'What you need is a wife who will stand, steadfast and strong, at your side… a supporter you can rely on. And I have fallen far short of being such a wife…'

'On the contrary,' I exclaimed, 'you have been all of that and more. I am the one to blame for being so foolish and selfish. This has been a harsh and savage experience which is beyond anything you had experienced before. No, no, it grieves me more than I can say that I failed to realise how much you needed my support too.'

Mared smiled at me through her tears. 'Those were the things that attracted me to you in the first place – your good nature and your kindness. And they are still your most lovable attributes. I know at least that will never change.'

I returned her smile but, as I looked into her dark eyes, I imagined I was staring into her very soul. I was shaken by the vulnerability I found there.

13

I MOUNTED LLWYD y Bacsie in the crowded courtyard of Dolbadarn while my personal guards lined up in six ranks of ten, waiting for me to lead them out of the fortress. Banks of white cloud high in the blue June sky hid the sun for a few moments and I was glad, for it had been difficult, despite squinting, to see Mared's face properly in a window of our quarters, high up in the gatehouse wall. She looked very lonely up there and her words a few hours earlier had disturbed me: 'I shall miss you more than I can say, my love. I have prayed to God to send a guardian angel to protect you till you return safely to me once more. Don't worry… I shall be brave.'

But I also remembered her words of some weeks before when she had wrung her hands before blurting out, 'It gets worse every time you go to war, for I now know how terribly capricious battles can be. There is savagery and slaughter so intense that even the bravest and best warriors need a great deal of luck to survive. How can any wife not feel fearful when contemplating such a thing?'

Since then she had said no more in that vein. Instead, she spent all her time trying to convince me that she was now reconciled to being without me for most of the summer. Now, as I looked up at her, she waved brightly, but though she was too far away for me to see them, I knew the tears would be welling up in her eyes. I swallowed hard as I turned away and, when I ordered my men to follow, the command was uttered in a harsh bark, for I did not want them to hear tremors in my voice. I did not look back.

Down in the valley along the banks of Lake Peris the combined forces of Rhys Gethin, Rhys Ddu and the Tudur brothers were waiting. The four leaders were in high spirits, for they were tired of the often boring duty of castle sieges and wanted to get involved in some 'real' action. So too my sons Gruffudd, Madog and Maredudd. They were itching to engage the enemy following the razing of Sycharth and Glyndyfrdwy. A member of *Y Cysgodion* had arrived in camp the previous evening with news that the men of Flintshire had left their homes in numbers and were coming to join us.

I decided not to take the coastal route south, for we did not want the English garrisons at Harlech and Aberystwyth to discover that we were on the move. We wanted to strike at the chain of castles in the rich agricultural land of the Tywi valley which ensured that the King and his local representatives grew wealthy from rents and taxes. Stealth was vital to avoid giving them no time to prepare their defences, so it made sense to take an inland route and gather experienced warriors and untried youths along the way.

At last the country was increasingly gripped by the belief that, with strong support, their Prince really could drive the English out of Wales. As we approached the small village of Corwen, close to the boundary of the lands of my ancestors at Glyndyfrdwy, I felt a coldness in my gut and a tension through my arms and shoulders. I hoped that no one would ask whether I wanted to visit my torched home and those of my tenants. Mercifully, they had the good sense not to. Miles before we reached Corwen, a stream of men armed and dressed for war came to meet us. The warmth of their welcome was a bittersweet pleasure as, among them I recognised many of my tenants whose homes and livelihoods had been destroyed by Prince Hal. They all chanted my name, smiling joyfully when they saw me riding Llwyd y Bacsie at the head of the army, and begged to be allowed to join us. I felt humbled by their loyalty and enthusiasm and I had to struggle to try and keep the emotion out of my voice as I addressed them.

'You are the most loyal of men. I welcome you into this army and I want you to know how proud I am of every one of you. Many of you are seasoned warriors and my captains will designate you to their respective companies. Those of you who are not experienced in war will be given intensive training in weapons' skills and in basic soldiery at every rest stop. You will need to learn quickly and there are plenty around you who can help. Never be afraid to ask if there is anything you do not understand or if you need more advice. Meanwhile, you can turn around and have the honour of leading the army to the outskirts of Corwen where we will make camp for the night. My senior commander, Rhys Gethin, will call you to order.'

Rhys, face expressionless but loving the title I had given him and being seen by all as my most senior captain, kicked the flanks of his mount and trotted forwards before turning his horse to face the expectant newcomers.

'Listen and listen well. You are now soldiers in Prince Owain's army. You have just given up your rights to loaf about and do what you want. From now on, you will do what I want. And believe me, I want discipline and I want willingness to learn. Anyone who is not prepared to lay down his life for his comrades had better leave now… immediately… I will have no frightened rabbits in this army!'

He paused, staring balefully at the recruits. I heard several of my regulars coughing to stifle their chuckles. Rhys spun around to glare in the regulars' direction. All coughing ceased as if by magic. The senior commander turned back to the newcomers.

'Very well. You have all decided to stay. I take that to mean that you are fully signed up to the life of a soldier. A soldier does as he is told and he does it as bravely and efficiently as he possibly can. Let us see how you respond to my first order… I want you to form up in rows, six abreast… no… no… Stand still, you lazy layabouts! I am telling you what to do. You will wait for the order before you begin! We will try again… form up in rows, six abreast… *now*!'

And so we went to Corwen, headed by several hundred men in loose rows, six abreast, many of whom had yet to learn the basics of marching, but bursting with pride and with spirit. It was well past midnight when a horseman arrived at our camp, escorted by twenty armed men. As they rode into the light of our campfires we could see that the escorting group was English. They were immediately made welcome though, for they wore the colours of Henry Hotspur. Their leader, who had spoken in Welsh, was Edmund Mortimer, my son-in-law returning from his meeting with the Percys in Northumberland. I had approached Edmund a few days before Christmas to see whether he would be interested in representing me in the proposed meeting with the Percys to outline the terms and timing of an alliance to overthrow Henry IV. His response had been positive and enthusiastic. He made light of the personal dangers he would face travelling in England as a traitor who had joined the Welsh rebels and was confident that his brother-in-law, Hotspur, would guard him well. It would also be a rare opportunity to see his sister again. The two had always been very close and he wanted to reassure her that he was being well treated in Wales. Catrin was considerably less impressed. She feared for his safety and thought I must be quite mad to send her new husband straight into the lion's den. How could I put my own daughter through weeks of worrying for her husband's safety?

Apparently, the concept of a ruler's duty to his people and his country was lost upon Catrin when it spelled absence and danger for Edmund! Now, thank the Lord, he had returned safely. He looked tired but in good heart and I decided that I could wait till morning for his report. We would both be rested physically and mentally and I would ask my captains and advisers to join us. Breakfast proved a cramped affair with twelve of my leading captains and counsellors crammed into my campaign tent. Nobody ate very much – we had feasted well the previous evening and a fair number were suffering from sore heads after acquainting themselves with the heady local beer.

I briskly dispensed with the servants as soon as I could and asked Edmund to report on his meeting with the Percys. He spoke with his usual unaffected eloquence in English, for he was still some way from being fluent in Welsh. He spoke for ten minutes and left us all feeling greatly excited. It sounded very much as if we were being invited to be part of an alliance powerful enough to have a better-than-even chance of defeating Bolingbroke and Prince Hal once and for all. I breathed deeply, trying to compose myself.

Suddenly, Maredudd was on his feet asking leave to speak. I hid my surprise. Though by now my son was an accomplished warrior with a gift for meticulous planning when preparing military attacks, I had never known him to stand to express a view at top-level meetings. Perhaps it was time he showed everyone that he was now a grown man.

'You wish to speak, Maredudd?' I asked politely, giving him a brief smile to settle his nerves.

'Yes, Father.'

'Very well. Let us hear what you have to say.'

'My Prince,' he hesitated and I struggled to hide a grin. My son obviously found the unfamiliar experience of addressing me formally just as incongruous as I found it to listen to.

'My Lords, gentlemen, may I say that I do not, as a rule, offer my opinions when in the company of such distinguished and experienced men. This morning I have been so excited and encouraged by Edmund's disclosures that I have broken that rule, so strongly am I in favour of this alliance. Firstly, I would like to congratulate my brother-in-law for having the courage to undertake this mission and secondly, for coming back with such favourable terms. Am I right to think that should our joint armies defeat the English King, England would be divided between the Percys and Edmund, Earl of March, our Edmund's young cousin; while my father would be granted sovereignty in Wales?'

I turned to Edmund for his reply.

'Yes, sire, Maredudd is absolutely correct.'

'Then,' Maredudd gasped, 'we must grasp the opportunity with both hands. It is exactly the boost we need and by far the best situation we are ever likely to be in to gain Wales its freedom... surely you must see that! I... I... thank you for listening.'

He sat down suddenly as if amazed that he had stood up

in the first place. I was proud of him, as almost everyone around the table applauded him loudly.

Only one did not and his face was wreathed in a dark scowl. My eldest son, Gruffudd, was not pleased and I was shocked by the hatred in his eyes as he stared in impotent rage at Maredudd. I sighed and gazed hurriedly around the company but, as far I could tell, I was the only one who had noticed the incident. I had never managed to feel much warmth towards Gruffudd despite the enormous efforts he had made to be a firstborn I could be proud of. Certainly he lacked ability in thought and deed though that, of course, was no fault of his.

Yet, despite the fact that my coolness towards him had caused much sorrow to him and to Mared, I had never completely succeeded in overcoming it.

The remainder of that week passed quickly as we marched south towards our chosen battlegrounds along the Tywi valley where, hopefully, we would overwhelm a string of castles including the regional administrative centre at Carmarthen. We did not run into any enemy patrols or foraging parties. The English garrisons seemed content to stay within the safety of their strongholds. In contrast, the countryside was buzzing with excitement and a constant stream of volunteers joined us every day to swell our ranks.

Occasionally one of these recruits would be dragged before me, more often than not by his own companions who had reason to believe that he was spying for the English. Several of my captains wanted summary execution for these men as a warning to others who might be tempted by English gold. I flatly refused. They were made prisoner until we reached our first targeted castle. A time and place would be chosen for a fair trial and, if a person was found guilty by a just court, yes, the punishment would be death by hanging. Until then, they would be kept under guard and treated humanely.

Our arrival in the Tywi valley was a new and magical experience. The sense of expectancy and hope among the inhabitants was palpable. I was treated like some kind of god who would be their deliverer from the economic and political stranglehold of the English oppressors. I was the prince who would bring back the glory days of Rhys ap Gruffudd, Prince of the kingdom of Deheubarth throughout the second half of the twelfth century, but now revered as Yr Arglwydd Rhys (the Lord Rhys). Everywhere we went we were greeted with smiles and happy laughter while scores of warriors, experienced and untried alike, begged to be allowed to join our army. It was a thrilling experience for all of us but not without a heavy sense of responsibility for me. Would I be able to deliver the success and the victories they craved? But any doubts were kept under wraps; I was determined to play the part of the courageous, confident leader.

If any of my commanders were aware of my inner turmoil they gave no indication. There was only one man who always seemed to know my every thought and that was Gruffudd Llwyd. He was constantly at my side, ensuring that everything ran smoothly and generally being a pillar of support. On the first day of July, we made camp a few miles from the castle and small town of Llandovery. Those of us who had made the journey from Snowdonia were much in need of a rest and my officers needed time to assimilate the huge influx of new men, sharing the experienced and the raw recruits equally among the various companies in accordance with their weaponry skills.

We arrived at Llandovery early in the afternoon of 3rd July, launching an immediate attack on the settlement outside the castle. Most of the inhabitants had already left for the castle itself, so the torching of the little town was accomplished quickly and with no loss of life. Before surrounding the castle I lined up all my men in front of the gatehouse and addressed them, mounted on Llwyd y Bacsie. I did so as loudly as I could so that those inside the fortress could hear me too, for my words were actually intended more for those within than our own troops. I began by intimating that this was an English settlement which had a great deal to answer for. When the English King was last here he had executed one most loyal young, local supporter in the most foul and barbaric manner…

'He was executed on the very spot on which you now stand. His name,' I yelled, allowing the orator's emotional tremor to creep into my voice, 'was… was the bravest of the brave. Not only did he refuse to reveal my whereabouts to the English King but he defied him, dubbed him a murderer and called on him to do his worst.'

I paused theatrically, and the silence was absolute.

'And then, that cruel despot had the courageous young man hanged, drawn and quartered. Not only that, but he instructed the hangman to ensure that his death should be as slow and agonised as possible or he too would be executed in the same way.'

There were howls of rage and disgust from my men, while within the castle there were shouts of alarm, for they could see that I was rousing my men to a fighting fury. But I was not finished yet. I continued in a quieter, almost sorrowful tone and everyone was straining to hear my words.

'And let me tell you, my friends… when this brave

youngster was screaming in agony as he was slowly butchered, these worthy English burghers… yes, these very same people who are hiding like startled rabbits behind the walls… they were enjoying this horrible slaughter and shouting encouragement to the executioner.'

For a moment I thought I had overdone my theatricals since my captains were having difficulty restraining some of the troops from advancing on the castle immediately. I could also hear much wailing and alarmed shouting from behind the castle walls.

'Hold!' I roared to my men, 'you are soldiers, not some wild mob. You will attack when you are ordered to attack!'

'But there is more. The next day, Bolingbroke had the local Welsh lord, a kind, elderly gentleman and good friend of mine, Llywelyn ap Gruffudd Fychan, put to death in the same way. He too was a martyr to our cause, refusing to reveal my whereabouts. I have two of Llywelyn's sons still serving in our army and we shall join them in a new encampment tonight only a few miles from here.'

Again I paused at a sudden murmuring among the ranks as dozens of arms pointed at the ramparts behind me. This was what I had been waiting for. I slowly turned Llwyd around and was not surprised to see a tall man in a fine suit of armour standing on the ramparts. At his side was a retainer holding a white flag which shook visibly, and the terror etched on his chubby face would have been comical in a different setting.

'Sire, by your leave I request a secure parley with you under a flag of truce.'

The speaker, though tall and slim, had an unexpectedly deep voice. His tone was neutral and reasonable, with no trace of fear.

'A parley would be a reasonable way forward,' I replied evenly. 'Who may I ask is making this request?'

'I am Sir Giles Mountford, in the King's name, Constable of this castle.'

'Then I suggest, Sir Giles, that you rid yourself of your sword and any other weapon on your person and meet me outside the gatehouse in five minutes. I too shall come to meet you unarmed and on foot.'

Sir Giles turned out to be a forthright, but fair-minded officer who recognised the hopelessness of his position as he had just fifteen professional soldiers at his command to defend the castle, not counting some thirty men from the settlement who were already scared out of their wits. His major concern was the safety of everyone within the castle walls after my colourful account of their alleged complicity in Henry's barbarous executions.

'The truth, sire,' Sir Giles could not hide his indignation, 'is that these burghers were sickened by both those executions as much as the Welsh onlookers were. Both were well-known and liked locally by both Welsh and English and were much moved by the bravery and loyalty of both young and old Lord Llywelyn. It would be a travesty if your angry followers were to murder them all after hearing a tale which is simply not true.'

'Are you calling me a liar, Sir Giles?' I asked quietly, secretly admiring the man's courage in speaking up for the people he was there to protect.

'All I know is that your account of their behaviour was very wide of the mark, sire. It could be that you were misinformed by others.'

For a moment he hesitated before continuing quietly: 'However, it could be that you coloured your account in order to whip up your men's resentment deliberately, so as to put the fear of God into everyone within the castle.'

The Constable cleared his throat, the only sign of nervousness as he stood grim and pale-faced, awaiting my reaction. I waited a moment to prolong his moments of tension, then I smiled at him.

'You are as perceptive as you are brave, Sir Giles. I salute you as an honourable adversary.'

The young officer returned my smile with some surprise. 'Thank you, Prince Owain. My sovereign would not be happy that I acknowledged you as such, but this short conversation has convinced me that you are an honourable man, worthy of that title.'

'Thank you, Giles. Now here are the terms of your surrender. You and your small band of soldiers are free to leave here and you can keep your arms. All the burghers of Llandovery are now under my protection. I shall announce that to my troops soon. Rest assured, none will be harmed and I shall also ensure that my men get to hear of the true reaction of the burghers to those executions.'

A little over an hour later Sir Giles Mountford and his small force left, heading for Brecon and escorted for the first ten miles by fifty archers from the main body of my army now encamped on the outskirts of Llandovery. During the night several hundred of my followers from the Conwy valley arrived to swell our ranks even further. Early the following morning hundreds more arrived from Ceredigion and Cydweli.

Some hours were spent assimilating all the new arrivals into the various sections of the army. I ordered a head count and we eventually discovered that we now had more than 8,200 men, armed and eager to fight. Late that afternoon we headed for one of the main castles in the area, Dinefwr, whose Constable was a Welshman, Jenkyn Havard. As we approached this daunting fortress, two of my scouts captured a messenger sent by Havard to his counterpart, John Fairford in Brecon. The messenger was a Welsh youngster, petrified that he would be executed. He begged me to let him join our army and handed me the letter he had been meant to deliver to John Fairford.

I read the note with interest. It was clear that Dinefwr would not be overcome easily, for the garrison of fifty-eight would be quite capable of keeping even our large army at bay from behind the castle's formidable defences for many days, if not weeks. Their problem would be supplies, particularly of food which were, apparently, already running low. Jenkyn was clearly very worried by the size of our forces and in his letter he beseeched Fairford to let King Henry know that 'all castles and towns in the area, and your loyal subjects within them, are in great peril'.

That evening, after enjoying a meal featuring the excellent local venison, I informed my commanders of my intention to press on with the bulk of the army to seek quick success attacking other castles, leaving a force of 2,000 to lay siege to Dinefwr commanded by my brother, Tudur, supported by old Henri Dwn of Cydweli and Philip Scudamore.

In the morning my main army was on the march again, heading for Carmarthen but following a route which would take us to Dryslwyn castle on the way. The Constable of Dryslwyn was another Welshman, Rhys ap Gruffudd ap Llywelyn Foethus. To our surprise and delight, as we neared the castle, we were met by a messenger from Rhys ap Gruffudd informing us that he and his garrison of Welshmen welcomed us and would throw open the castle gates to us in the hope that he and his men would be allowed to join us. There was no denying now that we were cresting a great wave of support and self-belief, with even those Welshmen who had previously been steadfastly faithful to the English King now rushing to change sides. I first saw the imposing relief of the castle at Carmarthen perched on a hill above the tidal river Tywi with the small but significant quayside below bristling with the masts of several ocean-going merchant vessels. The tide was on the turn and several ships were being steered hastily downriver, for news of our coming had obviously arrived ahead of us. By early afternoon we had surrounded the town wall. I could see a defensive force being organised and my offer to surrender was refused.

I had expected this, for the town was the King's administrative centre for the area and well defended. Its loss would be an embarrassing disaster for Bolingbroke. However, we were not going to be denied and by now I had a very powerful army at my command. Hundreds of bowmen were lined up around the town and our assault began with several volleys of arrows that rained a hail of death and severe injury on its defenders.

Then I ordered scores of siege ladders to be set against the town wall. I now directed my bowmen's volleys at the higher castle walls to prevent the garrison's archers from picking off my infantry as they climbed to engage the defenders in fierce hand-to-hand fighting. Thanks to our overwhelming numbers we were soon inside the town in strength. A hand-picked detachment secured the area around the main gates which were flung open so that many more of our men poured in to join the struggle. Within half an hour the town was ours, with several civic buildings and shops on fire and the golden dragon standard flying proudly in the breeze above the town hall.

Fifty-eight of the town's burghers had been killed and dozens more injured in the short but fierce battle. We had suffered a dozen fatalities and around twenty injured, though none seriously. The King's colours were still flying impudently above the castle and Rhys Gethin was chafing at the bit to mount a concerted attack on the English stronghold. In late afternoon I sent a message to Henry Wygmore, the castle's Constable, advising him that I would receive the keys to the castle from him at nine o'clock on the morrow. I pointed out that he was in no position to refuse as there was no chance of a royal relief force arriving for a very long time and he was vastly outnumbered. If he did not surrender I would launch the strongest attack we could muster and no quarter would be given. I had heard that Wygmore was a brave man but also a pragmatist. I hoped my reports of him were correct, for the sake of everyone involved.

On 6th July I lined up my bowmen in front of the castle gatehouse. At five minutes to nine I mounted Llwyd y Bacsie and stood at the head of my men, flanked by Rhys Gethin and Rhys Ddu, and waited. It was a fine, sunny morning and, listening to the birdsong, it was difficult to believe that within the next few minutes I might be ordering my men to begin another cycle of death and destruction. As the time passed I glanced at Rhys Ddu but his face was impassive, the black-bearded jaw set and ready. Rhys Gethin was alert and expectant, willing the Constable to defy us. At last I glanced across at Ednyfed who was standing by the crude metal sundial on a stand at the river end of the castle square. He slowly raised his arm. It was time. I was getting ready to order the first volley from my bowmen when the great gate swung open and the portcullis grated and squealed. The short, stocky figure of Henry Wygmore rode out on a coal-black destrier clasping a large bunch of iron keys…

Two days later we had secured the castles of Llansteffan and Newcastle Emlyn as part of my strategy for cutting off the Englishry of south Pembrokeshire from the rest of Wales. At the same time I had messengers from south-east Wales reporting that the Welsh populace had risen in those areas led by local commanders such as the colourful Cadwgan, Lord of Glyn Rhondda, who fought with a battleaxe, and was known as Cadwgan of the Bloody Axe. This rising in my name resulted in the surrender of several royal castles in the Vale of Glamorgan, Cardiff and Monmouthshire.

Another piece of exciting news came from one of the *Cysgodion*, who brought me a letter hot-foot from Robert Puleston. It instructed me to prepare for major action with the Percys in a few weeks' time when their great 'crusade' would be launched from Shrewsbury and our combined might would set out to secure 'our rightful mission'. The coded message left me in no doubt that we would shortly be embarking on the most fateful campaign of our lives, one which would provide the best opportunity I was ever likely to have of toppling Bolingbroke and securing independence for my beloved Wales.

First, though, I needed to capture Laugharne castle to complete the isolation of the English and Flemings of south Pembrokeshire before returning to the Llandeilo area to overcome the castles of Dryslwyn and Carreg Cennen. Jenkyn Havard was still defying my brother and his forces at the siege of Dryslwyn. Carreg Cennen too would be a tough nut to crack standing in all its majesty above a 300-

foot precipice which had an eagle's eye view of the lazily meandering Tywi in the valley below. The Constable of Carreg Cennen was Sir John Scudamore, from the noble Marcher family of that name of Home Lacey and Kenchurch in Herefordshire.

They had mingled with the English and Welsh of the area for at least two centuries and most of the family spoke as fluently in Welsh as they did in their mother tongue. Sir John had been put in charge of Carreg Cennen after the previous Constable, his brother Philip, had deserted to join our cause. It was rumoured that John was in line for appointment as Sheriff of Herefordshire, but I was one of a very privileged few who knew that he too was a secret sympathiser of ours. For now, however, it suited him, and us, that he remain an apparently loyal servant of the Crown. The castle of Laugharne proved a much more difficult proposition than we had originally thought. It was only when we started our journey there that I was appraised of the name of the castle Commander. It was Thomas, Lord Carew, a name I had heard discussed as that of a gifted military strategist. Apparently, he was now Bolingbroke's military leader for the entire area east of Laugharne including Pembrokeshire. We also heard, as we travelled, that he had responded swiftly to my Ystrad Tywi campaign by mobilising a large force of his own to resist us.

This unwelcome news created a real problem for us. I did not want to commit my forces to a major action in this locality when so much depended on my ability to reach Shrewsbury quickly in response to a sudden call to action from the Percys. When we reached St Clears and rested for the night I sent a messenger to Laugharne to ask Lord Carew to meet me under a flag of truce to discuss the situation.

The following morning the messenger had not returned, so I sent a small force of seventy archers to Laugharne with orders to learn as much as they could about Carew's deployment and strength but to avoid engaging with the enemy. As the morning wore on it became increasingly likely that the lone messenger had been killed or held captive and I called a meeting of my senior officers to plan our response. It was soon apparent that there was sharp disagreement on what to do next. One group, led by Rhys Gethin, wanted an immediate all-out attack on Laugharne castle while another, headed by Rhys Ddu and Ednyfed, were concerned that we might be dragged into prolonged conflict which could delay or even prevent us from joining the Percys in time to play our part in the campaign to topple the King.

The decision would be mine but, for once, I would not enjoy unanimous support whichever course of action I chose. The meeting was still in progress when we heard shouting from the camp perimeter and we all rushed out of the campaign tent to investigate. We stared in alarm as we saw half a dozen bloodied bowmen displaying a variety of injuries helping each other along. Finally, they stood in front of me, some swaying as they struggled to stand upright. I recognised one of them, a seasoned warrior who had been with me at Sycharth.

'Llŷr ap Goronwy... tell me, faithful friend... what happened... how were you betrayed?'

'I am sorry to have to tell you but we had barely journeyed halfway to Laugharne when we were ambushed... no one could have foreseen that the enemy was lying in wait for us, and so close to our camp... I fear that... that we are the only survivors, my Prince. We have failed you... and we are ashamed.'

'No,' I exclaimed sharply. 'I do not want to hear any talk of shame. You are all the bravest of men. Unfortunately, in war disasters sometimes strike us. We have known each other a long time, Llŷr, and you have risked your life for me on many, many occasions. Tell me, how did this happen?'

'We were riding through a wood, the moon serving as a bright lantern for us. Then, without warning, we heard the hiss of arrows filling the air and our friends…' his voice cracked as he struggled to control his emotions '… fell all around us like leaves in the winds of autumn. The silence of the night was rent by the cries of the injured. From the sheer blanket of arrows filling the air there must have been hundreds of enemy archers in the undergrowth all around us… within minutes most of our number had been downed. The only way out was to retreat but even that avenue was fast disappearing as the enemy closed in on all sides. There were only a dozen or so of us still mounted and we charged back along the path, cutting down the archers facing us on foot. By the time we got out of that hellish trap there were just the six of us…'

Llŷr stopped abruptly, his face screwed up and close to tears.

'Sire, with your leave, I would like to take these men to my sick bay. They are all in need of medical attention and rest.'

I asked Ednyfed to take them into his care and thanked the men for their bravery in such a testing encounter.

I watched the poor wretches being helped to the sick bay and turned back to my tent. Before I could enter there was fresh shouting from the sentries and a lone figure appeared, sitting head bowed on his horse but tied to the saddle, facing backwards. It was Alun, the messenger. I ran towards him and saw that it was only the rope which held him from falling, for his body sagged and he was barely conscious. Eager hands quickly untied him and laid him gently on the ground. I stared in disgust at his badly-beaten face. I called for Ednyfed who ran across to us.

'This man has received a vicious beating,' he pronounced at last. 'And, what's more, his right arm has been deliberately broken in two places… probably to ensure that he will no longer be able to use a weapon effectively.'

Ednyfed gave a short, mirthless laugh.

'Ironically, the broken arm will have little bearing on his ability to wield a weapon when he has recovered. You see, I happen to know that Alun is left-handed!'

As he undid Alun's shirt to examine his ribcage, the doctor found a roll of vellum strapped to his chest. He swiftly removed it and handed it to me. I opened it up and studied it in silence. It was a letter to me signed by Thomas Carew. It was direct to the point of rudeness.

He described my 'treasonable revolt against the English King's God-given right to rule these islands' as 'pathetic and deserving of the ultimate penalty for high treason' and counselled me to steer clear of the south-west corner of 'this infernal land' or he would have me hanged, drawn and quartered as a 'barbarian and a traitor.' However, if I agreed not to attack Laugharne and points west, he would refrain from launching an attack upon me which would result in catastrophic defeat for me and 'my band of thieves and ruffians'. Despite his rhetoric, Lord Carew clearly did not relish extending his military brilliance beyond his area of responsibility. This gave me the opportunity to return the favour as it was virtually impossible for me to press west, with my promises to the Percys needing to be honoured any day now.

I gathered my senior officers once again and explained my intentions to them. They all agreed, though Rhys Gethin was seething after hearing the tone of Carew's letter and had to be persuaded that first capturing the abrasive lord and cutting out his tongue was not currently in our best interests. In the end I rode to Laugharne with 5,000 men, directing the rest of the army to start the march back to Llandeilo. Our arrival at the castle on the shores of the Tywi estuary caused some alarm within the fortress, for we heard harsh notes of bugles and saw hurried movements of men to the battlements. We stopped several hundred yards from the gatehouse and I walked Llwyd y Bacsie casually to a position within one hundred yards of the entrance, with Rhys Ddu at my side bearing a white flag. We were both alert and ready to take evasive action, well aware that we were within longbow range.

After several minutes the portcullis was raised and the massive doors opened to allow a lone rider wearing a full suit of armour, including the helm, to emerge. At first I thought it must be Lord Carew himself. Then I realised that the horseman was nervous, holding the horse's reins very tightly and causing the animal some discomfort. He came to a halt some twenty yards away and mumbled something from the depths of his helm which was quite unrecognisable as any language I had ever heard.

'We cannot hear what you are saying... could you remove your helm so we can have a normal conversation?' I asked helpfully.

After some hesitation he slowly removed it and I almost laughed aloud. The great Lord Carew obviously regarded me as totally unworthy of his personal attention. The lad facing us was no more than sixteen years old and scared witless. He kept looking back at the castle as if entreating someone to come and support him.

'Who… Who are you?' he managed at length. 'And why do you c… come with a great army… do… do you mean to attack us?'

'I am Owain, Prince of Wales, and it is not my intention to attack you… at least not at present,' I replied evenly. 'I had hoped to have a discussion with Lord Carew but he is obviously scared of us! Who are you, young man?'

'I am Geoffrey Stoodley, Lord Carew's personal squire,' he replied, beginning to relax. 'And… and he… my Lord… is not afraid of you, sire.'

His face reddened as he realised that I might take offence at his temerity. I laughed.

'No, you are probably correct. My guess is that he regards himself as too superior to be seen meeting a Welshman on equal terms… even if that Welshman is having a good deal of success against his kind on the battlefield. But let us not waste time on Thomas Carew's opinions. As you know, he has agreed not to seek military engagements with me as long as I do not invade his area of control in the south-west. Tell him that I am agreeable to such an arrangement… for the present. But he must also agree not to send his soldiers on forays outside his own area of responsibility while this agreement exists. Now go back and tell him exactly what I said. If he is satisfied and agrees these terms have your bugler give three sharp blasts on his bugle and we will withdraw. If I have not heard the three-note bugle salute within the hour then the agreement is null and void and I shall resume hostilities as and when I see fit.'

Young Stoodley seemed glad that his ordeal was over and hurried back to report to his master.

'Do you think Carew will honour the agreement?'

Rhys was dubious.

'Oh, I think he will…' I responded confidently, though I too had my doubts. Soon after we had rejoined our men three loud bugle blasts rang out.

A short while later we began our march back up the Tywi valley following a route which would take us past Carmarthen and on to Llandeilo. I was angry and disappointed at having to leave the gloating Lord Carew safely ensconced in his castle, no doubt thinking he had browbeaten me into retreat. But I really had no other option. Teaming up with the Percys was my best chance of securing the whole of Wales in one mighty battle. That was something that no other Welsh leader had ever managed. After that there would be time enough to deal with the Carews of this world.

14

I SAT AT the roughly-made wooden campaign table in my tent cradling a pewter pot of ale in my hand, lost in thought. It was late and through the canvas flap I could see a fine star-speckled, night sky bathing the riverbank in a silvery light. Then the magical moment was shattered by the shouted challenge of a sentry.

The guard outside hurried into my tent, 'Are you all right, sire?'

'Yes, of course. Was that a sentry getting nervous?'

Before he could reply we heard the sound of running feet and Maredudd burst into the tent narrowly avoiding the guard's swiftly-drawn blade.

'I'm sorry to barge in, Father, but there is an Englishman at the gate who claims to be the Constable of Carreg Cennen castle. He says he is Sir John Scudamore. Strangely enough, he told me all this in fluent Welsh!' Maredudd's astonishment made me laugh.

'Well, I happen to be acquainted with Sir John,' I grinned. 'So we will soon find out whether he spoke the truth. Bring him here and if it is he, I shall be pleased to offer him refreshment.'

'He has a retainer with him, sire.'

'In that case bring them both here. If it is the real Scudamore I will invite him to my table and you can take the servant away for refreshment. Oh, and make sure you keep him away from loose talk among the men. I do not want him to learn anything about our strength or our plans in this area.'

'Of course, Father.'

Within minutes I was looking at a tall, good-looking man in his late twenties sporting a flamboyant black moustache who unbuckled his sword belt, giving it to Maredudd without being bidden, before stepping confidently into my tent. Behind him shuffled an elderly retainer clutching a white flag.

'Scudamore,' I exclaimed. 'So it really is you. Maredudd, take Sir John's companion with you and make sure he gets somewhere comfortable to rest and whatever refreshment he requires.'

'Ah, Glyndŵr… or should I now call you Prince Owain…' Scudamore beamed, a mischievous glint in his eye.

'Enough of that, you scoundrel. You can call me whatever you like in private, but Prince Owain would be appropriate in more formal surroundings.' I smiled. 'Come and join me at this table. Are you hungry? Your supplies must be getting low in the castle by now…'

That is for me to know and you to guess,' he assured me as he sat down.

'But seriously, John, I'm sure you could do with a square meal and a tankard of good Llandeilo ale.'

'Ah well… if you insist…' he responded.

We both laughed, at ease in each other's company. I had got to know his father, Jenkin Scudamore, during my service in King Richard's armies and we had become good friends. In later years I had accepted hunting invitations to the Scudamore estates in Herefordshire on numerous occasions and always received a warm welcome from Sir Jenkin and his Welsh wife, Alys. I had first met John as a jovial youngster and had seen him develop into a fine hunter, like his father.

'What news of Philip, then? The downside of his joining your army is that I have heard nothing of him since.'

Philip was the previous Constable of Carreg Cennen and John's brother, who had defected to us the previous year.

'To the best of my knowledge he is alive and well. At present he is helping my brother Tudur and 2,000 men at the siege of Dryslwyn.'

'Well, it is a relief to know that the old rascal has managed to survive so far.'

I called the guard and ordered him to organise a meal for John. For a moment he stared dubiously at me and inclined his head towards our visitor.

'No, it's all right, Gerwyn. I shall be perfectly safe until you return.' I smiled. He left with doubt still clouding his face, a fact which John clearly found amusing.

Gerwyn was back in quick time and later, after an obviously ravenous Scudamore had eaten his fill of the Tywi valley's finest beef, we filled our tankards and got down to some serious discussion.

Apart from his brother Philip, I and a very small group of my commanders were the only ones who knew that Sir John Scudamore was one of our sympathisers and a more than useful source of information. Now we were about to attack his castle, it was very much in our interest that he be kept alive and that he should somehow 'escape' our clutches when Carreg Cennen fell. For his part, his main concern was that his wife and his mother-in-law be given safe passage before we mounted serious attacks. I had been giving much thought to this already, and his plea for safe passage for his wife and her mother gave me an idea which might make his subsequent escape from the castle more credible.

'No, no,' I said firmly. I cannot allow your wife and mother-in-law safe passage from Carreg Cennen.'

'What? You are refusing my request?'

There was a look of blank disbelief on John's face.

'But Owain… if you refuse, they… you… will be placing them in mortal danger.'

His words were clipped and a look of genuine annoyance spread across his face. I sat quietly letting him stew. Such a display was rare indeed for the normally jovial John, and I enjoyed his discomfiture for several moments.

'Cool down, my friend, and let me explain,' I said soothingly. 'That is my official answer which I want as many people as possible to know about. If my official answer were to be yes, how do you think that would look to your King and many others who may harbour doubts about your loyalty to the Crown? Surely it would look as if we were in each other's pockets. By refusing your request I am showing that I do not give a damn about you or the safety of your wife and her mother. It would also suggest that I am not trying to win you over to our cause. However, if I were to devise a secret plan which would allow you and everyone in the castle to escape, it could be made to look as if you proved to be very resourceful in the face of overwhelming odds. You would have managed to escape from the doomed castle, securing deliverance for yourself, your family and all your surviving retainers…'

John breathed a sigh of relief but looked distinctly embarrassed at having allowed himself to lose his temper. I laughed good-naturedly and, after a brief hesitation, so did he.

'It sounds good,' he affirmed. 'But I cannot for the life of me see how you can plan such an escape. By the time I am officially aware of your imminent onslaught, you will have several thousand men surrounding three sides of the castle with a 300-foot drop on the fourth. And, of course, you will not be able to appraise your own men that we are to be allowed to escape, or the truth will soon become common knowledge.'

'How well do you know your castle, John? You have been Constable there for a year… maybe a little longer?'

'The first duty of any castle Commander is to acquaint himself with every aspect of his castle. He must know every stone in every wall and he has to assess its strengths and, even more importantly, its weaknesses,' Scudamore replied, looking at me quizzically.

'Then you will be aware of a small but well-constructed iron gate set into the wall overlooking the precipice, only a few yards from the corner where the precipice wall joins one of the castle's side walls.'

'Yes, I am. I was perplexed when I first saw it, for I could not imagine what its purpose might be. After making enquiries I was told that it is sometimes used to get rid of any rubbish like broken weapons or furniture we no longer need, which is broken up and thrown out of the gate to hurtle down into the valley below. However, it once had a far more sinister purpose. Legend has it that it was first used, centuries ago, to throw miscreants or enemy captives who could not be ransomed, to their deaths. And that is the point… It is directly above 300 feet of empty air. We are hardly going to escape with our lives if we jump out of it, are we?'

'I have to concede you would need to sprout wings to succeed with that endeavour,' I grinned.

'But, of course, there is more, and the great magician,

Glyndŵr, is about to cast a spell… maybe…' he offered sardonically.

'Actually, I am about to offer a much more practical course of action. How closely have you examined the immediate area outside the gate?'

'If you mean, have I peered out through the iron bars… well no, I have not.'

'Let me explain to you then that while by far the greater part of that wall is built on the very edge of a rock ledge, the last twelve feet to the corner I have referred to is set on a kind of spur or projection of the rock giving a foothold of about two feet. This would allow brave men to step out of the gate, admittedly with mere inches between them and the precipice, but sufficient for them to ease themselves slowly, by hugging the wall, some six or seven feet, to the corner where the two castle walls meet.'

'What a wonderfully appealing prospect. And, assuming that we managed to reach the corner, we would gleefully dance around the side into the arms of your men? How is that going to help us?' John's voice was heavy with sarcasm.

'What if I were to withdraw the company guarding that area of the curtain wall and relieve them with another?'

'What would be the point of that?' He was getting exasperated.

'Ah, but what if I were to order the withdrawal at an agreed time and refrain from ordering another company to replace them for, say, half an hour. In fact that would give you the best part of an hour to make your getaway before the relieving force was effectively in position. And if it were to be done just before dusk, you could perform the nerve-wracking crawl from the gate to the corner in daylight then hide in some cover till darkness fell before making a break for it…'

'By the gods of the ancients.' John's face was a picture, at first incredulous but slowly transformed to one of hope and excitement. 'So you are a wizard, after all. Why did I not believe it before?'

'Now Sir John, less of the mockery. We still have some issues and a lot of detail to work out,' I said firmly.

'Yes, you can say that… and not least how I am going to persuade my wife… and… and my mother-in-law, for God's sake… to make that daredevil tiptoe journey from the gate to the corner.'

I laughed.

'That, my friend, is your problem. However, you could impress upon them that it is my practice, when a castle has refused to surrender, to kill everyone within when I do storm it. Furthermore, as women they might face a fate worse than death… How many of your garrison are left?'

'All of them. We have not had to withstand a siege this year yet. Mind you, there are only ten archers and six pikemen… and our food supply is now very limited.'

'Are any of them Welsh?'

'Not in Carreg Cennen I assure you; no, they are all English, so no one is likely to defect to your side.'

'Good. Any Welsh members would be sorely tempted to switch allegiance to save their hides, because in this area they would not be readily forgiven for supporting Bolingbroke.'

The following morning I sent the bulk of the army, led by Rhys Gethin, to attack the castle and town of Brecon, while I led the remaining 1,000, comprising mainly archers, to lay siege to Carreg Cennen castle. When we arrived I sent a message to the Constable demanding the garrison's immediate surrender. I received a short, blunt refusal. In late afternoon I sent another message warning Sir John Scudamore that this would be his last opportunity to surrender. If he was still determined to defy me, then we would storm the castle the following day and no quarter would be given. This time they did not bother to answer and my demand was ignored.

After the evening meal I instructed my commanders to pass the word for everyone to be ready to attack the castle an hour after daylight the following morning. Later, with dusk less than an hour away, I sent an instruction to Gwilym Tudur, commander of the company guarding Scudamore's escape route, to stand down for the night. They were surprised by the late decision but glad to be given a chance to sleep before the following day's attack on the castle. I then instructed my eldest son, Gruffudd, to ready his company for night duty.

An hour and a quarter later Gruffudd came to see me showing some irritation, as he had still not been informed where his men should be positioned. I apologised for my waywardness and sent him and his detachment to replace Gwilym's men, hoping that all had gone well for the escaping fugitives in the meanwhile.

When we attacked the castle in the morning there was no resistance, and all we found inside was a group of petrified servants. A few days later I discovered that there had been one casualty of the escape, when the body of an English soldier was found in the valley directly below the precipice. He had fallen to his death. Initially everyone was baffled as to how Sir John, his family and the garrison could have escaped, but the discovery of the dead soldier led to a thorough search of the castle wall directly above the precipice at every level and eventually the small gate near the servants' quarters in the lower basement was discovered. It was still open. The narrow, dangerous footholds leading from the gate to the corner were also discovered. Still, everyone wondered at the incredible bravery, or desperation, of the escapees which had led to freedom for at least eighteen people and death for one less fortunate soul.

That night we dined in the great hall. There were far too many to accommodate at one time so the men dined in relays. The top table, however, was of ample proportions for my officers and me, and we all dined in very good spirits after a campaign that was more successful than we had dared hope. But the gods do not like mere mortals to have too much happiness for long and take great delight in striking us hard, often when we are at our happiest.

After restocking Carreg Cennen castle we left a small garrison of twenty there and moved on to Dryslwyn castle where Jenkyn Havard was still holding off Tudur's force of 2,000 after more than two weeks. Despite having only a few dozen soldiers, the castle's defences were such that they were sufficient to hold off an army. The only way to take the castle was to starve them out. Tudur and Philip Scudamore had tried hard, even using fire arrows to set the timber roofs of several of the castle's buildings alight, but the formidable defences were constructed of stone and in the warm summer weather the burnt-out roofs were not a major concern for the garrison.

I now needed as many men as possible to join me on the march to Shrewsbury, for I knew that the summons to war from the Percys would reach us soon. So I was glad when Rhys Gethin returned from Brecon with the bulk of the army, having ravaged the town but failed to take the castle. Thankfully we had suffered only light casualties. I left a fresh company of 600 archers under the joint command of Philip Scudamore and Henri Dwn to continue with the siege of Dryslwyn, and incorporated Tudur's 2,000 men into the army before turning northward towards the looming conflict which I believed would define my destiny.

We were camped outside the tiny hamlet of Llanelwedd when Robert Puleston's first messenger from *Y Cysgodion* arrived. It was a balmy July evening and we were in good spirits, relaxing tired muscles around our campfires in anticipation of the evening meal. I was savouring the mouthwatering aroma of roast pork when sentries challenged a lone horseman and led him quickly to me. I could see that the horse had been ridden hard, its sides heaving as it fought for breath. I called for an ostler to take the animal away to be watered and fed and turned my attention to the messenger.

'*Henffych*, my Prince.' The man bowed awkwardly. He was small and wiry, ideally built for riding a horse for long distances. His pale blue eyes were almost lost in the weathered face which indicated that he was well past his middle years. His demeanour was respectful but confident.

'I am Derwyn ap Emrys and I have a letter for you from the Master. My orders were strict. I have to deliver it to you personally'.

'I thank you for carrying out your orders so diligently, Derwyn. I will see the letter right away. You are most welcome to rest with us tonight. You are probably famished. Tell the cooks that you are to have as much as you want to eat and the best ale too.'

I went to my tent to read the missive from Robert Puleston, always referred to by his agents as the Master, gesturing Gruffudd Llwyd to come with me. I read it quickly and then a second time more slowly, consumed by a nagging disquiet.

My face must have been an open book, for Gruffudd grasped my arm and exclaimed, 'What is it, Owain? Why the frown?'

'The Percys are on the move but there is a problem… the Earl of Northumberland is ill. Hotspur has started to march from Berwick to Chester with about half of his father's army together with his own and the Scottish earl, Archibald of Douglas, who was captured by Hotspur in the battle of Homildon a while ago. When they get to Chester they are hoping to recruit Cheshire archers and supporters of ours in Flint and the surrounding areas. Presumably they will rendezvous with his uncle Thomas, Earl of Worcester, and his army following the muster in Chester. We will then join them in the Shrewsbury area before we march on London. But, with half of the powerful Northumberland army still moribund in the north of England, we will be understrength… Also, without his father's steadying influence, I am concerned that the impetuous Hotspur may be tempted to deviate from the plan…'

'… And do something stupid.' Gruff finished the sentence for me, grimly. I was thinking furiously, for the hot-headed Hotspur was not one to have in charge of such a campaign. Could he be relied upon to stick to the plan and wait for his father to join him with another large force from Northumberland? Would he wait patiently or would he fill his head with plans for some madcap adventure which would put everything in jeopardy?

'Gruff… would you get that messenger back in here. He has delivered Robert's letter which was what was required.

However, he may know something more which could be important, though it may not seem so to him. Oh… And let's get Edmund to join us as well.'

Minutes later my son-in-law, Gruffudd, and I were seated at my table with Derwyn ap Emrys standing before us looking mystified.

'Derwyn, have you eaten yet?'

'No, sire. I was about to when you sent for me.'

'Not to worry. We will only keep you for a short while longer. Derwyn, I have read the letter but I thought you might cast your mind back to when you went to pick it up, just in case you may have heard something, anything, which you feel would help us to understand the situation in Chester a bit better?'

Derwyn thought for a few moments before shrugging. 'I'm sorry, but I cannot think of anything which would interest you, my Prince.'

'Tell us a little about the pick-up,' Edmund asked encouragingly.

'Where did you go to get the letter, for example, and who gave it to you?'

'I am based in Flint, sire. Another member of our local team told me to be at the Red Lion tavern, which is in a little alley not far from Chester castle, at midday two days ago. It would require a fast horse and a long journey to reach Prince Owain with a letter to be delivered as soon as possible.'

'Describe to us what happened at the Red Lion,' said Edmund.

'I got there early. I wanted to eat a good meal before being given the letter so I could be on my way at once. The place was full of noisy soldiers wearing Hotspur's colours. They were boisterous but in good spirits, so I was able to eat my meal and drink some small beer unhindered,' Derwyn remembered.

'So there were soldiers all around you,' I mused. 'Do you remember what they were talking about?'

'Oh yes, sire. The big topic was the war against King Henry and how Hotspur would soon hammer him and his soft southerners into submission, sire.'

Derwyn smiled appreciatively as he remembered.

'And did anybody know how Hotspur would set about defeating the King?'

'Well, most said that he would not make his move until his father, the Earl, arrived with his troops. Then they would meet up with the Earl of Worcester and his army and with you, Prince Owain, and your army, before seeking out the King and challenging him to battle.'

'And that was all... nobody thought Hotspur might switch to some other plan?'

'No, they all seemed pretty sure... no, there was nothing else you would regard as important, Prince Owain.'

'You hesitated a second then, Derwyn. Are you sure that no other plan of action was mentioned.'

'No, all the soldiers seemed pretty sure of what would take place... the only reason I hesitated was because of the ramblings of a halfwit at the bar. He said something rather silly which made all the soldiers laugh. I'm sure the lad regretted opening his mouth, for he had to endure a lot of ribbing from the soldiers.'

'Do you remember what the halfwit said, though?' I tried to keep the edge out of my voice.

'Well, he seemed to have trouble getting his words out, sire, but he claimed that he was cleaning the fire grate in Hotspur's bedroom that morning when he heard him telling one of his captains to gather all the officers, for he wanted to announce something to them.'

Derwyn paused, as if unsure of what my reaction would be to his next words.

'Well? Come on, man, spit it out…'

'He… Hotspur had said that he thought the war would be over much quicker if he could attack Prince Hal at Shrewsbury and capture him before the King could get to there, sire. He said that most of Prince Hal's garrison at Shrewsbury had deserted him because they had not been paid for months. He was going to march to Shrewsbury as fast as he could to capture the Prince… Of course, none of the soldiers believed him … he was talking rubbish.'

'Yes… well… That will be all I think, Derwyn. You can get back to your quarters now to enjoy that meal. Thank you. That was very helpful.'

After he had left, the three of us stared at each other, aghast. Nobody said a word for a long time. Our worst fears had been realised.

15

I T WAS 20TH July 1403. We had made camp a few miles south of Welshpool and the following morning we awoke to a dismal, dark morning with a thin veil of light rain falling steadily. Nevertheless, we made an early start, desperate to reach Hotspur before he committed himself and his men to do battle with the King, whose army would inevitably be much larger. We were soon soaked to the skin but I hardly noticed because, for once in my life, I was in very low spirits. It was pretty clear that we would be far too late to make a difference to the result of any battle in Shrewsbury, but we had no choice other than to make the attempt.

For the past three years I had hoped and prayed for the help of an ally or allies powerful enough to make defeating Bolingbroke a practical proposition. The alliance with the Percys had been the answer to my dream and our success over the past month or so had really buoyed us all up as a prelude to the final titanic struggle which we were confident would end the war conclusively in our favour. Now, suddenly, the whole enterprise was in imminent danger of collapse – and all because of the foolhardiness of one man. And I was powerless to prevent Hotspur from throwing away the best chance we would ever have of toppling the King of England. It all seemed unreal – a dreadful nightmare.

As the day wore on the weather improved and by the time we made camp south of Oswestry the skies were blue and the sun was a fiery red ball beginning to slide to its rest below the western horizon. Surely the fates were laughing at us, mocking our human frailties. My gloomy frustration had been transferred to everyone else and even the horses seemed to be hanging their heads.

The exception was Llwyd y Bacsie who was loath to leave me as my servant came to lead her away. She was obviously conscious of my rare, dark mood and neighed gently, tossing her head and stamping a front hoof to show her concern. I patted her neck briefly, whispered in her ear and smiled for the first time that day. I watched her as she was led away, marvelling at her intelligence, her protectiveness and the strength of her powerful body. She was now in her prime as a warhorse and I wondered how I would cope in battle without her reassuring presence. Our hopes were finally shattered at breakfast the following morning.

Having slept badly, I got up early having decided that as Commander-in-chief I must fight my demons and present a more confident Prince to my followers, starting with the other commanders. When they were all gathered, a subdued group around the breakfast table, I clapped my hands and launched into a spirited tirade chiding them for their forlorn faces and demanding that they show their mettle and professionalism. We would have no more long faces.

After breakfast we would address all our respective companies with a message of hope and confidence. We would remind them of our victorious exploits over the past two years and vow that, whatever may have happened at Shrewsbury, we were here for the full course of the struggle. We were Welshmen, the tried and tested warriors who wore the leek in our caps and our heritage and pride in our hearts. The general mood visibly improved around the table, and as we ate our breakfast of stale bread and cheese there were even a few jokes being bandied about. The sudden sounds of raised voices outside the tent broke the spell and the guard brought in a tough-looking but clearly exhausted man whose clothes were splattered with mud and what appeared to be dried blood.

For a while he was too breathless to speak and I rose quickly to help him into a spare seat at the table. He was Hefin Glanddwr, who had been one of my gamekeepers at Glyndyfrdwy before the rebellion and who was now a lieutenant in Robert's spy ring. I insisted that he have a mug of small beer and some bread and cheese before addressing us. He accepted the drink gratefully and gradually his breathing slowed so that he could speak coherently.

He had ridden all night from Shrewsbury after having been attacked as he began his ride by one of the King's cavalrymen. He had managed to wrestle the man to the ground before stabbing him to death with his dagger. The tale he told was not a pretty one. Bolingbroke had been travelling north with an army of 14,000 to help the Percys wage war on the Scots. When he reached Burton-on-Trent, the King was astonished to hear that the Percys had denounced him as a traitor and started a rebellion.

Since the Percys had been mainly responsible for installing him on the throne four years before, this was a real shock. He had, of course, neglected to pay Hotspur for keeping the Welsh in check in north Wales which had left the hot-headed Percy heir significantly poorer. Recently he had also refused to ransom Hotspur's brother-in-law, Edmund Mortimer, making it clear that no one else could do so either. On hearing that Hotspur had marched to Chester to recruit more men to his banner, Bolingbroke realised that he would be bound to attack Prince Hal and his weakened force in Shrewsbury. He therefore made a forced march to Shrewsbury to try and get there ahead of the rebels.

Hotspur too was heading there in a hurry and was joined by his uncle Thomas Percy, Earl of Worcester, with his army, along the way. Unfortunately for Hotspur, the King reached Shrewsbury an hour ahead of them, saving his son, Henry of Monmouth, from probable defeat and capture. Hotspur commanded a force of 10,000 men. Bolingbroke's army outnumbered his by 4,000 and between them the two armies included the flower of England's nobility and leading knights. Hotspur's army now included hundreds of Cheshire bowmen and hundreds more from north-east Wales, still loyal to King Richard II, who had been deposed before being murdered or starved to death at Bolingbroke's command in Pontefract castle in 1399.

Most of the Welsh bowmen were led by an ally of mine, John Kynaston, steward to the lordship of Ellesmere. He had enlisted many by telling them that King Richard was still alive and would be leading them into battle. Most of them fought with Richard's white hart badge on their shields and tunics. On arriving at the gates of Shrewsbury, Hotspur, who must have been profoundly disappointed to see the King's Lancastrian banners draped along the castle walls, took his army a few miles to the north and camped for the night near the little village of Berwick.

The following morning, Saturday, 21st July, the King brought out his army in three divisions led by the young Earl of Stafford and chose a position at the south end of a large, flat area of land near Haytley field. On hearing that Bolingbroke was marching out of Shrewsbury, Hotspur and his forces set out to meet him and eventually found him at Haytleyfield. He took up a position on the northern end of the area on slightly higher ground. Hefin Glanddwr, who had attached himself to Percy's army, was perfectly placed to view the day's events. Some hours were spent in negotiation after Henry invited Hotspur and Thomas Percy to discuss ways of avoiding bloodshed and sent the Abbot of Shrewsbury, Thomas de Prestbury, to offer redress of grievances, a full pardon and peace.

Both armies had large numbers of archers so that any battle was certain to be a bloody affair with very high losses. The Percys, familiar with the King's reputation for duplicity, refused the terms. A battle was now inevitable. It began in late afternoon, heralding three hours of bloody savagery. The King ordered his vanguard to advance and Hotspur set up his archers in lines several rows deep. In minutes the air was black with thousands of arrows whistling skyward before dipping with deadly accuracy into the leading royalist troops. It was a swift, murderous death for scores of men while several more equally deadly salvoes produced a scene of utter carnage.

The Earl of Stafford, Constable of England, was an early victim as was the King's standard bearer, Sir William Blout. The fallen standard was trampled upon as survivors of the death-dealing arrows tried to turn to find cover. Henry was forced to ride up and down the flank of the leading division exhorting his men to hold their ground for the early fall of the standard and the huge loss of life which had stunned and demoralised them.

His troops, seeing that the King was still alive, rallied and made a determined advance using their superior numbers to force the leading ranks of the Percy army to give ground. Meanwhile, Prince Hal had been injured when an arrow struck him a glancing blow in the face, causing serious bleeding. He gamely refused to leave the battlefield, apparently to demonstrate to his men that he was still alive. Hotspur and Douglas led a determined charge and the Scottish earl felled two knights wearing the King's distinctive dress, mistakenly rejoicing twice that he had killed the King.

It became apparent that the wily Bolingbroke had made several knights wear the royal battle dress so that he would not become such an obvious target. Unfortunately for Hotspur, their charge had not been well supported and the royal lines regrouped and closed behind them cutting himself, Douglas and thirty or so of his troopers off from the rest of his army. They fought furiously to carve out an escape. It was a warm evening and, at one stage, Hotspur paused and lifted the visor of his helm to gulp in some air. As he did so, a chance arrow tore into his face, piercing his brain.

The force of impact caused him to fall backward off his mount and he was dead before he hit the ground. Douglas and a few troopers managed to fight their way back to their own men, but the news of Hotspur's death spread rapidly through both armies and the forces of Percy quickly lost heart. The King's men, knowing that their enemies had lost their charismatic leader, waded into the fray with new heart. Within the hour the survivors of Hotspur's army had fled to the north and east, leaving thousands of their comrades dead at Haytleyfield.

The King had also suffered heavy losses with several thousand having been killed on the battlefield. It was also rumoured that Lord Archibald Douglas and Thomas Percy, Earl of Worcester, had been captured. Hefin was convinced that the loss of life must have been the greatest in any battle ever fought in these islands.

The defeat of the Percys at Shrewsbury was the worst blow we had suffered during the rebellion so far. While it made little difference to my current position and authority in Wales, it meant the end of my one golden opportunity to rid England of an unlawful tyrant, create two lesser kingdoms with more benevolent rulers while at the same time extending my own territory into a 'greater Wales'.

I conveyed my views to a few of my commanders that evening. I was so wrapped up in the significance of the battle for me that I had not thought of its effect on another.

'I understand and sympathise with you, Owain,' Edmund observed sombrely. 'But spare a thought for your son-in-law. That was my last chance to rescue even part of the Mortimer heritage, which was nothing less than the English Crown. I too am greatly saddened by that and of course by the death of Hotspur, which has now made my young sister a widow.'

'Forgive me, Edmund. I was so selfishly concerned with my own disappointment that I did not appreciate what a personal and political disaster this is for you. Still, we must fight on to secure our dream for Wales. And as my daughter's husband and a man of integrity in your own right, I will ensure that your future in the new Wales will be an honourable one.'

16

GRUFFUDD LLWYD AND I rode into Dolgellau at the head of *Y Cedyrn* late on a wet and windy April morning. The horses' hooves clattered and slid on the cobblestones as we approached the old meeting hall where my newly-formed, enlarged council was meeting for the first time. We were soaked to the skin. I entered the dimly-lit old hall and paused to allow my eyesight to adjust to the gloom. There was one long table taking up most of the space available. Around it sat some forty men, many representing communities from all over Wales. When they saw me enter, followed closely by Gruffudd, they stood as one, cheering loudly.

'I give you Prince Owain ap Gruffudd Fychan, the one true Prince of Wales,' Ednyfed ap Siôn announced, bowing low. The others hastily followed suit and as they straightened the cheering and clapping redoubled. I walked to the head of the table at the far end while Gruffudd took an empty chair to my left. I lifted my hand for silence. For a moment I glanced around the faces, seeing my commanders, a goodly number of senior clerics and the majority, the representatives invited due to their commitment to the cause and their influence in various parts of the country. I knew many of them already but there were several whom I had not met, although I knew of them by reputation.

The wind swirled in gusts against the panes of three small windows facing the street, while the glass was rattled frequently by the irregular hammering of hailstones. There was a smoky log fire struggling to stay alight in the ancient fireplace and, every few minutes, the capricious wind would howl around the chimney top, reversing the smoke's normal upward progression, blowing thick, acrid blankets of it back into the room. The wax-soaked torches lining the walls did little to alleviate the gloom, producing their own smoke to blend with that of the fire.

As I rose to my feet there was an expectant silence. I was aware of being closely scrutinised by those who had never seen me before. I wondered whether I actually matched up to their expectations. I decided on a no-nonsense approach.

'There is only one reason why we are gathered here this day.' I paused theatrically. 'Due to our successes in the struggle against the enemy we have reached a position of strength. We are now ready for many major developments which are necessary to enable us to form an independent state in which we ourselves will rule; we ourselves will decide what is best for us; what our laws will be; how we will administer the new Wales; how we will educate our people and how we will plan a better future for our children.'

The words seemed to stir my listeners intensely, for they were greeted with loud enthusiasm.

'That is why I have decided to form this new, greater council with members drawn from all over our country. I want everyone to be part of *Y Gymru Newydd*, the New Wales. I want all of our people to know what our intentions and ambitions are and I want everyone to feel that they are involved in our great adventure.' I paused again, and raised my hand to silence the fresh applause.

'In another month or two I hope to be in a position to organise our first parliament, a *Senedd* in which we can really begin to organise ourselves as a country and show the whole world that we are self-governing. Before that though, there are several key objectives we must achieve. As you know, we are now in control of most of Wales and the great majority of Bolingbroke's former castles. We are also controlling virtually all of the March on the English side of the border. We have agreed separate local treaties with the counties of Shropshire, Herefordshire and Montgomeryshire. Those counties are now paying us… that's right, *paying* us… for not causing further destruction in their areas. The King is unable to defend them as his Exchequer is bereft of funds and he cannot pay for an army to take the Marches out of our control. Indeed, he has been forced to accept Parliamentary control over spending and even over his own council. Also Prince Hal, having been given control over all English garrisons in Wales in January, is still not back in action, for he is not fully recovered from a serious injury to the face he sustained in the Battle of Shrewsbury last year.

'It is fair to say that, so far, our hit-and-run tactics, mixed with a few well-chosen stand-and-fight battles, have confused and dismayed the noble Bolingbroke. Even his large royal expeditions into Wales, and there have been four so far, devastating though they were, have failed completely in their purpose, which was to bring us to battle and destroy us.

'There remains one essential task for us. Despite taking most of the inland English castles, we have failed to capture a single one of the mighty coastal castles – though let us not forget the Tudur brothers' cunning occupation of Conwy castle for three months, three years ago.'

At this there was a ripple of approval and I saw the pleased grins on the faces of Rhys and Gwilym Tudur.

'It has not been for want of trying, as you all know. But the English fleet of warships has been beyond our powers. They enter our bays and harbours with impunity to reinforce these castles with troops and supply them. As I say, beyond our powers – until now.

'Last year, many of you will remember that we asked our Celtic cousins, the Bretons, for support. You will remember that Breton ships and warriors landed on the west Wales coast to aid my friend and ally, Henry Dwn, to attack the borough and castle of Cydweli.'

Here I paused to acknowledge old Henry who looked somewhat embarrassed by the sudden clapping.

'Later more Breton ships with Welsh and Breton troops on board attacked Plymouth and several other places on England's south coast, causing damage and much alarm to both the inhabitants of these areas and to Parliament in London. Well, I have sent two more missions to seek naval support, one to the Bretons and the other to the French King. This time their role would be to prevent English ships from bringing supplies to their coastal castles. I am pleased to tell you that both have agreed to help us. The Breton ships are already on station to guard Aberystwyth and Harlech castles while the French will be with us in a week or so to blockade Cricieth, Caernarfon and Beaumaris castles. Harlech and Cricieth have been under siege now for several months and we will have forces to begin sieges at Aberystwyth, Beaumaris and Caernarfon within weeks. Now we need quick success by taking Harlech and Cricieth swiftly, to destroy the myth that they are impregnable.'

Again I had to pause to allow enthusiastic cheering.

'Finally, my friends, may I inform you that a few days ago I chose my first chief minister to begin the process of creating the administrative offices of state befitting a self-governing country. He is Gruffudd Yonge, Doctor of Canon Law and presently Archdeacon of Meirionnydd, who will be my Chancellor. I now call upon Chancellor Yonge to address you.'

As I sat down all the council members rose in a standing ovation. Gruffudd Yonge stayed seated for several minutes, allowing the applause for my speech to run its course. When he rose, dressed as usual in black, he cut an imposing figure. I smiled inwardly, pleased with my choice for this pivotal role.

After some fine words of introduction, my new Chancellor was not slow to get to the point.

'I know that Owain has a great vision. Every country needs to have a vision – it is what gives its people their national pride and what earns the respect of other nations. We also need to develop a strategy for creating pragmatic alliances with powerful neighbouring countries, for after removing our oppressors we will need to make them realise that if they attack us again in the future they will be risking war with other, equally-powerful nations.

'Finally,' and here he turned to look at me with a slight grin and a somewhat irreverent bow, 'we really need to think about how we project the image of our Prince. Owain is not the sort of man who takes delight in ordering people about or preening himself in front of a mirror. He is a man of action. Or so he has been.

'However, he is no longer Owain ap Gruffudd, Lord of Glyndyfrdwy and Cynllaith. He is our royal Prince of Wales, proclaimed by his own people and by the grace of God. All Christian monarchs make that claim. Charles VI of France does, so do the Kings of England... even the usurper,

Bolingbroke... has the nerve to do so. Yet it is something which no other Welsh Prince has ever claimed before. Proclaimed by God – and we, the senior clerics in Wales, confirm it. The Deans and Bishops here present confirm it.'

Several tonsured heads around the table nodded vigorously.

'That is why I am determined that later this year, once we have gained control of a suitable castle, he will hold court with all the pomp and ceremony of a true monarch: he will hold his first Parliament; he will be crowned before God and man at that Parliament; and foreign potentates or their representatives will be invited.

'I am sure you will all go back to your respective homes knowing that there are now important and ambitious plans afoot to consolidate our position in this struggle which, as you must realise, is still far from over.'

The Chancellor turned to me and bowed before resuming his seat. For a moment there was complete silence as the audience absorbed the significance of his words. A Prince before God. A nation before God. Then there was enthusiastic clapping and stamping of feet as they all rose to their feet.

A few days after the meeting in Dolgellau, Gruffudd Llwyd and I were back in our headquarters tent at the siege of Harlech castle. It was a sunny, mild, spring morning and everyone's spirits had been given a boost by the news, delivered in the early hours, of the capitulation of the English garrison at Cricieth castle the previous day. At last, one of the coastal castles had succumbed to deprivation and hunger, for the winter storms had ensured that no provisions had reached Cricieth by sea since the previous autumn. The sight of newly-arrived French warships a few miles offshore had been the last straw for the beleaguered defenders. Now we were in high spirits, aware that conditions inside Harlech castle were very similar to those at Cricieth. Harlech had also been denied supplies for some months by the winter storms and now the remaining defenders could observe, with trepidation, Breton vessels blockading the seaway to their fortress.

The previous year Harlech's garrison had numbered fifty-seven – twelve men-at-arms and forty-five archers – to defend its stout walls, which were up to twelve feet thick in places. At that time the commanders were Richard Massey of Sale, and a local Welshman calling himself Sir Vivian Collier. Massey was replaced by John Hennore during the summer but he was captured soon after taking up his post by my loyal supporter, Robin Holland of Eglwys Fach. Before Christmas he had been replaced by a William Hunt via the sea route, who gained entry to the castle through a small but well-guarded sea gate. He found a much-reduced, starving garrison. The situation seemed so hopeless to Hunt that he indicated his intention to surrender immediately. Vivian Collier was made of stronger stuff and would have none of it. He ordered his troops to lock up William Hunt and charged him with treason. Resistance continued under Sir Vivian but, we are reliably informed by 'friends' among the remaining castle servants, due to deaths, injury, sickness and malnutrition the available fighting men were now sixteen Welsh and five English soldiers, with most of them in a pretty parlous state.

The end, when it came, was so mundane and low key that, for a while at least, it took away the excitement and exultation we had expected to feel when we finally gained control of one of the greatest of all the English castles in Wales.

One miserable morning in mid-April, with Harlech engulfed in steady, dispiriting drizzle, I was summoned from my tent by news of movement at the castle's imposing main entrance. I hurried to the drawbridge to find a large group of my followers, including several of the commanders, watching as the great portcullis rose very slowly, its heavy, rusty chains squealing in protest. After it had finally been secured, the iron-studded oak doors began to move and now the squeals were replaced by the loud creaking of seized-up hinges.

There were no defenders stationed on the curtain walls or the towers and there were just three sorry figures standing miserably in the rain at the entrance. I found out later that the short figure in the middle was William Hunt. He was flanked on either side by two unarmed pikemen. I gestured to Rhys Gethin and gave him quick instructions to send half a dozen men to escort the three to me. We entered the castle with a squadron of armed men to secure it before sending out all survivors, giving them whatever assistance was required. They were to be taken to Ednyfed ap Siôn in his hospital tent.

'Remember,' I reminded Rhys, 'these are brave and loyal men who have done their utmost to protect the interests of their master. They are to be treated with honour and with dignity.'

I returned to my tent accompanied by the Tudur brothers, Rhys Ddu, Gruffudd Llwyd, my sons Gruffudd and Maredudd and my brother, Tudur. When the three prisoners were escorted in I quickly ordered an extra chair for Hunt. It was pretty clear that he was having some difficulty in standing. A quick glance at the faces of the two pikemen standing stiffly to attention convinced me that their pride would not allow them to accept seats.

'Master Hunt,' I began, not unkindly, 'I appreciate that the decision to surrender must have been difficult for you and that you are all in urgent need of sustenance. You can rest assured I shall make this as brief as possible.'

'That is appreciated, sire.' The man spoke through dry, caked lips after swallowing several times.

'How many of your garrison are still alive?'

'Twenty-one, sire.'

'Why is your fellow commander, Sir Vivian Collier not with you?'

'He died last night.'

I did not fail to notice the hesitation before he answered and decided that I would not pursue that line of questioning, at least for the present.

'So you, as sole commander, are surrendering Harlech castle to me.'

'There was no point in doing otherwise, Prince Owain. In a few more days we would all have been dead and you would have gained the castle in any case. There is no virtue in… causing… pointless deaths…' Hunt would have slid out of his chair onto the floor had one of his pikemen not grabbed hold of his arm.

'Thank you. That will be all, Master Hunt.'

I turned to the guards and ordered them to escort the pikemen to Ednyfed's sick bay and bring back a litter to carry their commander over there. Meanwhile, Maredudd pressed a goblet of water to the sick man's lips.

I sent a message to Rhys Gethin to take the strongest of the castle's survivors to search for the corpse of Sir Vivian

Collier. Rhys visited my tent some time later. He had found the body of Sir Vivian and had it identified, separately, by three reliable witnesses. As far as anyone could tell, the man had died of natural causes. There were no wounds or marks on the corpse to indicate otherwise.

17

I WOKE UP suddenly, prising open my eyes to be blinded briefly by a shaft of bright, May sunshine streaming through the narrow window in the eastern wall of the bedchamber. We had now occupied Harlech castle for several days and Mared and I had chosen the Constable's former quarters in the massive gatehouse as our private chambers. They were warm and spacious, providing the kind of luxury and comfort we had not experienced since being forced to abandon our home after what seemed an age ago.

Easing away the blanket and rising cautiously so as not to awaken my slumbering wife, I padded across the rich square of carpet to the tiny window, moving slightly to one side to escape the sun's glare. I caught my breath as I stared at the glorious, majestic grandeur of Snowdonia with its array of snow-capped peaks in the distance, reaching confidently into an azure sky. It was a moment of wonder which will stay with me as long as I live. I was prince of all I surveyed, and a great deal more, ensconced in a formidable castle, staring at that magnificent mountain range. And then I saw another prince, a monarch of the skies, though from this distance merely a dark speck in the cloudless sky, soaring effortlessly above it all. A golden eagle was gliding, seemingly disinterestedly, high above the caps of glistening snow. Its mind, however, was intent on feeding itself and possibly its young, and the huge raptor had the power, the speed and the murderous weapons to fulfil that urge. The nobility and artistry of its flight would quickly be transformed into instinctive and merciless savagery with no thought for its unfortunate prey. Food was a basic necessity – without it the eagle and its young could not survive. The prey, be it small animal or bird, would be food… just food; there was no room for any other thought or sentiment.

I sighed as I felt the cares and the weight of my princely responsibilities falling firmly back onto my shoulders. I turned and walked over to the larger square window in the west wall. Unlike the slit windows in the outward-facing east wall, the windows facing the inner ward of the castle were of more normal dimensions. I looked across at the tower which Catrin and Edmund had chosen as their quarters, then let my eyes roam to the great hall where my new Chancellor, Gruffudd Yonge, was engaged in a rapid transformation of the building. On the day after we moved into the castle I was amazed to see an army of stonemasons, carpenters, tilers and labourers streaming into the great hall. In a matter of days they had already effected essential repairs and improvements to the inside, including a raised dais at the far end on which it was planned to erect a throne with two lesser, elaborately-carved chairs, one on either side. Meanwhile, on the outside, the roof was being renewed with best-quality slates.

The following day Gruffudd Yonge came to our daily morning conference with ideas for setting up a small privy council chosen from members of the Prince's council. Its members would be used as a sounding board for new social, economic, political and fiscal policies and for practical adjustments to existing ones, as well as debating and suggesting improvements to the fulfilment of those policies by the new offices of state. They would also advise on all aspects of the conduct of the war with England.

'You see, Owain,' Gruffudd explained smoothly, 'the world we now live in has become too complex for any one man to control without giving day-to-day control of many things to trusted advisors… people carefully chosen for expertise in the field they will administer.'

'I understand what you say, Gruffudd,' I responded. 'However, I doubt that Henry Bolingbroke is very happy to see his Parliament developing its power to the extent that they have now taken control of his finances and even his own council. You cannot claim to be King by the grace of a God on the one hand and then find yourself having mere mortals as your masters.'

For a moment, my Chancellor reddened, his face registering shock and concern.

'Oh no, my Liege. Pray, do not misunderstand me. No, no, under my plan you would still be our Prince, exactly as you are now, and with the same powers to veto any suggestions from the counsellors.'

'I do not doubt your intentions, my dear Gruffudd. What you are suggesting makes sound sense.'

My Chancellor's list of proposed counsellors was well thought-out – a mix of senior clerics, highly-educated and articulate, several with practical experience in dealing with senior figures at the English court, in Parliament and with foreign envoys. It also included my brother Tudur, several of my commanders as well as wise and faithful friends who had been with me for most of my adult life such as Gruffudd Llwyd and Ednyfed ap Siôn. But there were two more I wished to add.

'I would have the captain of my guard, Gerwyn Dal, a

skilled and thoughtful soldier who can represent the views of middle-ranking officers and the men; and Thomas Easton, the husband of my wife's lady-in-waiting, a carpenter and common soldier who has shown great understanding of life and the soldier's lot. He has also displayed considerable acumen and quick-thinking in emergencies.'

Gruffudd looked up in surprise, eyebrows raised.

'You would have an Englishman as a member of your privy council?'

'This Englishman, most certainly. He has proved his worth and his loyalty to me time and again. I would value his advice and his insight into the thinking of ordinary people… of whatever nationality,' I responded firmly.

My Chancellor picked up his quill without further comment.

A week later, on 9th May, my privy council met for the first time. I had met Gerwyn Dal and Tom in my private quarters a few days before to inform them of their nomination. Both were concerned, as ordinary freemen, that they would not be sufficiently aware of the niceties of rank and order expected within such a body; but more importantly, that they might not be accepted as full members by the others.

'I assure you,' I told both tersely, 'every member will be there for one purpose and that is to offer views and sound advice to me and my Chancellor. When they sit on this council everyone will have equal status and will behave accordingly. Apart from me, of course.'

Apart from settling the protocols and procedures that are always required in the first meeting of any new committee, there were two matters for discussion. I invited the Chancellor to introduce the first.

Gruffudd beamed as he got up, went to the large cupboard against the wall behind him and brought out an ornately-carved wooden tray, setting it on the table. Then, his face wreathed in a broad smile, he placed his hands either side of a polished lid on which the Prince's coat of arms, the red and gold lions rampant, were painted within a black-lined, rectangular border. He turned a small key and opened the lid to reveal a shining metal object which he picked up reverently before handing it to me. It was my new great seal of state. Henceforth I would have two seals – the great seal, held by my Chancellor, and my private seal, already kept by my personal secretary. I studied the great seal with interest. On one side it showed an illustration of me as an armed warrior. On the other side I was a seated prince with a sceptre, orb and crown. I was pleased with it. It was handed around so that everyone could see it in detail to a chorus of acclaim. I thanked Gruffudd Yonge for designing and securing the finished article so efficiently and within such a short timespan.

'Now that the great seal has been given back to our Chancellor for safekeeping I wish to move on to the only other item on today's agenda.'

I paused for their full attention.

'I refer of course to the urgency of seeking alliances with friendly countries to support us against the English. As you know, the French and our Breton cousins have already provided warships to blockade several coastal castles and have, I believe, had a big influence on the surrender of both this castle and that of Cricieth. I also think we should now seek a formal alliance with King Charles VI of France. To that end, I intend to send envoys to France tomorrow. Before I finalise that decision I wish to seek your views on the matter. Unless someone raises a vital issue which would cast doubts on the wisdom of sending envoys to the French king at present, I shall confirm it in this meeting.'

I leaned back in my chair, glanced around the table and suggested a short break to give them time to think.

When we reconvened it was clear that all were in favour. I declared that we would send a delegation of two led by Chancellor Yonge. He would be accompanied by my brother-in-law, John Hanmer, whose legal training would be invaluable. I had already primed both envoys; all that was required now was for Dafydd to pen a formal document with my proposals bearing the great seal, and a less formal letter to Charles VI, bearing my private seal. Before closing the meeting I informed them that the Chancellor and I had discussed the possibility of holding our first *Senedd* in the mid Wales town of Machynlleth in the latter part of June. While Gruffudd and John were away in France I would be holding further meetings of the privy council, enlisting the help of various members in the planning and organisation of a *Senedd* to sit for several days. It would conclude with my official crowning as Prince of Wales in a religious ceremony in Machynlleth.

One evening, a fortnight or so after our delegation had left for France aboard one of the French warships which had blockaded Harlech, Mared and I were seated at the top table in the castle's great hall, replete from consuming one of the best meals I had ever tasted. It was a remarkable dish of roast venison smothered in honey with root vegetables, followed by various delicious sweetmeats which I had not had the opportunity of savouring for several years, Eating fare provided by the nobles of the Harlech area was a special luxury – all the more delicious after months of warfare on very basic rations. We were being entertained by the doyen of all the bards, our great friend and Mared's personal guard, the hairless but unsurpassed Gruffudd Llwyd, with velvety voice and sonorous harp. We listened to the exploits of our ancestors, faithfully delineated in magical verse to stirring music and, of course, culminating in fulsome praise of the current Prince and his armies.

We were applauding Gruffudd's virtuoso performance when the hall's doors were flung open and a guard came rushing in followed by a travel-stained messenger. I motioned the exhausted man to approach me. The breathless man gulped.

'My Liege, I bring you good news from Chancellor Yonge in France.'

He rummaged in a soiled travelling bag and carefully brought out a scroll encased in a protective leather tube. I thanked him and sent him to the kitchens for sustenance, ordering the guard to go with him to find the man a comfortable bed.

The news was good, very good. Our two ambassadors had been received by King Charles VI on 20th May. It was a warm and friendly meeting. Charles was accompanied by his brother, the powerful Louis, Duc d'Orléans, leader of an influential group of nobles already pressing for all-out war with England. The French king had also pointed out one interesting historical fact concerning the Welsh nobleman known as Owain Lawgoch (Owain of the Red Hand), who with his followers had served as mercenaries for the King's predecessor, Charles V. Owain had signed the Treaty of Paris declaring friendship between the two countries thirty-two years before, on 10th May 1372. As my current request for a treaty had also been signed on 10th May, Charles was convinced that the coincidence was a favourable augury for the new treaty, which spoke of an agreement to provide strong support against our mutual enemy, England. He also informed me that, as a token of his admiration and goodwill, he was sending me a suit of armour designed for a prince aboard the French warship that had carried the messenger home.

18

W HEN THE SUIT of armour was brought to me the
following day I thought it a most amazing gift.
The metal plates shone and sparkled in the early summer
sunshine and the workmanship was of the finest quality;
easily the best I had ever seen. It was far too refined to
be risked in battle, for it was nothing short of a work of
art. Moreover, it would be so conspicuous that the enemy
would know perfectly well who the wearer was and would
concentrate arrows and other weaponry upon it. Worn
on formal state occasions though, it would be extremely
impressive.

The two ambassadors returned from Paris at the end
of May to discover that preparations for our first *Senedd*
were well advanced. A new guildhall in Machynlleth had
been hired for the duration of the *Senedd* which would
commence on 20th June. Most of the privy council had
been dispatched to the little mid Wales town two weeks
beforehand to ensure that this first senate, lasting several
days, would be organised to perfection. I had invited
noblemen known to be supporters of our cause and four
freemen from every commote, or administrative area, in
Wales. Gruffudd Yonge, who had overall responsibility
for the event, had decided the *Senedd* would, in fact, be in
session for three days, culminating with my coronation on
the fourth day.

He had planned a religious service emphasising how my

temporal powers were presented to me with God's blessing. The coronation would take place just outside Machynlleth in a large marquee donated to us by King Charles VI, and the Chancellor was intent on crowning me with as much pomp and splendour as he could muster. We had also invited envoys from several countries and had already received affirmative responses from France, Scotland, Castile and the Duchy of Brittany.

On the eve of our departure for Machynlleth, Mared, Gruffudd Llwyd and I were having supper in our private dining room in the castle gatehouse. Gruffudd was displaying considerable anticipation and kept referring to 'this historic event' and a 'turning point in the history of our people'. I could imagine the patriotic fervour that he would instil in a post-event ode which, no doubt, would captivate audiences for a long time to come.

'What troubles you, Owain? You do not seem to share Gruffudd's enthusiasm for the week ahead. I thought you would be delighted… After all, we have lived through some pretty hard times praying for the good fortune which would allow you to be confirmed as undisputed *Tywysog*.'

I saw Gruffudd staring at Mared in surprise, for it was very unusual for my wife to display signs of irritation towards me.

'My Lady, I am sure that Owain is looking forward to it all just as we are. Perhaps we are forgetting that despite his many attributes, Owain is as human as everyone else. I would not be surprised if he is getting a little nervous… a sensation which is foreign to his nature.' The big man chuckled softly at the thought.

I looked from one to the other and sighed.

'You are right, Mared. This is a time for celebration and

I should be feeling delighted with what we have achieved so far. You speak of nervousness, Gruff… well maybe so. I do feel something… but I would not call it nervousness… more a sense of foreboding. It is like a dark cloud at the back of my mind. It is totally unreasonable but I cannot shake it off. Is everything going too well for us at present… and are we too ready to take our luck for granted, perhaps?'

'Oh, my love, you must not think like that,' Mared said soothingly. 'I can see no reason to fear any change in our luck at present. You are in your strongest position since the war started, and now we have gained control of two of the mighty coastal castles, with Aberystwyth likely to surrender to us soon.'

'Absolutely,' Gruff confirmed confidently. 'Why, you are now ruler of almost the whole of Wales and even the Anglo-Flemings of southern Pembroke are paying you not to attack them, not to mention several of the English border shires. No, I can see nothing that could cause us a setback in the foreseeable future.'

There was a knock at the door. I called the visitor to enter. It was my secretary, Dafydd.

'I have brought you the list of confirmed attendees for the *Senedd* sessions, my Liege. More than three-quarters of the invitees have confirmed their attendance.'

'Indeed,' I exclaimed. 'That is a very good response, especially when you allow for the distances involved. You seem a little troubled, Dafydd. What is it that concerns you?'

'There is one name on the list, sire, which I am unsure of. This man was certainly not on the list of named invitees.'

'His name?'

'Dafydd ap Llywelyn ap Hywel Fychan.'

'By the bones of the saints,' Gruffudd gasped incredulously. 'It is that traitorous lover of the English, Dafydd Gam, who had the nerve to attend our meeting at Sycharth four years ago and argued against starting a rebellion. He and your late cousin, Hywel Selyf, were the only two to speak against the proposal. Now he has the nerve to attend a *Senedd* he does not believe in and to which he was not invited!'

I, too, was shocked, though I tried to show a total lack of concern. The hunchback was a direct descendant of the Princes of Brycheiniog. He and his immediate predecessors had been effective puppets for their English masters in south-east Wales, administering lands on their behalf, making themselves indispensable to the smooth running of those areas and the effective collection of local taxes. As a result, several prominent family members, and not least Dafydd Gam, had been rewarded with lands, generous annuities and the patronage of the ruling English. If Dafydd Gam was intent on attending the *Senedd* it was certainly not to support our cause. His would be a completely disruptive influence at the very least, and he might even be planning something more dangerous.

'Can you not ban him from the sessions, my Lord?' Mared broke my reverie. 'Surely you would be fully justified in imprisoning him as a traitor.'

'No,' I replied firmly. 'I would not give him the satisfaction of being taken so seriously.'

The following morning we set out for Machynlleth. I was accompanied by several of my leading privy councillors, commanders and senior officials, with Mared and her ladies-in-waiting travelling in a beautifully-furnished coach drawn by four horses. I was escorted by my personal guard company, *Y Cedyrn*, and by a hand-picked force of 600 of my most loyal soldiers. Another 400 were already in Machynlleth commanded by Rhys Gethin, charged with providing organisational support and maintaining law and order.

I had been invited to bring the royal party and *Y Cedyrn* to the home of my friend, the local nobleman Rhun ap Gwynfor, some miles away, with the main body of my force travelling on to join their fellows at their encampment outside Machynlleth. Rhun had ensured the presence of 200 of his own men close to his moated hall to provide support for *Y Cedyrn*, though it was not expected to be required.

Rhun, obviously pre-warned of our coming, was waiting for us with studied formality, flanked by a small group of his senior retainers and domestic staff. He greeted us affably, staring in undisguised admiration at Mared, whom he had never met before. I glanced across at Gruffudd Llwyd whose face was set in a frosty frown. I struggled to control the beginnings of a grin. Gruffudd was always extremely protective of Mared when there were strangers around and the great love he bore for her was well understood by both my wife and I – though he was, thankfully, unaware that we knew.

'You honour us with your presence, my Prince, and we are doubly honoured to be hosts to your gracious wife. My Lady, I am delighted to make your acquaintance and I hope you will enjoy your stay with us,' Rhun beamed.

'The honour is all mine, my Lord,' Mared smiled. 'I owe you a great debt of gratitude for the complete and unconditional support you gave Owain at the battle of Mawddach Bridge. Without your help he would have been in huge difficulties that day.'

'It was the least I could do for my lawful Prince. I like to think that he now regards me as a faithful friend, and that is a privilege which I value greatly.'

As Rhun ushered us to our quarters, I could not help thinking that he was not totally at ease. Despite his usual warmth and straightforward manner he seemed to have something on his mind. I resolved that I would speak to him alone as soon as I could. The opportunity came sooner than I expected. As he ushered Mared and Gwen, her first lady-in-waiting, into our chambers he asked if he could have a brief word with me and we went into a small sitting room only a few yards away.

'Owain…' he hesitated before taking a deep breath. 'Last night I was presented with a situation which put me in a very difficult position. Dafydd Gam and another man called here and asked for food and shelter for a couple of nights, for they had failed to find lodgings in Machynlleth for the *Senedd*. As soon as they find alternative accommodation in town they will be leaving.'

'I hear what you say, Rhun.'

Rhun took another deep breath. 'I know how much you dislike him and his views. However, as you well know it is our custom to grant hospitality to any stranger who is in need of shelter…'

'Absolutely,' I interrupted. 'You have done no more and no less than I would have done in such circumstances. I won't pretend that Dafydd's presence will not be a nuisance but I am sure we can manage.'

'However, I have made it clear to Gam and his henchman that they will not be seated at the top table for supper. In fact, I intend to ensure they are sitting at the far end of the great hall. I have also warned him that I am totally loyal to my Prince and any attempt to disrupt or interfere in any way with you or any of your party and the two of them will be cast out of this house immediately.'

'Then, my friend, you have done all you can to minimise any unseemly confrontation,' I assured him.

There was a frown of concern on Mared's face when I told her. I moved quickly to reassure her. I called for Gerwyn Dal and Gruffudd Llwyd. When they arrived I invited them to join us at our modest table and filled two pewter jugs with Rhun's best ale for them. They both stiffened on their chairs when I informed them of Gam's presence.

'Rest assured, I will sleep on a blanket outside your door tonight, my Lady.' The words were spoken in a cold, quiet monotone which resonated as if it had been a shout.

'No, you will not, Gruff,' Mared retorted, though her gratitude shone through the sharpness in her voice.

Gruff made to protest but I cut in quickly.

'Gerwyn, I want you to detail two fully-armed men to stand guard outside this door all night. There will be a change of guards every two hours. I want them to be alert to the slightest indication of danger. If an intruder is identified as Dafydd Gam or his associate, your men's orders are to kill them immediately. I shall inform Rhun that I am taking this unusual step. In the circumstances I'm sure he will see it as something we cannot afford to ignore. As for you, Gruff, you are sleeping in an adjacent room in any case and you have my leave to keep that axe of yours at your side all night.'

'My Liege, all of *Y Cedyrn* are elite soldiers. Tonight I shall pick the best of the best, be assured. With your leave, I will also post a brace of guards outside every entry point to this building.'

'There you are, my love.' I turned to Mared. 'I believe

you and I will have the most secure sleeping chamber in the whole world tonight!'

Later that evening the meal in the great hall passed without incident. From my vantage point next to Rhun I could see Dafydd Gam and his companion seated at a distant table. They both behaved impeccably. Similarly, the night also passed without incident. Indeed, Mared and I slept well.

We were enjoying a quiet breakfast in our quarters when Gerwyn Dal came to see me. There was a crumpled note in his outstretched hand with no covering or seal of any kind. I spread it on the table. It was of low-grade animal hide, written in the smeared ink from a badly-worn quill which, on top of its crumpled state, made reading it very difficult. It took me three attempts to decipher the English words…

Glyndŵr, you and I need to talk. I know I am at risk coming here, for you could imprison me at any time should you wish. On the other hand, you know that I can be a considerable nuisance to you at your so-called Senedd… *quite an embarrassment in fact. All I want is one final private discussion with you to see if we can come to some agreement or arrangement whereby you relinquish all your claimed rights to rule the lands of my ancestors in the south-east so that I can continue to control those lands for King Henry and his nobles in the manner in which my family has done so successfully for more than a hundred years. In return, I will agree to cease all attempts to dislodge you as ruler of the rest of Wales. A reasonable offer, I think. I am sure you will agree that it is worth talking through.*

I invite you to join me on foot for the first few miles of the journey to Machynlleth tomorrow. You could send your entourage ahead to the little hamlet of Craig y Ddafad where they could wait for us to join them, horses ready to mount. By then you and I may well have come to a mutually beneficial agreement and, instead of causing trouble in your Senedd, *I will be on my way south immediately!*

Your fellow uchelwr,
Dafydd ap Llywelyn ap Hywel Fychan

I handed the note to Mared and told Gerwyn Dal: 'You may send a message to Dafydd Gam telling him that I will walk the first few miles of tomorrow's journey with him but I shall be leaving here promptly at the hour of nine.'

'What is this foolishness?' Mared, her face cloned with the same incredulous expression as the captain of *Y Cedyrn*, ran over and clung to me for a second before pushing me abruptly away.

'Why on Earth would you agree to that cunning devil's request? Apart from the fact that you have no intention of making such an agreement, the risk of walking some miles in open countryside alone with that monster is immense. He probably wants you alone so he can murder you. Oh Owain, please think again about this, for my sake if not for your own. Have you already forgotten your cousin Hywel Selyf and his trickery?'

But I remained adamant. I have always believed that a true leader does not hide from those who disagree with him – or from the dangers he asks others who support him to face also. Nor had I forgotten the treachery of my cousin Hywel – the scar on my shoulder reminded me of that – but I had dealt with men more powerful and more able than either Hywel or Dafydd Gam, and I had learned the lessons also. Although she soon accepted that I would not be persuaded otherwise, she found it hard to hide her fears from me that evening.

I awoke on 20th June to blue skies and a gentle southerly breeze. It was a pleasant early summer's morning and one that would undoubtedly get hotter as the day wore on. I took my leave of Mared with a jaunty wave. She smiled too, trying hard not to show her concern.

As I stepped out onto the main courtyard I saw Dafydd Gam approaching from the other side. He was short but broad, with a barrel chest, leaning to one side because of the misshapen lump on his right shoulder. His gait was uneven as his physique forced him to drag his left foot slightly with each step. As he got closer I saw the marked cast in his left eye. I also noticed something which I had not remembered from our few previous meetings; his good right eye was hazel while his weak right eye was a watery blue.

'*Henffych, Dywysog,*' he hailed me, the overly-obsequious tone serving to remind me of how much I disliked this man. My feelings had nothing to do with his physical imperfections… No, it was the twisted personality, Dafydd the twisted individual, who made my stomach heave whenever I met him. Here was a descendant of the royal house of Brycheiniog who had sold his birthright, as well as his soul, to foreign masters.

As we walked onto the drawbridge over the moat, most of our conversation centred on the glory of the morning and the distance to Craig y Ddafad. We soon ran out of things to say and walked on in an awkward silence. I was determined that, since this walk was his idea and the subject was of his choosing, then it was up to him to raise it. After several minutes he did. His main theme seemed to be that everything in life is a compromise. None of us can have everything we want, and sometimes it is better for people of opposing views and interests to try to resolve their differences through a little give and take. In this instance there was nothing to stop me from calling myself Prince of Wales even though, in reality, he would be ruling in south-east Wales as my vassal.

'An interesting proposition, Dafydd,' I said, my voice heavy with sarcasm. 'I wonder what your English friends would think of that? Do you think that your master, Bolingbroke, would continue to pay you upwards of forty gold marks a year if he heard that you were holding the lands he claims as his own in my name?'

'Oh come now, Owain; King Henry would not know that I was, in truth, acting on your behalf.'

'I don't think you could keep that sort of arrangement secret, Dafydd. You would be taking an enormous risk every day trying to please Henry and me...'

I stopped and stared at the man. Did he really believe that I would fall for such a silly, impractical plan?

'The King,' he drew himself up stiffly, 'trusts me implicitly.'

'Then the more fool he,' I snapped. 'Just answer me one question. Who would you be collecting the peoples' taxes for in your dual role as my vassal and the King's seneschal, or whatever he calls you? Would they be taxed by the King of England... or by the Prince of Wales?'

'Owain, Owain, we are at the beginning of our conversation and you start asking questions which are for later, when we work out the details.'

He blustered before pausing to stare keenly at a thicket of trees lining one side of the road. After a moment he turned to me and said, 'Did you hear anything then? I could have sworn I heard someone shouting from somewhere in those trees.'

As if on cue, I heard a man's voice shouting in fear, 'Help me, help me. For the love of God, someone help me.'

After tailing off, the voice screamed desperately as if its owner was being tortured, before finally subsiding into helpless sobs.

I drew my sword and entered the trees at a run, my heart pumping as I dodged around the gnarled trunks. I found him almost immediately, a dishevelled figure roped securely to an ancient oak. I kept a sharp eye open for his captors but saw nobody. I could hear Dafydd thrashing about behind me as he sought to catch up. I ran over to the oak and saw that the man's head was hanging forward onto his chest as if he had lost consciousness. In two strokes of my sword all the binding slithered to the ground and the man crumpled and fell rolling onto his back. I sheathed my sword and knelt at his side. Then I stopped in shock and knew that I had been conned, for the face staring up at me was very much awake. It was that of Dafydd Gam's companion of the night before. As I prepared to leap to my feet the back of my head exploded with pain and I sank into impenetrable darkness.

Distant voices, faint, far away were slightly irritating. All I wanted was to rest in the comforting darkness. But the voices were still there, getting closer… more insistent. I was suddenly aware of a throbbing pain at the back of my head. Then, without warning, I received a hard slap across the face which raised the level of pain in my head by several notches. With the pain came a sudden anger and I opened my eyes to see who my assailant was so that I could return the favour. I was halted in my tracks as the glare of summer sunlight seared my eyes, blinding me for several moments. Someone laughed harshly.

'Looks like his Royal Highness is waking up and he ain't looking too happy, either.'

It was a voice I did not know. I ventured to open my eyes again, slowly this time. It was Gam's companion. I turned my head gingerly. My reward, apart from more pain, was the twisted face of Dafydd Gam grinning at me in triumph.

'Well, well. So our gullible Prince is back with us. I am sorry for the hard knock on the back of your head but I only had a fallen branch as a cudgel and I needed to make certain that you would stay down, quietly while my man, Islwyn, and I disarmed you and tied you up. I was quite surprised when you agreed to our little walk. Did you really imagine I would agree a deal to be your vassal, Glyndŵr? If so, you really need to sharpen up.'

My mouth and throat were dry and my tongue felt swollen. I had to clear my throat before I could speak.

'No,' I said huskily. 'I did not believe that half-baked story for one minute. However, I knew you were desperate to get me to stay away from your area and the problems I would cause… problems which your English masters would expect you to solve. So I took you up on the offer and I have succeeded in forcing you and your treacherous schemes into the open. What you hope to gain by capturing me and tying me up is a mystery to me… not that it matters a jot, for I have instructed my guards to come in search of us if I did not reach Craig y Ddafad by a set time. They should arrive at any time now, I think.'

'Which is why, my dear Glyndŵr, we must hasten away from here, before your uncouth retainers arrive. As to what I hope to gain…'

He paced over to me, jerking my head up by my hair.

'It is more a case of how much you are prepared to lose or suffer. You see, if you do not sign a proclamation stating that you are relinquishing all claims to being Prince of Wales, and conceding that the lawful Prince is Henry of Monmouth… then I shall kill you… very, very slowly… after putting out your eyes with a red-hot iron of course… If you are sensible, and accept the inevitable, I shall still kill you, but it will be humane… and quick.'

The hunchback stared into my eyes, the malice in his own eyes unmistakable. He noted the determination to resist in my own stare, and nodded coldly.

'I see you still want to play the hero, Owain,' he whispered. 'It will be interesting to see how long your pride will carry you. I shall be content to wait for the moment you break… I have seen many tough men broken, and it is not a very… edifying sight, shall we say. No, indeed. Pitiful – is the word which comes to mind.'

He called to his man to hurry up. My hands were tied tightly behind my back but I struggled to my feet swaying a little, for the pain in my head sharpened in the effort of rising, causing giddiness.

Then there were footsteps at the edge of the clearing and Dafydd Gam's face was a picture of rage and disbelief. I spun around, forgetting the pain and the dizziness as I recognised the comforting bulk of Gerwyn Dal standing less than twenty yards away.

'Stay exactly where you are or you are dead men,' Gerwyn called grimly. 'You are surrounded by archers and the slightest movement will spell your death.'

'Kill him, Islwyn… now,' Dafydd hissed, and in an instant the man was hurtling towards me, dagger drawn. I positioned myself to kick him but the air was rent with the deadly whisper of arrows and Islwyn was dead before he had made two yards.

My guards' captain strode over. 'Sire, you are injured. Let me look at that wound. We need to get you seen by Ednyfed as soon as possible.'

Before I could reply there was another man, even bigger than Gerwyn Dal, at my side.

'Owain, what have they done to you? Oh God, that looks nasty.' Gruffudd Llwyd gently parted my matted hair to examine my scalp and sucked in his breath. 'Where is that treacherous toad?' he roared. 'I will kill him with my bare hands.'

Before anyone could stop him he had reached Dafydd Gam and, with a vicious punch, caught the man high on the side of his head as he ducked. He went down hard, his body slamming into the ground and lying perfectly still.

The men shouted their approval. And Gerwyn breathed, 'By all the saints, he has killed him too!'

I shook myself, striving to clear my head.

'Gruffudd, come back here and cool down. Now listen to me everyone. I thank you for saving my life by arriving when you did but I want it to be absolutely clear that there will be no more physical attacks on Dafydd Gam. If he is still alive, he is to be treated as we would treat any other prisoner. He will not be harmed in any way without my explicit agreement. Is that clear?'

There were shouts of assent. Gruffudd apologised for his loss of control but, from the glances exchanged with Gerwyn, it was clear that both were far from unhappy with the action which had left Gam lying prone on the ground.

'Are you fit enough to ride a horse, my Liege?' Gerwyn Dal asked politely.

'Of course.'

I glared disapprovingly at the two giants before they walked away to organise a spare mount for me. I could not resist a brief, indulgent grin, for though they had their backs to me I was fully aware that they were both beaming like mischievous children.

19

T HE BRASSY FANFARE of ten trumpeters startled the large crowd of onlookers in Machynlleth. The *Senedd* had completed its three-day session and now, on the fourth morning, Mared and I waited for the signal to leave the hall and step into our coach for the stately procession. Our destination was the huge marquee where my coronation would take place, a mile to the west. Gwen, my wife's senior lady-in-waiting, appeared in the open doorway and curtsied, smiling happily. It was time to go. Mared gave me her hand and I gave it a little squeeze as I felt a slight nervous tremor. She looked up at me, her eyes filled with pride. It was a moment I shall always treasure and, as we stepped out into the sunshine in our long ceremonial robes of red and gold, we were met with the loud approbation of the waiting crowd. Never had Machynlleth seen anything like this. At the head of the royal entourage was Rhys Gethin, looking every inch a general on a perfectly groomed white destrier. Behind him came a cohort of sixty archers, marching in ten rows, six abreast. A few yards behind them came a dozen of my senior commanders, including my brother Tudur, in two rows, six abreast, their polished armour gleaming in the sunshine.

Then came thirty members of *Y Cedyrn* in their ceremonial, red-plumed helmets while behind them danced twenty young maidens dressed in knee-length, green tunics with flowers in their hair. Behind the dancers Mared and I sat in an elegant black, open carriage drawn by six horses, their black coats shining and their manes beribboned in red, white and green. We were followed by the remaining thirty members of my personal guard. Behind them was a coterie of a dozen clergy headed by Chancellor Yonge in his new purple bishop's robes, with a sprinkling of other bishops including Ieuan Trefor, Bishop of St Asaph; Lewis Byford, Bishop of Bangor; Hywel Cyffin, Dean of St Asaph and other representative clergy. Our strong supporters, the Cistercians and the Franciscans, were also well represented. Next in the long procession were the 120 representatives of the *Senedd*, including the privy councillors not already included in the procession. Finally, a company of sixty Gwynedd pikemen, commanded by Rhys Tudur, formed an impressive rearguard.

The whole route from the *Senedd* to the coronation marquee was lined by hundreds of waving, excited men, women and children eager to cheer us as we passed. For them, as for us, it was a truly unique and inspiring occasion. As we came to a halt at the entrance to the marquee I could see that the last two-thirds of the massive seated area was already full, with all the waiting guests craning their necks to catch a glimpse of us. Mared and I sat in the coach chatting quietly and waving to the exuberant populace as the distinguished guests and clergy left the procession and entered the marquee heading for the front seats. Then the ten trumpeters stepped forward to repeat their rendition of the stirring fanfare as Mared and I strode slowly forward, our robes billowing slightly in the breeze. As we entered the covered area we both gasped as our eyes met a scene we were totally unprepared for. At the front, facing the congregation, was a small altar draped in a beautiful cloth of white and gold. To one side was the intricately-carved throne I had seen a few weeks before in the great hall at Harlech castle, but now there were two slightly smaller, lower-backed chairs, similarly embellished, on either side.

Standing by the altar was the Chancellor in his purple robe, with a tall mitre on his head and a silver crozier in his right hand. Resting on the altar itself was a finely worked and polished crown. We had been informed that the coronation would be in two parts. First there would be a religious ceremony, for I was to be crowned in the presence and acceptance of God – the first native Prince of Wales for more than a century and the first ever Welsh prince to be crowned in the English and European style confirmed by the Almighty Himself. The second part would be a celebration of my coronation in music, verse and dance. However, nobody had warned us how long the religious ceremony would take.

After a succession of Bible readings and prayers we came at length to the coronation ceremony. Gruffudd Yonge launched into a long peroration describing the history of the various Welsh princes and concentrating on the thirteenth century when the princes of Gwynedd had gained ascendancy over other regional princes. He cited the two who had managed to gain authority over most of Wales, Llywelyn ap Iorwerth (the Great) and Llywelyn ap Gruffudd (the Last) who had laid claim to the title, Prince of Wales.

Then he described the English occupation lasting more than a century, the building of the great Anglo-Norman castles and the massive taxes levied by the English kings in the areas directly under their control and by the Anglo-Norman nobles in the Welsh Marches, leading to the extreme poverty of the country. He reminded the congregation of how English law denied the Welsh any meaningful rights and how they were forced to sell their produce in the English boroughs at a fraction of their market value.

Then he came to our rebellion and how I, Owain ap Gruffudd Fychan, had been recognised as the promised saviour of our people, the prophesied *Mab Darogan*. Now, with God's help, we would drive the English out of Wales and restore the traditional values, laws and government usurped by the oppressor for so long.

'Here,' Gruffudd Yonge exulted, 'is the man, supported by our all-powerful Christian God, who leads us into a new era where we will be governed according to the laws of Hywel Dda and where we will all be treated as equals for the purposes of law and order.'

The Chancellor turned to me, inviting me to stand facing the altar and to kneel before God in the presence of all the witnesses. He then made me swear an oath of fealty, promising to rule my people according to Christian teachings and standards and to take heed of the Almighty's advice when taking decisions which would affect any or all of my people. Afterwards I was required to stand and turn towards the congregation, with Mared on my left. Gruffudd retrieved the crown from the altar and placed it carefully on my head. I had forewarned him that my head wound, though much improved thanks to Ednyfed's very effective salve, was still tender. Nevertheless, it was a truly magical and emotional moment. As I led my Princess towards the throne, my heart was filled with pride for my people and my country; I had never felt so joyful and alive in all my life. I sat on my throne for the first time, with Mared taking the seat on my left.

Gruffudd Yonge stood in front of the chair on my right and whispered for me to stand.

'Distinguished envoys of France, Scotland, Castile and Brittany; my Lords, ladies and gentlemen.'

The Chancellor's voice was charged with authority and drama.

'I give you… Owain IV… by the grace of God, Prince of Wales!'

The entire congregation stood as one, clapping their hands and cheering, the celebration being taken up in like fashion by the multitudes waiting patiently outside the marquee. At last the Chancellor raised his hand for silence and, when order had been restored, Mared and I resumed our seats. Gruffudd announced that the celebration in song, verse and dance would now begin, and seated himself on the chair to my right. After the pomp and seriousness of the religious ceremony the celebration which followed was a delight which entertained and enthused everyone present.

Six leading bards sang a mix of traditional patriotic songs and items specifically composed for my coronation, to their own harp accompaniment. The last and best of the bards was, clearly, my old friend and comrade-in-arms, Gruffudd Llwyd. His imposing voice and dexterity with the harp matched the quality of his paeans of praise to perfection. He toyed with his listeners' emotions, invoking in them pity and sadness, joy and pride, humour and grief.

Then the maidens in their short tunics, who had danced in Machynlleth at the start of the day, now returned to entertain us in the marquee. There were twenty of them, all maidens of marriageable age who were daughters, nieces and granddaughters of *uchelwyr*.

The dancers were in the prime of youth, their tunics a beautiful green but of a very fine material which clung to their bodies like a second skin. And so it was that, though sophisticated and elegant, the dance was also a tantalising mix of the exotic and the erotic. And – as Mared took pleasure in wryly pointing out to me when I later praised its elegance and innocence – a golden opportunity for parents to have their daughters display their charms to many young, not so young, but often – and for different reasons – highly-desirable potential husbands.

At last the entertainment was over. The procession formed up again in the same order for the return journey to the *Senedd* house in Machynlleth where Mared and I were hosting a formal dinner for the foreign envoys and the privy council. It felt strange seated in the carriage wearing my crown. It also had an unexpected effect on the onlookers. Instead of the loud, abandoned shouts and cheers of delight which had marked our morning procession, they were now more respectful, almost awed.

These were people who had never seen a Welsh leader wearing a crown and they seemed unsure quite how to behave. Somehow I had, in the space of a few short hours, been transformed into an almost godlike sovereign. The story of the day, that they had seen a real Prince of Wales, would be told to their children and grandchildren for years to come.

A few days later, in Harlech castle, we were brought back to reality. I had called a meeting of the privy council to evaluate our first ever *Senedd* session. We were all in good spirits, for we all deemed it a great success. On the first day, many of the delegates had only the vaguest idea of the nature and purpose of a *Senedd*. It took the whole morning to reach a general understanding of what the gathering was intended to achieve and the remainder of the day to explain and practise the general rules and procedures for achieving an orderly discussion and voting method. Over the following days, apart from a few embarrassing gaffes, the great majority of members rapidly became adept at the required procedures.

The first and immediate concern had been for my state of health and how Dafydd Gam should be dealt with. On seeing me arrive swathed in bandages, most delegates were strongly in favour of executing the man immediately, preferably by burning at the stake. It took a great deal of persuasion from both Gruffudd Yonge and myself to turn that view around. Indeed I very nearly had to use my powers of veto to stop them in their tracks. However, since it was the first sitting of our first *Senedd,* I wanted to assure them that I preferred to carry them with me to a carefully thought-out and agreed decision. After much persuasion, backed to the hilt by the Chancellor and winning over the members of the all-important privy council, I managed to get them to agree to a short term of imprisonment in Harlech castle dungeons so that we could consider Gam's fate calmly in a few weeks' time. By then I calculated that I would only have the privy council members to persuade.

On the second and third days everything went smoothly. I spoke at length about the aims of the rebellion and how we were currently enjoying unprecedented success. I warned that we would have to gain the support of the French or the Scots or both to counter England's massive power in the long run and asked the Chancellor to report on the agreement he and John Hanmer had reached with the French in Paris. We had strong hopes that this would lead to significant practical military support from across the sea. It was essential we achieved our goals within the next two years, for the weakness of the English king would not last for ever. After the Chancellor's report on the Paris agreement I set out my views on the kind of independent country I wanted to see.

They were surprised and fascinated by the breadth of our thinking, particularly in our plans for the future of the Church in Wales. I explained how we could take advantage of the schism in the Church of Rome which had resulted in two rival Popes, one based in Rome and the other in Avignon. I reminded them that there had been a Christian Church in Wales long before the English became Christians and I could see no reason why Wales should be answerable to the Archbishopric of Canterbury. Instead we should have a Welsh Church headed by an Archbishop at St Davids where our patron saint had worked so hard to establish Christianity in our country. Since Canterbury was firmly in thrall to the Pope in Rome, the only way we could break free was to offer our allegiance to the Avignon Pope. This would also please our allies, the French.

The proposal was unanimously accepted. I then went on to describe my vision for education, law and order, taxation and the future of farming and trade. I promised that taxation levels would only be a fraction of the greedy demands of the English. On farming and trade in general, I outlined plans for seeking local agreements within communities and a drive to secure trade agreements with various friendly countries which would establish affordable and fair prices for food and other essential commodities.

Most pleasing was the reaction to my dream of establishing two universities, one in the north and the other in the south, which would eventually provide us with highly-educated graduates having a good command of Latin and the ability and expertise to become efficient civil servants, lawyers, teachers and administrators. And finally there was loud acclaim when I announced that English law would no longer apply in the new independent Wales, for we would return to the traditional, more equitable laws of the early Welsh king, Hywel Dda.

Several members of the council spoke of the progress made at the Machynlleth *Senedd* and of its value as a means of informing and gaining the support of leaders and ordinary people throughout Wales. It was enthusiastically agreed that we would hold another *Senedd*, probably in Harlech, a year hence.

Later that evening Mared, Gruffudd Llwyd and two of our sons, Gruffudd and Maredudd, had a quiet supper in our private apartments in the castle gatehouse. While we tucked in heartily to a delicious dinner of roast pork, Maredudd sat morosely toying at the meat on his platter with his knife. His uncharacteristic melancholy created an oppressive atmosphere.

'Maredudd…' Mared's voice was low and motherly. 'I seem to be the only one present who has only a second-hand account of your upsetting encounter earlier. Would you mind telling me what happened precisely? I'm sure the others won't mind hearing it again. It might help you too, my love, if you share the experience again with people who are close to you…'

Our second son looked at her doubtfully for a moment before nodding wearily in agreement. Gruffudd, our eldest son, nodded too.

'Mother is right. Telling the story again might help you to come to terms with it all.'

As if their permission had unlocked a dam, Maredudd's

story came in a flood: 'Tom Easton and I were coming back from hunting this afternoon with two plump boar carcasses. As we approached the drawbridge we saw a small group of people pleading with the guards to let them in. As we reached them I realised that they must be a family. The parents could have been any age, for they were shockingly thin and their clothing old and torn. The son and daughter, both around fourteen or fifteen years, were almost too weak to stand. In fact, the daughter slipped to her knees as we approached and started to weep silently. The four turned towards us, their faces pinched and eyes despairing. Worst of all...' Here Maredudd paused, struggling with his emotions, '... the mother was holding a babe in her arms. Hunger had made the little body very small and scrawny and the eyes stared dully out of deep hollows above protruding cheekbones. The tiny creature was wasted and obviously used to hunger pangs, for there were no tears... only those artificially large eyes filled with pain and suffering, the only kind of life that it had ever experienced.'

Maredudd suddenly banged the table with his fist, sending platters and bowls clattering and startling us all. He placed his head in his hands, his body wracked with deep sobs. His mother started to get up, but I gripped her arm and motioned her to sit. In a minute or two he had composed himself again.

'It is all wrong,' he exclaimed at last. 'No babe-in-arms... none... should ever be subjected to that. They have just entered our world for God's sake... they have not had the time or the capability to do anything wrong, so why should I have to witness a baby who should, in a fair and just world, be a small, beautiful miracle, looking like a starving... a starving... rat? So, what are you doing, Father? I hear you and your officials saying that we are winning this war. Are we? Who do you mean by "we"? I'll tell you who are not having fair play in our new free Wales… I'm talking about the ordinary people, the children, the babies, for most of them are worse off now than they ever were. Tell me, Father, do you have a strategy for improving the lot of the starving members of our society?'

'Enough. That is more than enough, Maredudd. I know you are upset but I will not have you speak to your father like that,' Mared snapped furiously.

'Now wait, let us cool down for a moment,' I interposed quietly. I was struggling to get over my astonishment. Maredudd and I were very close and he had never spoken to me in that tone before. The sight of that starving family must have affected him deeply. But he had raised an important point. How would we deal with the poverty and despair which I knew was the lot of a large percentage of the Welsh populace?

'It's a very pertinent question, Maredudd, but I would like to know how you dealt with the situation.'

'Well, when we arrived I shouted to the guards to open the gates, which they did, for Tom and I were returning from hunting. I shepherded the poor family in ahead of us and took them immediately to the castle infirmary. Ednyfed was not there but I instructed the man in charge to find him at once and ask him to examine these people to determine how best to help them. Then I asked Megan, a young scullery maid I know and trust, to take the infant to the kitchens and ensure that she was given some warm milk immediately. The mother became hysterical when she realised we were taking the baby away from her, so I quickly agreed that she could go to the kitchens as well. Finally, I organised a small, comfortable bedchamber for them in the guest quarters. They will stay in the castle until Ednyfed is satisfied that they are back to reasonable health.'

'I applaud you, Maredudd,' Gruffudd Llwyd said in a gruff voice. 'You are a good man, just like your father.'

'Yes, thank you, my son, for showing such kindness and Christian charity,' said Mared, close to tears.

I looked across the table at my eldest son, Gruffudd, and was saddened but not surprised when I saw his furious frown, for he hated hearing praise heaped upon any of his siblings. I glanced back at Mared. As her first-born, Gruffudd had always been the apple of her eye but my wife was not blind to her favourite's flaws. There was nothing we could do about his physical weakness, but we had both tried very hard to counsel him out of the insecurity which lay behind his blind jealousy of his brothers and sisters. There was a silence while we sat, nursing our own thoughts.

At last I returned to Maredudd's question and answered him as best I could.

The sad fact was that neither I nor anyone else had an instant, or even a short-term answer to the major economic problems facing us. Centuries of English occupation, the great plague which savagely reduced our populations – life for most people in Wales was pretty grim before our rebellion started.

War was a terrible thing and the modern scorched-earth methods forced upon us made it even more terrible. I hoped and prayed we would gain full independence within a year but still it would take many years to achieve the fair and prosperous society we wished for.

But I felt Maredudd's anguish also. These arguments

were little consolation to him or the poor families at our door.

'We do not, and will not have the means to help the hundreds of desperate families at present. But there are several smallholdings in this area which lie empty. I shall get riders to seek out a suitable home tomorrow. This little family will be granted full ownership and helped to move there when they are ready. They will be given some cattle, sheep and seed for sowing and our Exchequer will cover their food for the first year.'

Sleep eluded Mared and I for hours that night. We huddled together, both of us troubled by a host of disparate thoughts and concerns.

Sometime in the early hours Mared held me tightly in her arms and whispered, 'Thank you, Owain, for your compassion towards that family, and for dealing so wisely with Maredudd's outburst. Did you see his face when you told us about how you would settle them in their new holding? In fact everyone, even Gruffudd, our eldest, was pleased.'

Later that night I was troubled by strange dreams. I found myself at the head of a powerful force attacking an English borough. We had recently left a Welsh village, its dead bodies littering the streets, and we were in no mood for showing mercy. Our attack was a complete surprise and soon the borough was filled with the screams of the injured and the dying while flames swept swiftly through the wooden dwellings. My feet slithered along paths made slippery with the blood of our victims.

'Well done, lads,' I roared. 'Now let us take the castle, its not-so-mighty lord and his cowardly henchmen. Let them feel the cold kiss of our steel!'

But, no matter how hard we searched, we could not find a castle. I stopped in shock, my mind spinning with a horrible thought… No… please God, NO!

'Wake up, wake up, Owain. All is well, you have had a bad dream, that is all… please calm yourself my love.'

I awoke to find myself sitting bolt upright in our bed. Mared was holding me tightly by the shoulders. Then I heard a man's voice crying out in despair, and after a few seconds I realised that the voice was my own!

'Hush, hush, my love. You will awake everyone in the castle…'

I snapped my mouth shut to still the sound, then hurriedly opened it again, for I was breathing heavily with sweat breaking from every pore. I clung to my love in confusion. Then I remembered the cause of my horror and I struggled to master my shivering body so I could tell her.

'Oh Mared… I… it… it was truly horrible…'

She raised her hand and gently stroked my cheek, then brushed the hair from my eyes. 'There, my Lord, you are safe with me. It was not real, your mind can play terrible tricks with you in your sleep…'

'But it was so real… so outlandish…' I breathed. 'I was leading an army on a mission of revenge… we had discovered a Welsh village where everybody had been slaughtered. We rode to seek revenge on an English settlement. We entered the place, fired it and killed every man we could find… we gloried in our vicious revenge attack and turned to attack the castle…'

'And?'

'And there was no castle… no castle… no English! In our thirst for revenge we had… we had attacked a Welsh settlement in error... We had murdered our own kin... in an unforgivable, violent rampage... Oh, God forgive me!'

'But it was only a bad nightmare my love... only a nightmare...'

The dawn was breaking as we stared into each other's tear-streaked eyes. We both turned to look at the narrow window in the landward wall of our bedchamber. Silently we walked over to it. The bright orb of the summer sun was slowly rising behind the majestic, comforting bulk of Snowdonia, soon to bathe the steep, craggy slopes in warm sunshine, swiftly dissipating the early morning mists to reveal the ancient citadel of our ancestors in all its glory. We stood very close, bellies touching, arms around each other, gazing in wonder at the stunning scene unfolding before our eyes, both ready to march towards our destiny.

Whatever that might be...

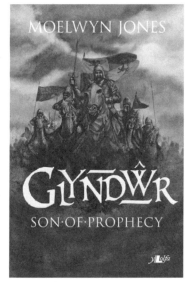

£6.99

£7.99